VOL. COMPLETE

[PRICE ONE SHILLING ... D.

(6)

NED NIMBLE

AMONGST THE CHINESE
OR
THE SECRETS OF THE PURPLE PAGODA

EDWIN J. BRETT, "BOYS OF ENGLAND" OFFICE, 173 FLEET STREET, E.C.

NIMBLE SERIES. VOL. 8.

NED NIMBLE

AMONGST THE CHINESE;

OR,

THE SECRETS OF THE PURPLE PAGODA.

BEAUTIFULLY ILLUSTRATED.

VOLUME I.

LONDON:
"BOYS OF ENGLAND" OFFICE, 173, FLEET STREET, E.C.,
AND ALL BOOKSELLERS.

"' ATTEMPT TO DRAW A WEAPON AND I'LL STRIKE YOU TO THE EARTH,' CRIED NED."

NED NIMBLE AMONGST THE CHINESE;

OR,

THE SECRETS OF THE PURPLE PAGODA.

CHAPTER I.

IN WHICH NED NIMBLE AND HIS FRIENDS COMMENCE A SEARCH FOR BOASTER IN CANTON.

"MAY success crown your hopes, Ned. You have gone through many trials to attain them in other lands, and when they seemed about to be fulfilled cruel fate has blighted them; but I know your motto, dear boy is 'hope on, hope ever,' and so I drink success to your hopes."

And Harry Honour drained his glass to the dregs ere he set it down.

"I reckons dis 'lusterous inderwiderel ull take two drinks to dat ar bery fine toast, an' as I'se a meandering wid free tails, ob course de high position I occerpies in dis yer nation entitles me to double shares in eberyting."

"Where would I get my share then?" asked Charley. "You always was an avaricious beggar."

"Guess dat's trufe," said Jumbo, as he tossed another glass of liquor down his throat so rapidly that he was seized with a violent fit of coughing, which gave Charley the opportunity of landing him several heavy blows between the shoulders, under the pretence of desiring to relieve his friend.

Jumbo having at length got his breath, and Charley returned to his seat, Ned Nimble rose.

"Thank you, Harry—thank you all," he said. "But there have been times when I have forgotten that motto and almost given way to despair, and should I really be upon the track of Boaster and Minnie, and run him down and discover that he has indeed forced that poor girl to become his wife, I must, for her sake hold my hand. But my hope, my prayer is that he lied—that Minnie is still unwed. Then will I avenge her wrongs, and in that villain's blood wash out the indignities he has put upon her and me."

"But what makes you think you have so nearly run the fox to his hole?" asked Jack.

"While standing on the banks of the Bocca Tigris, watching the tea ships loading I felt a hand on my shoulder, and turning, saw my old friend and schoolmate, Dick Darewell."

"Dick Darewell?" echoed the others.

"The same. He is mate of the tea ship 'Speedwell,' and after our surprise at meeting was over, he told me he had seen on the wharf a man he believed to be Bill Boaster. He caught but a hurried glance of his features, when he turned, and darting from the wharf, dived into one of the narrow streets and was lost in the crowd."

"But he may have been mistaken," said 'Dolf.

"Possibly he was; but I have a feeling that he was not," returned Ned. "More than once on our way from Bokhara we have heard of him, or at least of one who answers to his description."

"That's true," said Harry. "There can be no doubt but that it was Bill whom we heard of at least a dozen times in the course of our journey; but he had a long start of us, and perhaps Europeans appear to be all alike to Asiatics, even as these Chinese seem to be all alike to us."

"But Dick would not be decieved," said Ned.

"Not if he had a good long look at him," said Harry Honour. "However, as I said before, may success crown your hopes—that you will soon run him down and wrest Minnie from his grasp."

"I shall not give up hope now of rescuing her," said Ned, "after we have travelled thousands of miles over mountains, across arid plains, and through many cities to reach this place, where I believe Bill is now hiding, and from where he hopes to escape to either England or America in one of the tea ships."

"Then we had better keep a good look-out on the tea ships," said Harry.

"I will get some of you to do so, while I will make inquiries in that part where Dick says he saw Bill disappear. There is only one drawback, and that is the dislike of these Chinese to afford any information to Europeans."

"They're a beastly lot," said Harry.

"Liars and thieves," put in Jack.

"That is the reason that Jumbo and Tilda have adopted their costumes," said Charley.

"Hole on dar," cried Jumbo.

"Anything to oblige a friend," said Charley, seizing a long plait of hair that was attached to Jumbo's head, and secured by a strap round his forehead. "I'll hold on like a bull-dog, never fear."

Twisting the plait round his hand, Charley gave it a fierce tug.

Back went Jumbo's head, up went his legs, over went his chair, and Jumbo lay on his back on the floor.

"Gor-a-mighty! dis yer neck ob dis magernanermous meandering am broked for suah."

"An' so am de head ob dat ar waggerbone," shrieked Tilda, as with her closed ivory fan, she dealt that festive young man a blow on the forehead that made him release his hold, and with a cry of pain leap to the other side of the apartment.

Smarting and indignant, Jumbo sprang up.

But his feet got entangled in the long and gorgeous robe he had assumed, and he pitched on to the overturned chair, crushing its slender frame to pieces by his weight.

All but Tilda roared with laughter.

Even Charley, smarting as he was from the blow of Tilda's fan, laughed loudly.

Tilda was too concerned for Jumbo to see anything to laugh at.

She helped Jumbo to struggle up, and when the negro got on his feet, instead of making a dash at his tormentor, as all expected he would do, he held up his silken and embroidered robe, and shaking his head solemnly, exclaimed—

"Brest if dese yer magernifercent close ain't got spiled afore I could show dis yer majestic pussonage to de ladies and gen'lem ob Canton."

"Shouldn't put yourself in petticoats," cried Charley, "or let Tilda wear the breeches either."

"I'll make breeches right frue dat ar body ob your'n, I will," cried Jumbo, making a dash for Charley.

"Stop it," cried Jack.

Out went the conjuror's hand and Jumbo was pulled up with a jerk by his robe collar.

"Dar goes anoder tear," cried Jumbo; "and dis yer splendifferous gownd cost me two hundred dollars."

"Peace, peace!" cried Ned.

"It am all bery well to say peace," cried Jumbo, "but dar's a lot ob pieces. Dar's about forty tears what de chair gib it, and dar's dis yer big un what Jack gib it. But de greatest tear ob all is in dis yer heart to see dis beautiful dress spiled, dat it am."

"Never mind, Jumbo; we'll buy you another," said Harry.

"Guess I doesn't want none ob your buying. I'se got plenty ob money to buy my own," said Jumbo.

"Sorry I spoke," said Harry.

"I 'cept's yer 'pology," said Jumbo "an' Tilda ull hab to sew up de holes."

"She'll only be too happy, I am sure," said 'Dolf.

"Come, no more wrangling," said Ned; "and let me impress on you all the necessity of keeping out of brawls with the natives, or we may be driven out of the place before I can discover whether Bill and Minnie are hiding hereabouts or not."

"That is good advice, Ned," said Harry, "for the Celestials are so suspicious of foreigners that they are only too glad to find an opportunity of expelling them from their cities."

"Now, Harry dear boy, will you and 'Dolf go down to the quays and keep a sharp look-out, and should either of you see him, follow him ? "

"Certainly we will, Ned," was the reply.

"Of couuse there you will see a good many Europeans connected with the ships at anchor, but I don't think you could mistake Bill."

"He must be altered if I do," replied Harry.

"As I said before, I have a suspicion he will try to get the captain of one of the vessels to take him on board. Of course that is supposing that Dick was right in the man he fancied was Boaster."

"And what will you do, Ned ? "

"I shall go and wander about the locality in which he disappeared from Dick's view, and a few dollars judiciously applied may get me some information respecting them."

"You won't go alone, Ned ? " cried Harry.

"Better that I did," said Ned. "Of course I shall not go unarmed, though I shall be careful not to show my weapons unless I find it necessary to protect my own life."

"Of course. And Jack and Charley ? " asked Harry.

"They will go on board any vessel nearly ready to sail, and make inquiries whether a young Englishman and woman have taken passage in her. I am sure they will so question as not to put Boaster on his guard, or let those whom they question suspect our desire to molest him."

"You may depend upon me," said Jack.

"I rather think I'm up to snuff," said Charley. "You don't see any green in my eye, I reckon."

"Well, that being arranged, I will set out. Of course we all meet here to supper, barring accidents."

"Ob course we'll all hab meat for supper," said Jumbo. "I guess yer don't cotch dis yer chile a-eating ob rats and puppies like de yaller-faced Chinee man, does yer ? But what'll I an' Tilda an' Sally do ? Dat's what I wants to know ? "

"Stop at home, and make love to Sally," said Charley. "Jack won't mind ; and if you'd run away with her, he'd pray for you night and day he would."

"Do you know what you are talking about, Master Imperence ? " said Sally.

"You don't think I'm a fool, do you ? " asked Charley.

"I know you're a rogue," said Sally. "There's a great deal more of the R than the F in your composition. Jack."

"Yes, my dear," said Jack.

"Punch his head."

"Really I don't think it worth my while to do so, as I know he's only chaffing."

"Quite right, Jack. Shows how much more sensible you are than your wife," said Charley, winking at 'Dolf. "Ah, it is sad to think that a poor man don't know what trouble is till he gets married. Don't you ever marry 'Dolf. Take warning by the sorrows of poor old Jack."

"I think you wart to know what sort of a woman I am," said Sally, rising angrily.

"Sit down, my dear woman," said Charley. "There's no need for you to tell me. I've got my eyesight and my hearing. Here, come on, boys, before she gets on the rampage."

And Charley made for the door, followed by 'Dolf and Jack.

"I need not advise you to be careful, Harry," said Ned ; "for I know for my sake, you will be guarded in your words and actions. I will send a telegram to my dear old uncle in England, and then I'll make for the street of the Purple Pagoda. Good-bye."

The friends shook hands and Harry went out, and Ned sat down to write a telegram to his friends in England.

CHAPTER II.

IN WHICH JUMBO AND TILDA RESOLVE TO ASTONISH THE NATIVES AND ARE A LITTLE ASTONISHED THEMSELVES.

IT was not within the walls of the city that the one storied house in which, for the present, Ned and his friends had taken up their abode was situated but about half a mile without the walls.

The street in which it was situated was long and narrow, and every building was a shop.

The only windows open to the street were the shop windows, the windows of the private apartments opening into courtyards, before the gates of which were screens to prevent passers-by gazing in.

The merchandise here sold was principally ship's stores, though one or two of the shop-keepers increased their incomes by lodging and boarding the barbarians, as they called the English and American sailors or traders.

Ching-Fow's shop was not a large one though it contained a good stock, but the remainder of his dwelling was large and could accommodate a goodly number of lodgers.

He was of the middle height, but shorter than the generality of his countrymen, and his yellow skin and little eyes showed that he was addicted to the use of opium.

Mrs. Ching-Fow had never been seen by any barbarian who had taken up his quarters in Ching-Fow's dwelling, but Master Ching-Fow was as a rule seen too often.

This young gentleman might have been either eighteen or twenty-eight years of age, for few, if any, Europeans can guess the age of a Celestial.

He had all the characteristics of a true Chinese.

He could lie without blushing, cheat without blinking, and find anything before it was lost with the most wonderful promptitude.

His father looked upon him as a perfect treasure, especially when dealing with Europeans.

Never was a Chinaman quicker at nipping a piece out of a silver coin, never

one who could so command his countenance or smile with his bead-like eyes as he gave it back to the purchaser with a regret that he could not take it as it was not of the full value.

And never was one more adroit in extracting from the parcel he made up some article or another without being detected or even suspected.

Ned Nimble having finished his writing, folded the paper, placed it in his pocket, and then examined his revolver.

Finding it all right, he placed it in his breast coat pocket, and advancing to the door, said—

"Jumbo, should the others return before I do, tell them to have no anxiety about me, at least not till very late, for I may glean something that may keep me away longer than I at present anticipate."

"Guess I'll not forget dat ar observation ob your'n, Massa Ned. But jest yer take preshus good care ob dat life ob your'n, acos I don't want to be left a widder, yer know."

"All right, Jumbo, I'll be careful. Take care of the ladies; good-bye."

"Tah-tah, as dey seys in de perlite serciety in which dis extinguished pussonage has moved along and felled down."

With a smile Ned passed out.

"Now den, Tilda, am yer sewed up dem ar holes in dat meandering's gownd ob mine?"

"I reckon I'se pinned 'em up," said Tilda.

"Den just chuck it ober here. Mind how yer frows it; I doesn't want dat ar gole lace knocked off de shoulders. Guess I neber looked better in nuffin dan in dese yer close. What's yer tink?"

"Oh, you'se all dar."

"Guess I am when I'se got 'em on," said Jumbo, putting on the robe. "Dar now, I calls dat spiffin', I does."

"Guess yer don't look no better in dem dan I does in dese," said Tilda.

"Well, dat's a matter ob 'pinion, yer

know. I finks yer shows too much ob de bottom ob dem ar trousers."

"Git out," said Tilda, "I'se ashamed ob yer."

"Git out—guess dat's what I mean ter do. Tink I'se going to stop in dis yer place an' not let de peoples see what a 'stinguished inderwiderel as has honoured dere country wid his presence? I'se going to 'stonish de natives, I is. What's de good ob habing close if yer don't show 'em?"

"Dat ar's my 'pinion," replied Tilda; "an' I reckons I can take de shine out ob any gal in China, 'specially when I puts on de ornaments I bought yesterday."

"What am 'em?"

"Guess dere silber bells to hang at de bottom ob dis yer hair ob mine."

And Tilda gave her head a swing round and struck Jumbo in the face with three long plaits of black hair.

The negro started back and rubbed his eyes.

"Your hair?" said Sally, with a toss of her head. "Oh, Tilda, I'm ashamed of you, everybody will laugh at you; a regress with long hair—whoever heard of such a thing?"

"When yer's in Chiner yer must do as Chiner does," retorted Tilda, "and so perhaps, Mrs. Jones, you'll just mind yer own business."

"Bah!" said Sally, "the Chinese don't cut off their pigtails and wear wool wigs when they go to Africa, do they?"

"Perhaps not, ma'am," said Tilda, freezingly; "it's wery likely if dey visited some parts of Africa dey wouldn't long hab any heads to put wigs on."

"Dat's trufe," said Jumbo.

"That shows the stock you come from," said Sally.

"Yer hasn't got anything to say agin it, has yer," said Tilda, firing up.

"Oh dear no," said Sally, "it would of course, be no good if I did, seeing as how cannibalism and ignorance naturally go together."

"Dat's trufe," said Jumbo.

"Does yer presume, ma'am, ter say as how I'se a cannerbile?" cried Tilda. "I neber put my teefe inter a human body in my bressed life."

"Guess yer's forgotten dat ar day when yer was mad about summat, and I looked hole ob yer. Didn't yer shove dem ar two rows ob ibery into dis yer arm ob mine?"

"Oh dat's nuffin," said Tilda.

"Guess I'll differ in dat ar 'pinion," said Jumbo. "But dar, am yer done tying dem ar bells on dat ar hair, acos if yer is, come on, or I goes widout yer."

"Wait till I make myself 'specterble; yer don't fink I'se going out as if I was as common a pussonage as Mrs. Jones, does yer?"

Sally curled her lip but said nothing.

Tilda having finished her toilette to her satisfaction, tossed her head disdainfully towards Sally and taking up her parasol, strode out of the room.

"Is yer going to stop here by yerself, Sally, or will yer come wid us?" asked Jumbo.

"It ain't the month of November, or I might perhaps exhibit you both for guys," said Sally, "for I never saw two greater guys in my life."

"Dat's trufe," said Jumbo, "so I'se off."

And he went out and joined Tilda in the court, where she was waiting behind the screen.

They passed along the alley formed by the centre and side screen and out into the street.

"I guess we'll hab a day to ourselbes," said Jumbo. "We hasn't had a bressed bit ob fun for dese yer many monfs, hab we?"

"We'se too 'specterble to play in dese yer streets," said Tilda; "yer forgets as I'se a lady."

"Guess dat's trufe; and ob course I'se a bery high pussonage. Ain't I a meandering wid free tails at de back ob my head?"

"How's yer a meandering?" asked Tilda.

"Why, dese free tails ob hair makes me one," replied Jumbo.

"Den ob course I'se a meanderiness," said Tilda. "Don't yer see I'se got free?"

And she shook her head and rang the three silver bells attached to the end of her false plaits.

"Dat's just what yer is ter be sure?"

"Ob course, when yer was a king wasn't I a kingess? and now yer a meandering, ob course I'se a meanderiness, and I guess dese yer people knows it; see how dey's a looking at us?"

The numerous pedestrians paused in their walks to stare at them and point them out to others whose attention they had not attracted.

"Tilda."

"Yes."

"Does a meandering bow to de common people when dey stops to 'mire him?"

"Guess I don't know 'bout dat ar; but den you sees we's so bery perlite dat I thinks we oughter."

"Why, ob course we oughter," cried Tilda, "and hain't yer neber seen how dey do it?"

"Neber," said Jumbo.

"What neber? an' yer been in de States, an neber seen 'em a-doing ob it in de windows ob de dry goods stores."

"Ob course I has, among de tea an' sugar. I reckons I'se stood a lot of times a-looking at 'em a-wagging ob dar heads, and a-wishing as I could ha' put my hand frue de glass and a-collared some ob de plums dey was a-bobbing at."

"Den as we's sartin sure now, just let us return de complerments what's a-being paid us."

Smiling at each other, the crowd—for a crowd there was by this time—pointing at Jumbo and Sally and wagging their heads, drew closer around them.

"Now den, Tilda, let's go it just like dey do in de shop windows," said Jumbo.

And then Jumbo and Tilda smiled graciously and set their heads wagging up and down at a furious rate, the bells on Tilda's hair ringing out merrily the while.

No longer was the mirth of the Chinese subdued.

They shrieked with laughter.

"We's just gibbing 'em fits ob delight by our connersension," said Jumbo. "Jus' look at 'em—dey is fit to bust, dey am."

"Golly, dey is tickled wid happiness at de sight ob us," said Tilda.

"I know'd dese yer close 'ud do it," said Jumbo.

"And I was sartin sure dese bells 'ud set eberybody dancing wid joy."

"He, he, he!" shrieked the Chinese, capering about and pointing and doubling themselves up in the exhuberance of their mirth.

But this soon changed; the crowd surged forward and began to jostle Jumbo and Tilda on all sides, jeering them the while.

"I guess we's made a mistake," said Jumbo.

"Guess we has," replied Tilda, as she pushed a fellow away as he pressed rudely upon her.

"Lookee, blackee Chinee manee-girlee!" yelled one; "let's chuckee in de roadee."

"What's dat?" yelled Jumbo, as he seized the speaker and another by their pigtails and brought their heads together with a crash. "If yer don't know how to 'spect dese high pussonages, den I reckons as I an' Tilda knows how to make yer."

CHAPTER III.

IN WHICH JUMBO HAS A NOVEL SWING—NED ARRIVES IN THE NICK OF TIME, AND CHING-FOW PAYS DEAR FOR HIS RUDENESS.

THE Celestials were not a little astonished and terrified when they saw Jumbo dashing the heads of the two men together and that astonishment was increased greatly when Tilda, grasping her umbrella tightly, made a grab at the pigtail of another, and commenced to belabour him over the head and shoulders most unmercifully.

"Wire in, ole gal!" yelled Jumbo. "Gib 'em toko! I reckon as how dey came to de wrong shop if dey tinks to 'sult us."

And again and again he dashed the heads of the two Celestials together, while they yelled and shrieked for mercy.

But Jumbo felt his dignity was hurt.

He had been laughed at, jeered at, and mobbed, where he expected only to meet with respect and admiration.

"Yer tink yer'll hinsult his magernanermous majesty, Jumbo de Onet!"

onth, does yer? By golly, I reckon I'll teach yer to 'spect de magernificent inderwiderels what 'ave honoured dis yer nation of rat-eaters by dere presence! Hole still dere, or I'll twist yer heads off, I will!"

And he gave the men's heads such a twist that they both fell on their knees at his feet.

Tilda's victim was meanwhile shrieking loudly for mercy, and calling upon the bystanders to rescue him from the hands of a she-dragon.

But Tilda's passion was as fierce now as Jumbo's, and she threatened all who attempted to approach her, and still continued to beat away at the head and shoulders of the shrieking Chinaman.

Jumbo, instead of releasing his prisoners, quickly tied the ends of their long pigtails together, and then jerked them both to their feet.

"I guess I'll make a 'zample ob yer bofe," he cried. "I'se a-going to chuck yer ober de fust rail I sees, and dar let you hang like two cats wid dere tails tied togeder. I will, by golly!"

"Take out knifees and killee blackees," cried a fellow in the crowd, and his hand went under his blouse as if he intended to grasp a weapon hidden there.

But if so, ere he could draw it, a hand dashed his arm aside, then fingers grasped his ear, and a small hard fist was raised to his nose.

"What would you incite your countrymen to slay those whom you have insulted, and who sought to do you no harm? Attempt to draw a weapon and I'll strike you to the earth!"

At the sound of the voice Jumbo looked up and saw Ned Nimble.

"Hurray!" he shouted. "Oh golly, dat's all right, an' as I can't find a rail to hang yer bofe on, I guess I'll hang myself on yer."

And grasping at the two Celestials' heads, he gave a spring and sat astride their fastened pigtails as if on a swing.

The yell those two men gave was more piercing than a railway whistle, and the roar of laughter that greeted them from the bystanders failed to drown it.

Ned released the man's ear, and the fellow, utterly cowed by his determined look, slunk away behind his companions.

"Hold," cried Ned to Tilda.

She dropped her umbrella and released the man's pigtail.

Then he turned to Jumbo, who was making frantic efforts to hold the two men up and keep himself from falling from his strange swing.

"Come down!" cried Ned, in a severe tone.

And down came Jumbo on the instant.

But not as he had himself intended to do.

The two Celestials suffered their legs to slip from under them, and down came Jumbo all of a heap between them.

He scrambled up and rubbed the back of his head and his thigh.

"I guess I'se broke ebery bone in dis yer body ob mine," he groaned. "What for, Massa Ned, did yer speak like dat ar? Yer frightened de beggars off dere feet; and jest as I was a-beginning to enjoy dat ar swing."

"Jumbo," said Ned, "you have excited the ire of these Celestials. Let's get home quickly, or they may take heart and attack us."

"Guess I'll want a lot of tacks to mend dese yer broken bones ob mine," said Jumbo. "But where's dat ar Tilda?"

"I'se hear," said Tilda. "I guess I gib dat fellow somefing for his check."

"Serb him right," said Jumbo. "I'll lurn 'em not ter hinsult de magernanermous——"

"Come," interrupted Ned. "Come away at once."

And taking an arm of Tilda and Jumbo, he led them towards their lodgings.

The Celestials moved aside to let them pass, but scowled at them as they did so.

Had they dared, how gladly would they have thrown themselves upon them.

But they could not screw up their courage to assail them.

So Ned and his companions passed along unmolested. But would the Chinese always be as timid and hesitating?

Ned feared not.

He believed that they had made enemies who would yet, if they got the chance, do them an injury.

It was, therefore, with no pleasant feelings that he accompanied Jumbo and Tilda back to their lodgings

While these events were transpiring,

Sally who had been left quite alone, thought that she would improve the opportunity by looking over her wardrobe and trinkets.

Her supply was a good one, for the liberality of the Amir of Bokhara had enabled each of the party not only to provide any luxury they might require for the present, but also for the future.

The gold and jewels with which he had presented them enabled them to travel the thousands of miles they had had to cover either on horseback or on foot in palanquin, or boats.

But theirs had been no journey of pleasure, wild and beautiful as the scenes they passed through, for they were hanging on the track of Boaster, and ever haunted with the terrible fear that Minnie would fall a victim to Bill's fury or revenge.

Sally had heaped her goods about her, and was admiring her trinkets, when looking up suddenly, she was surprised to find she was not alone.

Not three feet from where she sat, stood a young Celestial, his small dark eyes twinkling and his yellow face aglow with pleasure.

"What do you want here?" cried Sally, hastily concealing her jewellery.

Ching-Fow the younger's eyes sparkled more brilliantly as he bowed and said—

"Goodee mornee."

"Good morning," replied Sally.

"Hopee see ee wellee," said Ching-Fow.

"Hope you do," replied Sally. "But what have you come here for?"

"Comee to see de prettee ladee."

"Then the next time you come, perhaps you'll knock as civilised people do," said Sally. "So now you've seen me, you can just take yourself off."

"Takee selfee offee," said the Celestial. "No runee wayee when he comee see you."

"But I don't want you. You are an impudent rascal to intrude into this room without being invited."

"No wantee invitee," said Ching-Fow. "Me see prettee ladee. Me lookee long at her, an' me heartee go patee patee, and then me lovee muchee."

"Get out," cried Sally. "Get out, you yellow-skinned mongrel, or I'll show you

what kind of a woman I am pretty sharp."

The Celestial opened his almond-shaped eyes in surprise, and as Sally advanced upon him with clenched hand, he gave a bound backwards in his fright, lost his footing and sat down on the matting with a bump.

"Oh!" he yelled, "backee hurtee muchee."

"And I'll hurt it more," cried Sally, stooping down and thumping at his back and shoulders with no light hand.

"Oh, you hurtee, you killee! Stopee—stopee!" he yelled, as he writhed about on the floor and tried to rise to his feet.

But Sally rolled him over at every blow, till she was fairly out of breath with her exertions.

"There," she cried, "now you know what sort of a woman I am. Get up, and out you go, or as soon as I get my breath I'll be at you again, you parchment-faced mummy."

Ching-Fow struggled up, and rubbed his back ruefully.

"Clear out," cried Sally pointing to the door.

Ching-Fow backed slowly towards it.

"If you can't move any faster, I fancy I can make you," cried Sally, seizing a thick bamboo that stood in a corner of the apartment.

She made a rush with the stick at the smarting Celestial.

With a yell of terror he leaped back and came down on the very threshold of the doorway fair on the toes of Jumbo, who at that moment entered, accompanied by Ned and Tilda.

"Gor-a-mighty!" yelled Jumbo, "I'se killed for suah."

Then, raising his fist, he dealt the Celestial so fierce a blow between the shoulders that he not only knocked the breath out of the Chinaman's body, but sent him sprawling against Sally with such violence that that lady fell into a sitting position on the floor.

Down into her lap went Ching-Fow, and Jumbo forgot his pain and hid his annoyance in the sight of the way in which Sally held the Celestial down across her knees and laid into him with the thick bamboo.

CHAPTER IV.

IN WHICH NED BEGINS TO HAVE MISGIVINGS.

NED NIMBLE forgot all his annoyance, and, leaning against the door-post, shrieked with laughter.

Jumbo, in his delight, grinned from ear to ear, and capered about as though he had suddenly gone mad.

Tilda placed her hands on her hips, and swayed her body up and down till the silver bells at the end of her long false plaits rang out a perfect peal, which, mingling with her own and the others' laughter, Sally's threats, and Ching-Fow's cries for mercy, made up a sound that might have been heard for some distance.

"You'll make love to me, will you, you yaller-faced, pig-eyed, black-haired son of a she-dragon?" yelled Sally. "I'll teach you to knock me down. I'll lay into you as long as I can hold this cane. You'll know what sort of a woman I am after I've done with you!"

"Oh, whitee girlee, hab pitee on Chinee manee! You muchee hurtee Chinee manee's backee wid big stickee."

"I ain't hurt it enough yet," cried Sally. "You won't come here again in a hurry, sneaking in like a cat—you won't make love to me again."

"Never moree," shrieked Ching-Fow. "Me vere soree. Hab muchee mercee on poor Chinee manee, goodee girlee!"

"Golly! dis am as good as de penny show what dey hab in de States," said Jumbo; "on'y I guess de panterloon don't get it so hot from de clown as dat ar feller's a-getting it from dat ar Sally."

"I reckon dat Sally Jones does wire in when she gets wexation a-going. Guess as how, Jumbo, yer wouldn't like dat larruping would yer?"

"Guess I'd like to hab a pillar underneaf dis yer meandering robe ob mine fore dat ar wixen began de whackin'—trader!"

"In heaven's name, Sally," said Ned, advancing, "how has this young man excited your ire that you feel it necessary to so severely chastise him?"

"Goodee Engleemanee, savee poor Chinee manee. Stickee muchee hurtee backee. No sabee, girlee killee."

"Let him get up now, Sally," said Ned, arresting the cane in its descent. "Whatever his fault you have surely made him suffer enough for it."

"What! The audacious waggerbone, to come in here and make love to Jack Jones' wife, and when my Jack ain't here, too! You stand back, Master Ned. I ain't half done showing him what sort of a woman I am."

"I guess if he'd 'a known what a wixenish wixen yer is he wouldn't hab gone and done it," said Jumbo.

"Come, come, Sally, let the poor fellow get up," said Ned, keeping hold of the cane.

"I'll poor fellow him!" cried Sally. "The imperence of the thing, to come here when I'm alone and tell me he loves me!—me, a respectable married woman, whose had two husbands! He lubee muchee, does he? I think I've knocked all the love out of him with stickee whackee."

"Then let him get up. He won't dare to insult you again, Sally," said Ned.

"I reckon I've knocked all that out of him," said Sally, "as clean as you knock oust out of a carpet. Now, you yaller mummy, if I take my fingers out of your hair will you promise to behave yourself in future?"

"Chinee manee promise muchee, no moree hittee backee," cried Ching-Fow.

"Then get out of this, sharp!" cried Sally, giving him a jerk off her lap on to the floor, and rising to her feet, assisted by Ned.

Ching-Fow staggered to his feet and stood wriggling and twisting with pain.

"Got it hot, ole man, I reckon," said Jumbo. "Dat ar gal knows how to lay it on fick."

"Backee muchee itchee," returned the Chinese.

"Den I guess as how yer'd better go away and muchee scratchee," said Tilda.

"Dat's bery good adwice dis lady gibs yer," said Jumbo. "I'se a bery tender inderwiderel myself, I is; but when I lifts up dis yer foot ob mine dar's boun' ter be somefing run agin it, an' den dat ar somefing hurts itself."

As Jumbo raised his foot, Ching-Fow realised that to remain longer might be unpleasant to himself and painful to his body, so with a howl, he made a dash for the doorway.

"No kickee. No likee bootee," he cried.

But reaching the doorway, he turned on the threshold.

The usually expressionless face of the Celestial had undergone a change, as had his cringing manner.

Fire seemed to flash from his almond-shaped eyes, and the rage of a thousand fiends to be concentrated in his face.

Raising his clenched fist, he shook it fiercely at Sally.

"Beatee Chinee manee, willee?" he cried. "Chinee manee killee—killee!"

Then he turned and fled from their sight.

"Was dat conwultures or de croup him caught so quick, I wonner?" asked Jumbo.

"Guess it was a little bit of bofe, wid de backache put in," replied Tilda.

"I am afraid we are making more enemies than friends here," said Ned, solemnly. "This is a bad morning's work, and may defeat the object we have in view."

"How's dat?" asked Jumbo.

"The Chinese detest us barbarians, as they call us, and would at all times willingly drive us from their land. Knowing this, it becomes necessary to propitiate them, and if we cannot gain their friendship, at least do nothing to excite their enmity!"

"What! put up with all their cheek and not let 'em have it?" cried Sally. "Not for me. I reckon I ain't a woman of that sort."

"Dat's trufe," said Jumbo. "If eber dar was a debbil it am dat ar Sally Jones."

"Guess I knows it," said Tilda.

Ned gave them both a warning look, while Sally bit her lip and looked very much as if she would have liked to serve them both as she had served Ching-Fow the younger.

But Ned's presence restrained her, and she muttered as if to herself—

"What can you expect of such ignorance."

"Calm yourself, Sally," said Ned. "What's done can't be undone, so let's hope that no harm will come of it."

He drew back a step, and then, stooping, quickly picked up something glittering from the floor.

"Halloa!" he said, "what's this, and how came it there?"

It was a splendid ruby, of great worth, size, and brilliancy.

"Oh, it's mine!" said Sally. "Oh! and there's that yellow diamond."

"But how came they on the floor?" asked Ned. "You can't afford to throw precious stones about like this, Sally, for, rich as the amir's presents made you, riches, like all other things, have an end."

"Yes, I know that, Master Ned," said Sally. "Surely you don't think I was such a fool as to put them there intentionally?"

"We'se only got de bare word of yerself for de fact dat yer isn't a fool," said Jumbo.

"Silence!" said Ned. "You'll be getting your tongue between your teeth and pitching yourself over if you don't mind what you say."

"Dat's trufe," said Jumbo.

Sally thrust her hand into her pocket, drew out her jewels and trinkets, and looked about the matting to see if any were missing.

"You see, Master Ned," said Sally, in answer to his questioning gaze, "when you'd all gone out and I was here alone I thought I'd have a look at my treasures, and while I was doing so I cast up my eyes and saw that yellow-faced mummy of a Chinaman close to my side, with his eyes staring as if they'd jump out of his head."

"Did he see those jewels?" asked Ned, quickly.

"See them!" cried Sally. "I should rather say he did. Why, he looked as if he could have swallowed them. I tell you you should just have seen his eyes then."

"This is most unfortunate," said Ned, in a vexed tone.

"What is?" asked Sally.

"That the fellow should have seen the jewels," replied Ned.

"Why?" asked Sally.

"Because these Chinese are such thieves that I fear he will seek to rob us now that he knows we have such valuables in our possession."

"You don't think that, do you?" asked Sally.

"I do; and what is more, if he succeeded, I fear we should get but scant justice, so deeply are Europeans hated by these Celestials."

"I wish we'd never come here," said Sally.

"Guess he'd a-grabbed 'em if he'd got de chance," said Jumbo.

"Dat's what he was after," said Tilda; "an' he only pretended to lub Sally. 'Tain't likely a young feller like dat 'ud fall in lub wid an ole woman, am it now?"

"And why not?" asked Sally.

"A'cos it ain't nat'ral, ma'am, dat's why not," replied Tilda. "Now, if it had a-been dis young and graceful inderwiderel, you might hab fought he meaned what him said."

"You!" sneered Sally; "as if he would have even looked at you. You are ugly enough to frighten the old gentleman himself with that black face of yours."

"Heah dat, now!" said Tilda, addressing Jumbo. "Does yer hear de imperence of dat ole woman?"

"Guess I ain't deaf," said Jumbo; "but I'se dat used to de wishous wickedness ob dis world dat nuffin' s'prises me; so I hole's my jaw an' says not nuffin."

"A very good plan, Jumbo," said Ned. "Never quarrel with a woman. You're sure to get the worst of it if you do."

"Dat's trufe," said Jumbo, "as dat ar Tilda can't deny, seeing as how I'se sometimes been dat ar sore atwixt dese yer shoulders acos ob her wishous way of punching de argymints into me."

"Well, we shall have to keep our eyes open and be on our guard," remarked Ned, "or we may find ourselves one fine day minus of all we possess. I didn't like the look of that Celestial, nor his threat either. We've made an enemy of him, of that rest assured."

"If he comes any nonsense wid dis yer 'specterble cullered gen'lam." said Jumbo, "der'll be a row for suah."

"I can only repeat that it is most unfortunate that the fellow got a glimpse of Sally's trinkets; and we must be on our guard against him or others who may attempt to possess themselves of them."

"I reckons I'll carry mine about wid me," said Jumbo.

"An' I'se bound to do ditter," remarked Tilda.

"Then you had better be careful not to get into such a squabble as you were in this morning," said Ned, "or you may lose not only your wealth, but your lives as well."

"It's a beastly place," said Sally. "It's worse than Bokhara, I do believe."

"Dat ar's a fac'," said Jumbo. "Nobody neber laughed at me an' Tilda dere, but here dey's dat iggerant dat dey can't tell a gen'lam an' lady when dey sees 'em, can 'em, Tilda?"

"Ob course not, or dey'd all fell down flop on dere bressed knees and kissed de hems ob dese yer robes."

"Sartin sure dey would," replied Jumbo. "Where's dere eyes dat dey couldn't see de majerjestic majesty of such extinguished meanderiners as we is? But dar! what's de use ob hoping to ciberlise dese heathen Chinese?"

CHAPTER V.

IN WHICH CHARLEY ORDERS DINNER AND JUMBO AND HIS FRIENDS DON'T LIKE IT.

HAVING prevailed upon Jumbo and Tilda not to appear in the streets again that day, Ned was about to set forth once more, when Charley entered the place rather hurriedly.

"Ned," he said, "I didn't expect to find you here, but as I do, all the better. Harry has met Mr. Darewell on board his vessel, and has sent me back to tell any one who was here that if Darewell can get away to-night, he'd like to join us at dinner."

"I'm very glad," said Ned. "I am sure I shall be most happy to meet my old school-chum."

"And dem ar's my senterments," said Jumbo.

"He says they've nearly got in all their cargo, and only wait for the last consignment, which they expect hourly, and is likely to be all on board before night, in which case they will weigh anchor with the tide in the morning; and unless he takes this opportunity of cracking a bottle with you, it may be some time before he gets another."

"I shall be most happy to see him," said Ned, "and we'll give orders for a good repast to be served up. Or, look here, Charley. As I am anxious to get out, I'll leave you to arrange that with old Ching-Fow. Let it be the best that he can produce—a regular good old-fashioned English meal, you know."

"Trust me," said Charley, "to order a stunner."

"Of course, if nothing happens, we shall all meet at the usual hour," said Ned, as he left the apartment.

Sally was engaged packing away her trinkets, Tilda sat sulkily aside, and Jumbo was examining his garments to find out what injury they had sustained in the jostling he had received.

"Halloa, boys, another guy!" cried Charley, bringing his hand down heavily between Jumbo's stooping shoulders.

"What's yer arter?" cried Jumbo, straightening up. "Does yer want dis yer fist ob mine in dat ar eye ob your'n?"

"'Taint large enough to go in," said Charley.

"Den I guess it'll stop outside."

And Jumbo struck a blow at Charley's face.

Charley was on his guard, however, and ducked his head quickly.

"No, you don't," he said. "A good miss that, old man."

"I reckon dar'd be no miss if yer'd only stand still."

"Don't you wish you may get it?' laughed Charley, as he bobbed out of reach.

"Guess I does. How de debbil's I ter hit yer when yer goes dancing 'bout like dat ar?"

"It's a way I've got," said Charley, "I can't help it."

"Yer's like a basin ob jelly in con-wulsions, yer is. Dar's no laying hold ob yer, dar ain't."

"You ain't so nimble as you was, old boy; you surely must be getting older every day you live," said Charley, sticking his tongue in his cheek.

"I only wish I could get hole ob yer, dar'd only be a heap ob little bits in de middle ob dis yer floor," cried Jumbo.

"You old double-breasted assassin!" said Charley. "Not only want to kill a man, but cut him up too! Ah, how vain it is to hope to eradicate the old cannibal propensities of the negro!"

"I'll cannerbile yer!" replied Jumbo.

"All right, fire away, old man. Look here. Did you ever see comical Joey in a Punch and Judy show? You did? Well, that's me, and you are Punch. One, two three—fair on the top of your nose."

"Goramighty!" cried Jumbo, putting his hand to his nose; "yer's broked it."

"Not quite, only tickled it a little. You'll be able to smell your dinner after that. Good-bye, old boy; I'm off to order it—and oh, won't you all enjoy it!"

And Charley danced out of the room.

Out into the courtyard, round the screen, and through the gate danced Charley.

There was a peculiar smile on his face as he entered the shop where old Ching-Fow sat, with his little eyes vacantly glaring out into the street.

With his hands in his pockets, and a smile on his face, Charley entered the shop.

Ching-Fow senior looked up and smiled.

He had not yet heard of the treatment his son had received at the hands of Sally.

So he was in a good temper.

He rubbed his yellow hands together.

"Muchee gladee see-e," he said.

"Talk English," said Charley.

"Me mgchee talkee Englee—me muchee Enulee manee," said the stout Celestial.

"Glad to hear it, I'm sure," said Charley. "So now then, old kite-flyer, I've come to give you a stiff order."

"Much obligee."

"You see, we are going to have company to dinner to-day, and we want a regular out-and-outer. All the things in season, you know; everything that a

Chinaman delights in, you understand; none of your English dinners, but such a one as you would provide for a marriage feast for your own son. Plenty of money to pay for it, so don't stint anything."

"Obligee muchee, bery proudee," said the Celestial.

"You'll give orders to your servants to see that everything is ready to be served at seven."

The Celestial assured him that he would at once give the orders, and Charley took his departure, the smile broadening on his face as he went towards the water.

He found Jack on one of the quays.

"Did you see Ned?" asked Jack.

"Yes, and Jumbo."

"What's that old fool doing of?"

"Oh he's looking after his rents," said Charley.

"His rents?" echoed Jack, with a laugh. "If he has as much trouble to collect them as my old landlord did, it will take him a long time to get them."

"Get out," said Charley, "I mean the tears in that gown he wears."

"Oh, ah," said Jack, "I understand now. Which way shall we go?"

"Oh, I don't care," said Charley; "looking for Boaster is like looking for a needle in a haystack, so it don't matter which course we take."

They strolled along the quays, till seeing Harry and 'Dolf on board the "Speedwell," they went aboard of her.

"Mr. Nimble says he will be delighted to see you to dinner, Mr. Darewell," said Charley. "Time, seven."

"And I am very sorry to say that we have just received a notification that our last consignment will not arrive before that hour, and that I shall be unable to leave the ship this evening as I am to superintend the loading and stowing of the goods."

"That's confounded annoying!" said Harry.

"Can't be helped, dear boy; there are worse troubles at sea."

"I'm very sorry," said Harry.

"So am I," replied Dick. "I suppose you have discovered nothing yet to confirm my suspicions that it was Boaster I saw?"

"Nothing. Evidently no person answering his description has made application for a passage on either of the English ships."

"There are three Americans in port. Have you inquired of them?"

"Not yet, but shall do so during the day."

"That Bill was always an artful card," said Dick; "and he'll try any dodge to slip through Ned's fingers, if he fancies he is after him."

"No doubt of that."

"I hope he won't escape him though. If ever a fellow deserved hanging Boaster does."

"You may well say that. But I won't keep you longer from your duties. I hope to see you again before you sail."

"And I to see you. Tell Ned how sorry I am to be unable to join you to-night."

"I will," said Harry.

And shaking hands with Dick, the four friends went on shore.

Jack and Charley strolled about the quays watching every person they encountered, either English or American, but no sign of any one at all like Bill Boaster did they see.

Harry and 'Dolf visited the American vessels and prosecuted their inquiries aboard, but with no result.

"I begin to fancy Dick was mistaken," said Harry; "and I feel sure that he was, but for the fact that he knew we were on his track many times in the course of our long journey."

"I can't give up all hopes of my gentleman," said 'Dolf, "though we shall soon have to give up the search for to-day."

"Yes," said Harry. "Ned is sure to be punctual unless he has discovered something."

At the appointed hour all had returned to their lodgings, and great was Ned's vexation when he heard that Dick would be unable to meet them.

"Never mind," he said. "Charley, strike the gong as a signal for dinner to be served, for if the Celestials have one good quality, it is punctuality."

Charley struck the gong that hung beside the door.

"Ha, ha! walk up, we're ready to begin!"

"Guess I'se all dat," said Jumbo. "I'se dat ar awful hungry, I could eat a donkey, I could."

"Then you shall take the head of the table," said Ned, with a smile.

"I guess I'se all dar. Tilda, just yer 'sport me at t'oder end."

And Jumbo seated himself at the head of the table, and Tilda took the foot.

Charley took a seat at Jumbo's side, and four Chinese servants entered with the dishes, placed them on the table without any noise, bowed low, and glided from the apartment.

"Now, Tilda, yer dissect dat ar pie while I cuts up dis yer grub what smells so lubberly dat I could gobble it all up meself."

Jumbo took off the cover, while Tilda proceeded to bury her knife in a huge pie.

"Gor-a-mighty!" cried Jumbo, dropping the cover on the floor and gazing round the table; "am dis a wision?"

"Venison, you mean; no, you fool, ain't it sucking-pig?" said Charley. "I thought you was hungry. Why don't you fire away?"

"At dat ar ting," cried Jumbo, pointing to the dish. "What de debbil am it?"

"Food for niggers," said Charley.

"Den I guess yer'll hab to eat it," cried Jumbo. "Look here," he yelled, picking up the animal by its tail; "it am biled puppy."

A cry of disgust broke from all, and a perfect yell of horror from Tilda, who stood at the foot of the table holding up by their tails a rat in either hand, which she had extracted from the pie.

"You willing, you've done this!" cried Jumbo.

"Done what?" said Charley.

"Yer's had dis ting serbed up, an' by golly yer shall hab de lot ob it," cried Jumbo.

And swinging the animal round by its tail, the negro caught Charley so heavy a blow with it in his face, that he knocked him over, chair and all, to the floor.

CHAPTER VI.

IN WHICH TWO RASCALS ENTER INTO A BASE CONSPIRACY.

A HUGE junk, borne swiftly along by its matting sails, passed through the long lines of boats that contained some of the floating population, thousands of whom had never been on shore, whose families had been born in the floating houses, and who had lived and died therein, without having once set foot on dry land.

Curiously many a water resident gazed after the junk with its dragon-shaped head and the large eye, painted on its bows.

She was manned by a large crew of swarthy-faced Chinese, among whom could here and there be seen a Malay sailor.

In the stern of the vessel stood two men in deep converse.

One was a cruel, crafty and merciless wretch of middle age if his face was any index to his character.

In the belt which confined his embroidered blouse was stuck a pistol with a carved and inlaid stock, and at his side hung a short sword.

The other was many years younger and totally unarmed.

Evidently he was ill at ease, for ever and anon his hand would be pressed to his back, and he would writhe as if in pain.

Speaking in his own language, the elder, who was the commander of the vessel, laid his hand on the other's arm, and in a voice rendered low so that those about the deck could not catch what was said, exclaimed—

"How learned you this you tell me, Ching? If it be as you say, then we might possess ourselves of those precious stones, for they would yield us more wealth than would a dozen cruises."

"I tell you I saw them," replied Ching. "I stole into their apartment, thinking it was empty, and saw her gloating over her treasures. I had gone to see what was there, and did not expect to find her, and the sight of those sparkling gems made me forget what I was doing, and I drew close to her when I was discovered."

"What did you then?" asked the other.

He eagerly awaited the reply.

"'MUSSY ON DIS POOR OLE NIGGER,' CRIED JUMBO."

"I told her I had seen and loved her. I thought she would have pitied me, but she struck me, and then, others coming, I could not kill her, and so she beat me till I am a mass of bruises."

"I would have stuck my knife into her heart and taken the jewels from her."

"No, for that might have been ill for me. The mandarin rather favours these foreign barbarians. He has been to their country and says that they are not so bad as we believe; and many suspicions have been hinted to him of my father's doubtful trading and presumed wealth; and had I killed her then he might have made it an excuse to satisfy himself of my father's dealings and confiscated his gold."

"Your father should blind his eyes as I do with presents. Have not orders gone forth that such as I should be swept from the rivers and seas?—but what is the emperor's edict worth? He might save the vermilion pencil; its writing is worthless, because I close his governor's eyes and ears by presents."

"My father will not part with his gold, and I dared not tell him what I had discovered, or he would have stolen the wealth himself and kept it to himself; but you will share it with me, brave Chow-Woo.

"By the bones of my father, yes!" said the other. "I claim not all booty for myself, but share it with my followers. All that I demand is absolute obedience to my will, and but few have ever attempted to dispute it."

"And those?" said Ching-Fow shiveringly.

Chow-Woo, the Chinese pirate, tapped the hilt of his sword and the stock of his pistol, and then pointed over the side of the junk.

Then turning quicky to his companion he asked—

"What want those barbarians in the land of the brother of the sun?"

"Listen?" said Ching-Fow. "When they knew it not I have had my eyes upon them and my ears open, and what they have spoken I have treasured here."

And he struck his bosom.

"That is well," said the pirate. "Open your heart to me. You have known me long and how fair have been my dealings with friends, if not with foes."

"I do."

"Then what have you heard and seen?"

"That, though English and African, they have come across the mountains from the Asiatic city of Bokhara; that there they did save the king, and that he rewarded them all with gold and jewels of rarity and great value."

"I have heard of the city beyond the mountains," said the captain. "But why sought they not their own lands? What seek they here?"

"They have followed another Englishman who stole the wife or intended wife, of one of them, and they believe him to be in or near Canton. They are here in the hope of finding him and her. Such is what I make out from their talk."

"Said you that they all possess gold and jewels?"

"If what I overheard when I lay with my ear to the wall be true, all have great wealth and are willing to sacrifice much of it to overtake the man they come in search of, and get back the woman one of the Englishmen loves."

"By the bones of my father! but this wealth must change hands!" said the captain in a hissing whisper. "How many are there of them?"

"Five men and two women," replied Ching-Fow. "One of them a she-devil."

And he writhed again as he thought of the castigation he had received at Sally's hands.

"Seven of them," muttered Chow-Woo. "And these barbarians fight like dragons. Don't I know how nearly I lost my junk when they tried to board me, and how I only saved my ship and men by hurling stink-pots amongst them! We cannot do the work, you and I; we must have some of our men, and they must have their share as well."

"That will lessen yours and mine," said Ching-Fow.

"Better that than lose it all, and our lives as well," said Chow-Woo; "unless we kill them while they sleep, and you get rid of their bodies."

"No, no," said Ching-Fow, "they must not die in my father's house."

"Where then?" asked Chow-Woo.

"Could you not betray them to the Purple Pagoda? Once within that who would know their fate?"

"By the bones of my father, you must be mad," said the captain. "Shall I show to the barbarian the secrets of that place, secrets that I and my followers and friends have kept so long and so truly? Were a search made for them there, not even the governor could save me and my good men from death."

"Who shall know that they are there, or were there if we lay our plans well? Who dares enter some of it's chambers but you and your followers? Who knows the mysteries of its walls but you and those in league with you?"

"True," said the pirate, "none but those who are sworn to secrecy."

"Then the task is easy. You may obtain wealth, and I revenge."

"How?" asked the captain of the junk.

"Listen. You have in your crew an Englishman, or did have when you started on your last expedition, though I do not see him on deck?"

"No he is hiding lest he be recognised by some of the English now in these waters; for you know that he escaped after killing his gaoler, and that if he be re-captured he would be hung directly."

"If recaptured?" said Ching-Fow. "Little chance of that."

"Ay, little chance if his capture was sought by one of our people; but these English are dangerous, and were all the forts ashore to aid me, I might be unable to save him; and even if I did beat them off, those English have a way of making our emperor and mandarins listen to their complaints. No, no, it is only the fool who seeks his own destruction. But what of the Englishman?"

"He could write to these barbarians in his own language, and by pretending that the man and woman they seek have found refuge in the Purple Pagoda, lure them to it. Once safe within its walls their wealth is ours, and their bodies may feed the fishes that swim in the waters of our rivers and bays."

The pirate thought deeply for some moments, then he said—

"But if they brought not their wealth with them?"

"Then could I find it at home and share with you," said Ching-Fow.

"How know I that you would share fairly?" asked the pirate.

"Do I not trust you?"

"Yes."

"Then why fear to trust me?"

Bad as he was, the pirate captain had ever acted fairly by his lawless crew. He did not believe in thief robbing thief; but he knew well of the antecedents of Ching-Fow and his worthy son, and felt he could not place the reliance in either of them that he knew they could in him and his lawless crew of pirates.

The description Ching had given Chow-Woo of what he had seen when he stole so softly behind Sally," and what he had heard of the conversation of Ned and his friends when they believed no prying eye was near, and no eavesdropper to overhear them, set the captain's heart throbbing violently, and he longed to hold the wondrous wealth in his hands, even though to do so it would be necessary to imbue those hands in blood.

"Be it so," he said hoarsely. "I shall anchor opposite the pagoda soon, and then I'll think how best to bring these barbarians within its walls."

"No better plan than that I have suggested," said Ching-Fow.

At present I see none. But I must think for we know not the names of the man and woman they seek."

"But I do. I have heard them so often," said Ching-Fow exultingly.

"What are they?"

"I know not which is which, but one they call Minnie, the other Bill. The Englishman will know which is the man and which is the woman."

"You say well. Now get back to your father's house, and let not your eyes or voice betray your motives to these barbarians. When I send the letter my messenger shall see you."

He gave some rapid orders, and his well-trained crew soon brought the heavy junk almost stationary on the water.

Then Ching-Fow dropped into a boat with four of the men and was rowed on shore.

The boat returned, the sails were again spread, and, an hour later, the pirate junk was at anchor opposite the Purple Pagoda.

CHAPTER VII.

IN WHICH THERE IS A SMASH UP AND A FALL DOWN, AND THE CHINAMAN GETS THE MOST OF IT.

NED, with a shudder of disgust, plucked Harry's sleeve, and together they left the table and the apartment.

'Dolf quickly followed, but not until he had given Charley a kick as that sportive youth struggled to his feet, half-blinded by the gravy that filled his eyes, and smeared his smarting cheeks.

Sally also sprang up, and dashed into the next apartment with her handkerchief pressed tightly to her mouth.

"Here, I say, stow that, do you hear," cried Charley, mopping at his eyes with his coat sleeve.

"Guess I will stow it," replied Jumbo, "an' dat's whar I'll stow it to, an' dat's in de buzzim ob de wagerbone what had it stewed for our dinner. Yer shall hab ebery bit ob it. I doesn't go shares in dis yer ting, I tells yer, so yer habs de lot."

And Jumbo laid into Charley's head and bosom with the puppy till, the tail coming away, the body flew across the table, and catching Tilda on the chin, made her drop the rats, which she still held gazing at in stony horror, and bound to her feet with a loud shriek.

"Oh, murder!" cried Tilda. "I'se bound to hab hyderphoby arter dat, I know I is, yer willing. What for did yer frow dat ar dog in my face?"

"Hear dat now? I neber frowed it," returned Jumbo.

"Yes, you did," said Charley, wiping his face and bosom on the end of the table-cloth.

"Course him did," said Tilda, "didn't I see him frow it at me? Am dat de 'lection yer perfesses for me, to hit me on de chin wid a dead dog, an' while I was a-suffering from dem ar spagems ob sickerness, what dem ar nasty rats gib?"

"How'd I help it?" cried Jumbo. "It wain't my fault; de dead dog jumped away from its tail itself; an' no wonner. What more nat'ral den for a dog to jump arter a rat as yer was a-holding up for him? It's human nater, it am, an' nuffin more."

"I like the human nature," said Charley.

"I'se glad yer does," said Jumbo, "a'cos I reckons yer've had de biggest lot ob de animal, an' yer won't want not no grease for dat ar hair ob yours for a month."

"Nor his clothes either," remarked Jack. "They look as if he had fallen into a candle-maker's vat."

"Vat's dat?" asked Jumbo. "Am dat English?"

"English, you fool!" cried Jack. "Of course not; it's Greece."

And Jack jumped up to join the others in the next apartment.

"Here's a pretty mess you've made, you nigger-headed kangaroo," said Charley.

"Dat's trufe," replied Jumbo.

"You and Tilda between you have been and gone and spoiled the loveliest banquet that was ever enjoyed; you deserve to be stewed yourself, you do."

"Dat's trufe again."

"And this is your gratitude for getting old Ching-Fow to provide the finest of feasts for us!"

And Charley pointed to his grease-besmeared garments.

"I knowed as how yer were de willing what did it," said Jumbo; "I'd a swored to it if I neber seed it; yer always was de dirtiest wagerbone what eber 'graced dis yer worle; an' I'se a-going to hab it put to de wote ob dis 'lustrious assembly weder, to sabe our own 'specterbility, an' uphole de honour ob our digernerties, you shan't be pitched neck and crop out ob dis extinguished circle."

"I wotes dat he am," said Tilda.

"An' I wotes ditter," said Jumbo; "an' as dat am de frowing wote, I'se bound to order yer, Master Charley, to go away an' neber see us not no more."

"Dat's yer banishment," said Tilda. "So perhaps yer'll take yer wanishment."

And Tilda pointed to the door.

"Oh, I know your little game," said Charley; "you and Jumbo want to get rid of me the same as you have the others so that you may both gorge the lot between you. But what else is to be expected of those who come of a race of cannibals?"

"Tilda, frow dat ar pie at his head!" cried Jumbo, seizing the large dish and raising it. "Dat hinsult shall be washed out ob him in dese yer dishes."

Tilda seized the pie, and poised it for the throw.

"Yah, you'll break them," cried Charley, as he made for the door and dashed round into the passage, nearly knocking over the corpulent form of old Ching-Fow as he entered the room to ask if anything more was required.

The old Celestial had chosen a bad time.

As he crossed the threshold of the door, the large dish hurled by Jumbo caught him in the chest, and while the pie-dish struck him on the right knee-cap, causing him to utter a cry between a shriek and a yell and double himself up as though he were suffering the most acute pain in the region of the stomach.

There was a crashing of china as the dishes reached the floor.

Then Ching-Fow in his wriggling and twisting, happened to step upon a well-cooked rat, and the soft substance slipping from under him, he came down with his face and body in the *debris* of the dishes, and the paste, meat and gravy of that horrible pie.

"Oh golly;" cried Tilda, "I do beliebe he's a-going to eat it."

"I reckons he may if he likes," said Jumbo; "but I isn't a-going to stay here to look at him. Ugh! oh Lor'! I feels dat awful bad, I does."

"An' I'se about done up, too," said Tilda! "though when I was de stewardess aboard ob dat——"

But Jumbo was making for the door of the other apartment, and Tilda did not finish the sentence, but rose quickly to follow him.

"Oh, Chinee manee hurtee headee," cried old Ching-Fow.

At this Jumbo and Tilda turned.

The old Celestial had struggled to a sitting position, and was rubbing his nose and forehead, each of which had been cut by the broken china amongst which he had fallen.

"Muchee breakee, muchee payee, poor Chinee manee," moaned the Celestial, shaking his head at the wrecked crockery.

"Bigee platee costee muchee monee; dishee smashee have to payee."

"I guess yer no need to be afeart yer won't get de money for de smash," said Jumbo. "I reckons dat we 'lustrous inderwiderels ain't a-going to run away widout paying."

"Ob course we isn't," said Tilda; "de idea ob de ting! We'se too 'specterble we is for dat ar."

"Lovee foodee wastee muchee," said the Chinaman, pointing to the contents of the pie at his feet.

"You ole willing, yer!" cried Jumbo. "Yer ought ter be 'shamed ob yerself to send dat ar beastly stuff to dis yer room for our dinner. I guess I'd like ter make yer eat it, I would."

"Muchee likee eatee," said Ching-Fow. "Pupee goodee, ratee finee—nicee nicee."

"Oh, yer beast!" cried Tilda.

"Ratee muchee nicee; all the samee boilee, roastee, stewee," said Ching-Fow, forgetting his pains evidently in the prospect of a feast to his liking.

"Yer nasty dirty man!" said Tilda. "Yer don't mean ter say as yer'd eat dem ar tings?"

"Eatee allee."

"Den, yer ole cannerbile ob a yeller-faced Chinerman, just yer clean up de lot an' take it away wid yer: for if yer goes ter gobble any ob it here I'se bound ter be ill, I is, an' when I'se ill I'se awful wexed; an' when I'se wexed I'se bound to hit somefing."

The Celestial evidently perfectly understood what Jumbo meant, for he glided to the gong, struck it, and then bowed low to Tilda.

"Eglishmanee tellee me have puppee and ratee cookee for dinnee. Chinee manee obey Englishmanee. Chinee manee no blamee. Muchee sorry no likee. Gladee berree muchee, get what he likee."

"I reckons as how dis chile 'ull go widout anyfing," said Jumbo.

"I couldn't eben eat a sheep's head now, I couldn't, nor tripe and inguns, nor cow-heel, nor nuffin," said Tilda. "But dere's de oders, yer know."

"I'll go an' ask 'em what dey'll hab," said Jumbo.

And he went to seek Ned and the rest

of the party, who had retired in disgust from the table.

As he passed into the next apartment the Chinese attendants entered, grinned, and smacked their lips when they saw that the repast had not been tasted.

Here was a chance of some of it coming to their share, and eagerly and delightedly did they seize upon the dishes and bear them away, under the orders of their master, old Ching-Fow.

The fragments were picked and swept up off the matting, and longing eyes followed the man who carried the puppy from the apartment.

Jumbo returned.

Old Ching-Fow bent low before him, and waited his commands with the most obsequious attention.

"Dey's all dat ar upset, dey is, dat dey won't want not no grub for a week. Dat ar puppy an' dem ar rats did it; an' I guess dey won't none ob 'em suffer from ndergestion for a little while."

"Veree soree," said Ching-Fow.

"I reckons yer is," said Jumbo, "but guess yer'd been more sorry if we'd at dem ar tings instead ob leabing 'em or you to swaller."

"If dey calls dat awful stuff wittles," aid Tilda, "den I reckons de sooner it hokes dem de better."

"Englishmanee no likee because he don't tastee," said the Celestial. "How he know he no likee when he no tastee? Chinee manee tastee and like muchee— so Englishmanee."

"I guess yer'd better go after the wittles," said Jumbo, "or I'll be gibing yer a tastee ob dis yer footee at de bottom ob yer backee."

Jumbo raised his foot, and Ching-Fow the elder took two leaps towards the door.

"No likee ratee pupee, muchee foolee!" he yelled, and then dashed from the apartment.

"Dat's trufe," said Jumbo.

"Get out," said Tilda. "What's yer a-saying ob?"

"I reckons I doesn't know."

"Yer allus was a iggerant nigger," said Tilda. "Yer allus saying what yer doesn't mean an' what yer doesn't know."

"Dat's trufe," said Jumbo.

"Den just gib me dat ar arm ob yers," said Tilda, "an' we'll jine de ladies an' gen'lem ob dis yer interlecteral an' extinguished party."

Jumbo offered his arm and led her into the next apartment, where they were greeted with roars of laughter.

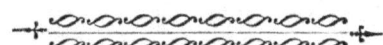

CHAPTER VIII.

IN WHICH POT AND KETTLE CALL EACH OTHER BLACK.

IT was a brilliant morning; the sunshine bathed the earth in gold, and the gilding of the pagodas and the burnished signs of the houses glowed as if on fire.

The rivers and canals looked like streams of gold, while the paint and gilt of junks and boats glittered and sparkled in the glorious sunlight.

On the waters the fishermen plied their trade.

On shore, those who had time, played shuttlecock and flew kites, the quaint devices of which, and the gilding thereon, made them look like fiends and fairies gamboling in the blue ether above.

Ned and his companions had made a hearty meal of rice and sweet potatoes, washed down with tea made in the thinnest of rice china, and having an aroma and flavour seldom discovered in the decoction brewed at home.

Jumbo and Tilda, who had, despite the chaff of Charley, 'Dolf and Jack, and the solicitations of Ned and Harry, resolved to attire themselves in Chinese costume, sat at the large open window fanning themselves with gorgeously-painted fans.

Charley had given great offence by his practical joke of the day before, and the whole company had resolved themselves into a committee to consider how best to punish him for the trick he had played them.

Of course his banishment by Jumbo and Tilda only amused him, and after about an hour, he had returned to the house of Ching-Fow and gone to rest as if nothing had happened.

"I think he ought to be well punished," Sally had said; "and if you'll leave it in my hands I'll soon show him what sort of a woman I am."

But Jack had told her to mind her own business, and Sally had sulkily retired.

At breakfast, however, the subject had been again mentioned by Sally; and Ned, finding that it was necessary to show the annoyance of all at the dinner provided by Charley's order of the previous day, addressing that young gentleman, remarked—

"It was too bad of you, Charley. You nearly made us all ill."

"Very sorry, I'm sure," said Charley, "but couldn't resist it, you know. I knew Jumbo and Tilda came of a cannibal race, and thought they would really enjoy the feast."

"Dat ar's a lie," said Jumbo.

"And a whopper," added Tilda. "My fader neber eat nuffin at all, an' my moder was a wegetablearian; so how's I come ob a cannerbile race? Tell me dat ar."

"Haven't got time," said Charley. "Perhaps I made a mistake with you, but I've heard Jumbo tell a fellow when he's been rowing with him that he'd eaten better men than him before breakfast. What better proof can you have of his being a cannibal than his own words?"

Ned smiled.

"You ought to be a queen's counsel, Charley," he said. "You would convict a man out of his own mouth. But look here, old fellow, they are all so annoyed at yesterday's freak that they insist upon your having to suffer for it."

"My back's broad," said Charley, "and I can take a lot of licking without holloaing."

"I guess dat de wotes ob me and Tilda has dispoged ob de case," said Jumbo, "and dat we dribes him out ob dis yer company as not fit ter 'sociate wid gen'lems an' ladies ob de dignerty ob ourselbes."

"What! turn your back on an old chum?" said Charley.

"Sar," said Jumbo, "I 'pudiates de chummy part ob dat ar observation. I'se not too proud to say dat 'n de nat'ral

'fections ob dis yer bery gentle heart ob mine I did 'low my generosity ter get de better ob my 'scretion, an dat out ob pity I did 'low yer to become de 'sociate ob dis yer extinguished cullered pusson; but I'se found yer ter be unworthy de 'spect as I conferred upon yer, and darfore I wabes yer off wid dis yer fan ob mine, and says ter myself, 'Jumbo, Jumbo, how could yer eber 'sociate wid such a wishous and contempterble pussonage?"

"Well, I do like that," said Charley, grinning.

"I'se berry glad ter know yer does," said Jumbo.

"I say, old man."

"Dat's me."

"How long have you been respectable?" asked Charley.

"I guess I was neber nuffin else."

"What! even when they clapped you into the state prison for taking away the child's penny his mother had given him to buy candies with?" said Charley.

"I tink dat dis suberjec' had better be changed," said Jumbo. "Dar ar some pussons who get pussonal in der remarks; an' I 'peal ter yer, Massa Ned, wheder it ain't better to drop de suberjec' den to get pussonal an' wound de feelings ob de bery sensitive buzzoms ob de highly interlecteral an' edercated ladies an' gen'lems ob dis yer party."

"I had you there, old man," said Charley.

"Guess dat's trufe," said Jumbo, fanning himself violently.

"What is?" asked Sally. "The stealing the child's penny and being put in the state prison for doing so?"

"I neber conwicts myself," said Jumbo.

"But somebody else did, said Charley, "and he was so satisfied with your honour, etc., that he——"

"Dar's no 'cesserty to go into dat ar painful suberjec'."

"But surely there's no truth in Charley's insinuation?" said Harry. "He's only chaffing you, Jumbo."

"Dat's trufe," replied Jumbo.

"Which?" asked Sally. "Charley's assertion or the chaff."

"Why, ob course, de chaff."

"Then you admit, Jumbo that you did take the child's coin?" said Ned.

"Bress my soul, what's yer talking 'bout?" said Jumbo. "D'ye tink dat dis yer 'spec'able cullered gen'lam 'ud go an' do dat ar? Just let me 'splain."

"Go on then, Jumbo; because if Charley has libelled you, we'll all kick him."

"Dat's jus' what he wants, Massa Ned."

"But the explanation," said Ned, smiling.

"De 'splanation? Jus' so. Well, de 'splanation is—— Yes, dat's it."

"What? You have not told us," said Harry, nudging Ned's arm.

"Dat's a'cos I wants to spare dat ar willing's feelings, yer know. I'se so tender-hearted I is. Ain't I Tilda?" said Jumbo.

"Or else yer a bery wicked-hearted ole waggerbone," replied Tilda.

"Dat's trufe. But dat 'splanation 'bout dat ar penny am dis yer," said Jumbo. "But dar, I don't s'pose yer'll care to yere 'bout it, as yer knows what a wishous and wengeful waggerbone dat ar Charley is."

"Yes, yes. Go on Jumbo," cried Harry, 'Dolf, and Jack, in chorus.

"Well, den, dis yer's de fac'," said Jumbo. "As I said afore, I'se got a bery tender heart in dis yer tender buzzim."

"Well, heave ahead," said 'Dolf.

"Don't yer be in sich a hurry. I'se a-trying to fink what I'se going to say, 'cos i can tell only de trufe. If I was a-going ter tell a lie I wouldn't keep yer waiting, but as I'se going ter tell de trufe, I'se got ter make it up, ain't I?"

The others could not help laughing at this, and Jumbo, after a pause, said—

"Now yer can b'lieve dis or not, but dis yer's what I says it was. Yer see, I knowed Charley an' Charley knowed me, so dat's plain we knowed each other."

"Quite plain," said Ned.

"Well, den, dat ar Charley was always a willing, an' I neber could break him ob dat ar willerny in spite ob all I could do to perwent him. So one day we sees a poor ole bline man and dat ar waggerbone ob a Charley tells de bline man dat he'd gib him tuppence only he couldn't get change for a shilling; an' den says if de ole man had got change he'd gib him de shilling."

"And did he?" asked Jack.

"Don't yer be in a hurry, 'cos I wants ter be bery 'tickler 'bout what I says. Well, de bline man had got de change an' he gibs it to Charley. D'ye see de willerny ob it?"

"Not yet," said Ned. "It seems to me that Charley was doing a kind action, for of course he gave the poor blind man the shilling."

"Ob course he did," said Jumbo. "But, den, stop a minute. Don't yer see dat ar shilling was a bad un?"

"Oh!" groaned the others.

"But where did he get the bad shilling?" asked Ned.

"Where'd he get it?" asked Jumbo. "Why ob course I gib it him, and tole him what to do wid it. Dat shows de difference atween us. I gib him de shilling for nuffin, but he gib de shilling to de poor bline man, and made tenpence by it; an' when I asked for my share, he wouldn't gib it me. Dat was de gratertood what I got. But dar, de guilty neber prospers, yer know. Wengeance was just behind him, an' he was collared, took afore de justice, and put in the state prison for free months."

"That was mean. But what has that to do with the penny and the child?" asked Harry.

"I'se going to 'splain," replied Jumbo, "though ob course I was wexed at not getting my share; yet dis heart ob mine in its tenderness made me determined ter rescue him; so as I couldn't get at him from de outside ob de prison I thought I'd get in. So I tooked away de kid's penny so as to make him kick up a row an' get myself collared, dat's de fac'."

"Whew!" whistled Charley.

"Oh!" groaned the rest in chorus.

"Did you succeed in rescuing your friend from durance vile?" asked Ned.

"How could I? Dey kept me dar such a bressed while dat dey let him out a long time afore dey did me, an' so I didn't get not no chance ter do it, and now yer sees de gratertood I gets for dat ar nobilerty ob soul which I showed in dat ar case."

"Jumbo," said Ned, "I'm afraid that both yourself and Charley have been two most infernal scoundrels."

"Well, dat's trufe," said Jumbo, fanning himself.

"A pretty pair," whispered Harry.

"Right you are, dear boy. But I

think we have reformed them. Look here, Harry, we must not be too severe on Charley for yesterday's joke, for we haven't forgotten our own schooldays. So I'll give him a quiet wigging when I get a chance. Halloa! who's here?"

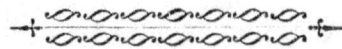

CHAPTER IX

IN WHICH NED RECEIVES A LETTER, AND JUMBO AND TILDA HAVE A STRANGE AND FEARFUL VISITOR.

It was one of Ching-Fow's servants that entered and stood bowing on the threshold.

"Well?" said Ned.

"Chinee manee wantee see Massee Nimblee. Got notee for he. Shall I send he to ee?"

"Yes," said Ned. "It is doubtless a note from Dick, for I could not expect any communication from England yet awhile."

"Well, then, Ned, I think we'll be off again on our search," said Harry, "and you can follow after us, as no doubt you will want to write an answer to Dick."

"Do, dear friend," said Ned.

"And I guess I and Tilda will go with you," said Jumbo.

"What! in that dress?"

"Ob course."

"No you won't," said Harry.

"No, no, Jumbo," said Ned; "you and Tilda in that attire will only excite the ridicule of the people as you did yesterday; and as I do not care that all are away from here at the same time, I beg you and Tilda will stay till our return."

"Well, I guess it's precious hot, and I don't care much 'bout going out just now," said Jumbo, "so I'll do me meandering where I is."

And Jumbo strode about the room, fanning himself, and thinking that he was a most charming figure in his quaint costume.

If other people could not admire him he could at least admire himself, and that was something.

Sally elected to accompany Jack, and while the Chinese servant went to bring in the messenger, the party attired themselves for their journey.

"We meet again at the usual time, I suppose, Ned, if nothing transpires earlier?" said Harry.

"Yes, dear boy," replied Ned

Harry shook hands with his friend, and followed by 'Dolf, Jack, Charley and Sally, left the house.

The next moment, a young, and not bad-looking Celestial was ushered into the apartment, and the servant bowing and pointing out Ned to him, retired.

"You have a note for me?" said Ned, holding out his hand.

The Celestial, without saying a word, handed him a letter.

It was addressed on the outside to Ned Nimble, and unfolding it, revealed a well-written letter in English.

"Pray wait till I read it," said Ned, "as you may require an answer."

So saying, Ned drew back to the wall, and began to peruse the letter.

Jumbo and Tilda crossed the large apartment, and stood fanning themselves near the window.

"Jumbo," said Tilda, in a severe, though low voice, "I'm ashamed ob yer."

"Guess dat's trufe," said Jumbo.

"So you'se been a tief, has yer? and Tilda Tompkins, has been an' lowered ob her digernity by connersending ter let yer make lub ter me?"

"What's yer talking 'bout?" said Jumbo hiding his face in his fan.

"De willing what yer is, dat's what I'se talking 'bout."

"Yer don't beliebe dat ar Charley does yer?" said Jumbo.

"If I doesn't I've got ter beliebe yer, I s'pose?" said Tilda.

"'Bout what?"

"Dat ar penny what yer stoled."

"Git out! Dat ar was only dis yer chile's nonsense. I neber stole no penny."

"And neber was put in prison?"

"Neber."

"What for yer say so den?" asked Tilda.

"Jus' ter make 'em laugh, dat's all," said Jumbo.

But he still kept his face hidden by his fan.

"Jumbo!"

"Dat's me."

"Where yes 'spect ter die when yer go ter?"

"All among de angels right up in de sky," said Jumbo.

"I reckons as yer'll go to dat oder place. Dey'll neber put wings on dem ar years ob your'n."

"Guess dey will, though."

"I tells yer what, Jumbo," said Tilda, "I beliebes yer's a bery bad man, an' dat one ob dese yer days de debil 'ull come an' run away wid yer, dat I does."

"De deb——Oh, golly! I'se a gone coon for suah!"

Tilda followed Jumbo's horrified gaze, then uttered a yell of terror, grasped at Jumbo's hand, and sank on her knees at his side.

Through the large open window floated a terrible object.

On it came towards them and hovered above them.

Jumbo, half paralysed with terror, put forth his fan to evade it, his trembling hand wafting the wind upon it.

The frightful object seemed to shiver as if with laughter, as with outspread wings it floated over them, its long, pointed tail just clearing the floor.

"Mussy on dis poor ole nigger, Massa Debil," gasped Jumbo. "I reckon I'll neber do wrong no more. Yer don't want me; yer's come for dat ar Charley, or else for dis yer Tilda. Oh, Massa Ned, Massa Ned, you'se a good man, yer is. Come and dribe him away."

Ned had looked up from his letter, and seeing the string attached to the object, which Jumbo and Tilda from their position could not, he guessed what it was in a moment.

But though he could not suppress a smile at the abject fear, and yet comical attitudes of Jumbo and Tilda, he did not open their eyes to the fact that the awful-looking demon was only one of those kites which the Chinese delight in making and flying.

The young Chinaman was fairly convulsed with laughter.

But neither Jumbo nor Tilda had eyes for anything but the terrible object before them.

Jumbo's terror at last became so strong that he too dropped on his knees, crying—

"Oh, gib me anoder chance, good Massa Debil, an' I'll neber tell no more lies, nor steal no more pennies from little children. Oh, hab mussy, good Massa Debil, hab mussy on dis poor ole brack sinner!"

"An' dis poor ole brack sinneress," whined Tilda. "I isn't wuff de taking away—oh, I isn't?"

Swaying from side to side, the horribly-painted kite descended till its pointed tail touched the floor, and then it fell forward on the heads of them both.

With one fearful yell, Tilda lay prone on the floor.

With one horrible shriek, Jumbo sprang to his feet and dashed to the window.

His foot was already on the sill, when Ned sprang upon him and drew him back.

"Oh, good Massa Debil—good—oh!"

"Fool! What would you do?" cried Ned in severe tones.

"Sabe me—sabe a poor ole nigger," gasped Jumbo.

"You insensate idiot!" cried Ned, angrily. "What is to harm you? Is your conscience so black that a kite can frighten the very senses out of you."

"A kite!" gasped Jumbo.

"Yes idiot; look at this string. The thing you fear is but paper."

He held the string and drew the paper figure from off the half-swooning Tilda.

Jumbo looked abashed for a few moments.

Then a light came into his terrified eyes.

A smile began to flutter over his lips.

"Ob course it's a kite, he said. "You didn't fink, Master Ned, as dis yer chile was afeared ob dat ar ting, did yer? I was only habing a lark wid dat ar Tilda."

A flush of anger leaped to Ned's face, but passed away in a moment, and he said—

"Jumbo, you are a frightful liar!"

"Dat's trufe," said Jumbo.

Ned strode back to where the young Celestial stood, and recommenced perusing the letter he held in his hand.

Jumbo kicked his foot through the kite.

"Dar," he said, "if yer tought yer could frighten dis yer 'specterble cullered gen'lam, yer's made a great mistook. I reckon yer's come to de wrong sbop to make peoples feel afeared. Just yer take dat for yer imperence, an' dat—an' dat!"

Jumbo kicked a hole through the large kite at each word, till it lay utterly wrecked upon the floor.

Then he turned to Tilda, who had so far recovered herself as to gain a sitting position.

"Gib us yer hand an' up yer comes. I'se done for dat ar fing. I'se ashamed ob yer to find what a fool yer's made yerself, a-screeching an' a-howling as if it was de debble hisself as had come arter yer, dat I is."

He drew Tilda to her feet, and that lady had no sooner reached them than, annoyed either at her own fright or Jumbo's barefaced falsehood, she slapped first one and then the other of the negro's cheeks.

"Yer disrepertable ole nigger!" she cried; "Yer wicked brack waggerbone, yer's de worstest man dat eber I see, an' I'se 'shamed dat I eber had anyfing ter do wid such a willing."

And Tilda flounced off into the next apartment, her nose high in the air.

"Guess dat's trufe," said Jumbo. "But I'se got somefing to hab my wengeance on, and by golly I'se de boy to hab it."

And he began smashing up the framework of the kite; then catching hold of the string, he looked round for a knife to sever it, but ere he could find one there came a fierce and sudden jerk, the bent and broken canes got twisted round his neck, and he was dragged to the open window.

"Gor-a-mighty," gasped Jumbo, "it's de debbil arter all."

The next moment he would have been dragged out of the window had not the string broken; and he fell on his back on the floor.

At the same moment Ned crumpled the letter fiercely in his hand, and shouted excitedly—

"A prisoner in the Purple Pagoda? Minnie, dear Minnie, I will rescue you or die!"

CHAPTER X.

IN WHICH DICK DAREWELL BECOMES A CAPTAIN.

THE vessel on which Dick Darewell was lieutenant, or more commonly called mate, having got the whole of her cargo on board, and safely stowed in the hold, only waited the tide to slip from her moorings and set sail for England.

But the tide would not serve for some three hours, and Dick approaching the captain, who was pacing up and down the bridge, saluted him in true nautical fashion.

"Captain Bennet," he said, "as the tide will not serve for three hours, and as I have friends ashore whom I should like to bid good-bye before we sail, will you give me permission to go ashore for an hour."

"With pleasure, Mr. Darewell," said the captain, "but you must return in two hours at the latest."

"Certainly, sir."

"Are all hands aboard?"

"Yes, sir."

"And sober?"

"As far as I can judge, they are," replied Dick. "Leastways, they are all fit for duty."

"Glad to hear it," said Captain Bennet. "If I could have my way, I'd have all hands aboard at least one day and one night before sailing. It is a lamentable fact that scarce a ship starts on her journey but half her crew are intoxicated."

"I think, sir, you will have no cause to complain of the hands. Some of them have taken an extra glass, but all are fit for duty."

"Very well, then, take the boat, and don't let the men land. Bid them return to the ship, and when you want to come aboard, I will send the boat for you."

"I will do so, sir. Ahoy, there, launch and man the captain's gig."

"Ay, ay, sir."

While the men where launching the boat—for the ship lay some fifty yards from the wharf—Dick again approached the captain and entered into conversation with him.

"Halloa! what do they want?" said the captain, suddenly pointing to a boat which came alongside, and which the men were making fast to the chains of the ship. "That's one of the 'Lord Warden's' boats."

"Yes, sir; and one of her men are coming aboard," said Dick, as a fine looking seaman came up a rope hanging over the side.

"Well, my man," said Captain Bennet, advancing, as the sailor dropped to the deck.

The man pulled at his hat brim.

"A letter, sir, from Cap'n Jones, of the 'Lord Warden'" he said, pulling a note out of his jacket pocket.

"For me?"

"For Cap'n Bennet." replied the sailor. "And I reckon I ain't far out of my reckoning if I say you are the skipper of this craft."

"You're quite right, my man," said the captain, opening the letter, as Dick went forward to where the men were launching the captain's gig."

The captain perused the letter and looked thoughtful.

"So bad as that," he muttered; "I'm very sorry to hear it."

Then looking up, he cried—

"Mr. Darewell."

Dick hurried to his side.

"Captain Jones is seriously ill, and desires me to let him have one of my officers who can navigate his ship to England. She will be ready in three days, and the state of his health utterly precludes his taking command."

"I am very sorry to hear he is so bad," replied Dick. "But surely his first mate can navigate the vessel."

"His first mate has been sent aboard the 'Sea King' that sailed yesterday, and he dare not trust the ship in the hands of his other officers. Therefore I see nothing for it, Mr. Darewell, but to send you on board the 'Lord Warden.'"

"I shall be very sorry to leave you, Captain Bennet," said Dick.

"And I shall be sorry to lose you, Mr. Darewell. But I know your abilities as a seaman, and you may not get such a chance again in a hurry of becoming a captain, for if you take your ship safe

into port, the company will recognise your services, depend upon it."

Dick bowed.

"As you say, sir, it gives me the chance of promotion; and if her crew only obey orders I have no fear of myself."

"Nor I," said Bennet; "and if we can get two of the 'Lord Warden's' crew to change ships, you can have Sam Splice and Tom Halyard in their place."

"Two good men, sir," said Dick, "and I thank you."

"Then I'll write to Captain Jones. Steward let the 'Lord Warden's' men have a stiff glass of grog."

"Ay, ay, sir," cried the steward.

The captain went to his state room to write his letter.

"Now, he's a skipper arter my own heart," said the bearer of the note, "and hang me if I won't be one to sail with him, if so be as he'll let me tramp these planks."

"Oh, he'll take you," said Dick. "Hoist in the boat, boys; I shall not go ashore."

The boat was again pulled up to the davits.

The sailors of the "Lord Warden" had their grog, and the captain wrote his reply.

Dick sought out Sam Splice and Tom Halyard.

They agreed to go on board the "Lord Warden," and set about looking up their traps.

Before the captain had finished his letter, two of the "Lord Warden's" crew had agreed to take their places, and promised to return with their chests before the tide was at the full.

Though Dick had expressed his regret at having to leave Captain Bennet, yet he was secretly glad.

On the "Lord Warden" he could do as he pleased.

Here he could not.

He had a superior, and that superior would never have permitted him to do what now he would be able to perform.

And that was nothing less than the carrying off of a young and beautiful Chinese girl.

Towards her Dick's intentions were pure and honourable.

In fact, he was madly in love with her.

Her father, Whang-Sing, was one of

the wealthiest tea growers and one of the most flourishing merchants in Canton.

He was a widower, with one daughter, named Gustee-Ge, whom he left wholly in the charge of a nurse, an old woman who rejoiced in the name of Chocklaw.

Whang-Sing loved but one thing, and that was his gold; and though he could have given his daughter enormous wealth, yet such was his greed that he resolved to marry her to the son of a man almost as rich as himself, though Gustee-Ge utterly despised him.

Tears, prayers, entreaties, all were unavailing.

He bade her receive the addresses of Bang-Wan, and prepare for their nuptials.

Whang-Sing, though a selfish man had an eye to business; hence it was that he had on several occasions invited the officers of the tea ships to his house, and on one occasion Dick had seen the daughter of the tea merchant.

So charmed was he with her that he resolved to meet her again.

Nor was he long in finding the means.

The girl on her part became equally charmed with the young English officer, and with the assistance of her nurse, many interviews were arranged between them, and it was with a feeling almost amounting to despair that Dick learned the resolve of her father to wed her to Bang-Wan.

How bitterly did he regret then that he was not master on board his ship, and as bitterly did Gustee-Ge regret that he could not bear her far away from her unfeeling father and his hated choice.

But now captain of his own vessel, and with three days to mature his plans, who was to prevent him carrying off the fair Chinese, and making her his wife at the first opportunity?

His heart beat high with hopes, and a smile wreathed his lips.

A hand was laid on his shoulder, and he started.

"Thinking of your promotion, captain?" said Mr. Bennet.

"I beg pardon, sir. I did not observe that you had come on deck," said Dick, flushing to the temples.

"Tell the men to sling your chest into the boat," said the captain, "and then come and drink a glass of wine with me."

"With pleasure, sir."

And Dick ordered Sam and Tom to put his effects on board the boat with their own, and followed Captain Bennet down the companion.

The captain touched a bell on the table.

The steward appeared.

"A bottle of port, steward, if you please."

The man bowed and disappeared, to reappear again almost directly with the wine.

Drawing the cork, and placing glasses on the table, he again retired.

The captain filled a couple of glasses, and raising his own, said—

"Dick, my boy, though I am sorry to lose so good an officer, yet I sincerely hope that you may have a prosperous voyage, and that we may meet in England possessed of both health and happiness. Here's God bless you, my boy."

"I reciprocate your good feelings, Captain Bennet, and should the company see fit to keep me out of command, I hope I may at least sail under you again."

"My lad, only take your ship safe to port, and depend upon it you'll ever after sail as first officer."

"Your health, captain," said Dick huskily, for he felt a lump rise in his throat. "May He who rules the winds and the waves have you in His keeping."

"Amen," said Bennet.

They chinked their glasses together, drank, and then grasped hands in a fervent and friendly grip.

"Chest's aboard, sir," said a voice. "Shall the 'Warden's' boat cast adrift or wait for you?"

"I'm coming," said Dick. "Once more, Captain Bennet, good-bye."

"Heaven bless you, my boy."

Another grip of the hand, and Dick mounted the companion to the deck, followed by Captain Bennet.

Sam and Tom had taken their seats in the boat, and were bawling out farewells to their late messmates, while the sailors on deck were giving them a parting cheer.

"I and Jack, here will be aboard with our togs within an hour, your honour," cried the sailor who had delivered the letter and now carried the reply.

"All right, boys," said Captain Bennet. "You won't regret the change."

Dick turned to the men.

"A fair voyage to you all," he said.

"Heaven bless you, sir," cried several.

Dick stepped over the side into the boat, and gave the order to cast off.

The next minute the boat was gliding from the ship, and Dick felt the tears rush to his eyes as a true and fervent English cheer broke from the lips of those on board.

CHAPTER XI.

IN WHICH DICK STARTS OUT ON A RISKY ERRAND.

THE captain of the "Lord Warden" had, under medical advice, been taken on shore, and Dick now reigned in his stead.

It was two days after he had gone on board as chief officer.

His late ship had sailed, and in another day his own vessel would stretch her white sails to the breeze and head for England.

Dick had found time to go twice on shore, and under pretence of transacting business with the father had managed to obtain interviews with the daughter.

And at each interview Gustee-Ge had appeared more loving and beautiful than before.

Had Whang-Sing only known what had been arranged at those interviews even he would have left his money-bags to keep a strict watch over his child.

Dick had been pacing the deck for some time in deep thought.

Suddenly pausing before a jolly-looking and powerful-built seaman, who was engaged in splicing a rope, he said—

"Sam."

"Ay, ay, sir."

"Come to my cabin."

"Ay, ay, your honour."

"And bring Tom Halyard with you. Not a word to any one else, mind."

"Trust me, captain."

And Sam, flinging down his work, dived into the forecastle, while Dick went towards the companion-way.

When Sam and Tom entered the captains cabin they found him girding a sword to his side.

"Merchant skippers don't usually wear side-arms," said Dick, with a smile; "but I am going on an errand that may prove dangerous, and I want you to accompany me."

"If there's going to be a fight," said Sam, "I reckon I can hold my own against most men."

"And I think it would take a little to knock the wind all out of my sails," said Tom.

"I have selected you because we have sailed together for a long time."

"You does us honour," said Sam.

"And because I know you both to be discreet," said Dick.

"If you mean we can hold our jaw, you're right there, captain," said Sam.

"I must let you into my confidence," said Dick; "and I'll take your bear words for it that your mesmates shall be none the wiser."

"Lor' bless yer we'd take our davy's if yer like, captain," said Tom.

"No, your promise is sufficient."

"Yer got mine afore yer asks it," said Sam.

"And mine as well," said Tom.

"Well, men, don't laugh at me," said Dick; "but I'm in love."

"Well, there's nothing unnatural in that," said Sam. "Why, when I was in Portsmouth I fell slap in love with a little gal——"

"Belay there, mate," said Tom; "don't get yer jawing tackle on about that gal; yer know she cleaned yer out to the last penny. Hang all the women, I say."

"Avast, messmate, avast; yer've got a mother and sisters," said Sam.

"Heaven bless 'em!" said Tom, fervently. "I didn't mean them' mate; only the sort as clean out a poor tar when he goes for a cruise ashore."

"As I said before I am in love," said Dick. "And, what is more, in love with a young Chinese lady."

"Oh, Neptune!" gasped Sam.

Tom nudged his mate to be silent.

"I thought you'd laugh at me," said Dick. "But I can't help it. She is as lovely as a houri, and her father wants to wed her to a man she hates. I have arranged to elope with her and bring her on board this ship, where she must be known to all but ourselves only as a lady passenger. Do you understand ? "

" Can a shark swim ? " said Sam.

" Do not imagine for a moment that you will aid me to wrong this girl," said Dick. " My intention is, when we reach England, if not before, to marry her. And she has consented to fly with me. Only her father and her lover stand in her way. Even her nurse is eager to assist her to escape from a fate to her worse than death. Will you assist me to get her on board ? "

" Will a shark eat pork ? " said Sam.

" Rather," cried Tom. " Captain, you give the orders, and we'll obey 'em."

" Hark you, not a word to the others —not even those who will pull us ashore."

" We're mum," said Sam.

" As silent as Jonah was when the whale gobbled him," said Tom.

" Then get out the pinnace, and when we reach the wharf we three will go to the house ; the others will remain in the boat to be ready to pull off should we be followed or molested. Let there be no violence if it can be prevented.

" And if it can't ? " said Sam.

" We must be ruled by circumstances," said Dick.

" Right, yer honour," said Sam.

" Of course if the rat eaters show fight we'll have to run foul of 'em," said Tom.

" If they do, but no blood-shed, mind that," said Dick.

" Of course, if a fellow—a yaller-skin, you know, captain—runs his nose again my fist and makes it bleed 'twon't be my fault, will it ? " said Tom.

" Of course not," said Sam. " If a fellow pokes his nose into other people's business, why, then that nose ought to suffer. That's only nat'ral, yer know, mate."

" As true as the compass," replied Tom.

" Then heave ahead, my hearties, and get the pinnace out," said Dick, " for my little girl will be waiting for me."

" Ay, ay, yer honour," cried Sam. " Heave ahead, Tom, yer lubber."

And away went the two men to the deck to superintend the launching of the boat.

Soon the voices of the sailors were heard as they lowered the boat from the stern davits, and the plash of oars in the water as the rowers took their places on the thwarts.

Dick was not long taking his seat in the stern and seizing the tiller.

" Give way, lads."

Out shot the boat from under the stern and headed for the shore.

There were so many vessels at that time loading that the " Lord Warden " lay out some distance from the wharves.

But the space was soon got over.

The shore was reached, and telling the rowers that his business ashore would occupy but little time, Dick bade them remain in the boat.

Then he stepped ashore, followed by Tom and Sam.

The hour selected by Gustee-Ge for her flight was one in which she knew her father was mostly engaged, and when she was least likely to meet with opposition.

Romantic as it might seem, the girl was desperately in love with the young Englishman, and could she have had her choice she would have preferred sharing a humble life with him to the great fortune which she knew the man of her father's selection would possess.

She had concealed about her what trinkets she possessed, and with her nurse awaited anxiously the arrival of Dick.

Strangers seldom pass the screen that hides the courtyard from the gaze of passers-by, hence little is known of the interior of Chinese dwellings.

There was no need for rope ladders to reach the ground, for the houses of the Chinese are only one story in height, and all that Gustee-Ge would have to do would be to step out of the window into her lover's arms.

" Follow me in silence," said Dick, as they stood on the shore. " You, Sam, enter the courtyard with me, and you, Tom, remain outside to give warning if any one should attempt to enter."

" Ay, ay, captain."

" A low whistle will tell us there is danger."

" I understand, captain. If I see a suspicious craft bearing down I'll make signals, never fear ; and if they don't sheer off sharp I'll lay broadside on and let 'em have a volley as will keel 'em over."

" Don't run foul of any one if you can help it," said Dick.

"'I SWAR I'SE DE DEF OB DE OLE LOT OB YER IF YER DON'T LET DAT BOY GO!' CRIED JUMBO."

"I won't if I can steer clear," replied Tom.

They had nearly reached the house, and Dick motioned for silence.

"I'll belay my jawing tackle," muttered Tom to himself; "but I reckon if any one runs foul of me they'll get their figurehead damaged."

Dick cast a quick glance round.

For a wonder, that part of the street was deserted.

"Come on, Sam," he said. "Quick!"

And he darted through the screen into the courtyard.

Sam followed him.

Several windows were open to the court, and the leaves of the trailing plants that grew up the walls glistened in the sunlight.

At one of the open windows sat Gustee-Ge and her nurse.

"My eyes!" cried Sam, "what a figurehead! She is a beauty!"

Dick did not hear him.

He bounded to the window.

The girl sprang up with a low cry and flung her arms around his neck.

"My darling!" said Dick, as he kissed her cheek, white almost as a Europeans.

"Oh, Gustee-Ge glad, much glad," murmured the girl. "I fear muchee you no come. My heart beatee with fear; but you come, and it beatee with joy."

"Yes, my darling, I am here. Are you ready?"

"Yes, yes."

"Oh, what I do?" moaned Chocklaw. "You go way your father beatee me. He say I help you go way. Then he beatee me with bamboo, and then I cry 'cos you go. Oh, what I do—what I do?"

And the woman, hitherto so eager to aid in her charge's flight, now wrung her hands in terror and despair.

"Peace, peace!" cried Dick. "Your sobs will arouse the household and bring her father to this spot."

"Oh, I no let her go without poor Chocklaw. Me her mother. She go away and I break heartee. Takee me—takee me too!"

"Impossible," cried Dick. "Come, my darling, come!"

"Me go—me go; takee me—oh, takee me!" yelled the nurse.

Then she gave a spring out of the window and clasped her arms tightly around Sam's neck, almost hurling the startled tar to the earth.

CHAPTER XII.

IN WHICH DICK CARRIES OFF ONE MORE THAN HE WANTED

WITH difficulty retaining his balance, Sam, with an oath, tried to free himself from Chocklaw's grasp.

"Shiver my timbers!" he cried; "fling off your grapnels! What do you mean by boarding a fellow like this here?"

"Me muchee love you. You takee me, I no stay here. I go on ship with you."

"If you do may I be hanged!" cried Sam. "Sheer off, you sea-pirate, or damme, I'll sink yer!"

But the woman only squealed and clung the tighter.

Gustee-Ge in her agony of terror, clasped her hands.

"Oh, what I do—what I do?" she cried wildly. "She scream—my fader come—he killee you—he killee me. Oh, what I do?"

"Oh, takee me—takee me too!" cried Chocklaw.

"Oh, take her—take her!" pleaded Gustee-Ge.

"There's no help for it," said Dick. She must go with you, and perhaps it is best she should."

"Oh, tankee muchee—tankee muchee!" cried the nurse, her sobs turning to smiles, and impressing a kiss on Sam's cheek that took the old tar quite aback.

"Yes, yes," cried Dick. "Come my darling, before we are disturbed. Take the old woman, Sam. You'll have to carry her, or we shall be overhauled before we can reach the boat."

He was helping Gustee-Ge over the window-sill when there came not only a whistle from Tom outside the screen, but the rough tones of the sailor as he shouted out—

"Port your helm, yer lubbers, and sheer off! Yer don't run into that harbour, I tell yer! Sheer off, I say, or I'll be aboard yer afore yer can say Jack Robinson."

"Stand aside! Dare you block my way into my own house?" cried a voice in good English. "Your captain shall hear of this, so that he may never again allow you on shore."

"Look here, old pig's-eyes," roared Tom. "I'm ordered to sink all strange craft as steers this way; so sheer off, the pair of yer, unless yer want a broadside poured into yer ribs."

And Tom began to take off his guernsey.

"My father—my father!" moaned the girl, shrinking back.

"Whang-Sing—Whang-Sing!" cried the nurse.

"Quick, quick—before he can obtain aid!" cried Dick. "Up with the old woman, Sam. We must run for it, now."

"Here, come on, you old cat!" cried Sam. "None of yer squealing! I'll have to hold yer on by yer pigtail, but I won't hurt yer if ye're quiet."

And placing his back against Chock-law's, he stooped and lifted her on to his back.

"Oh, muchee glad—muchee glad!"

The girl again placed her arms round her lover's neck, and Dick drew her towards him.

But at that moment Whang-Sing and Bang-Wan, taking advantage of Tom trying to get off his guernsey, dashed past and round the screen into the court-yard.

"Hold, Barbarians! What would you with my daughter?" cried Whang-Sing.

"And my promised wife!" yelled Bang-Wan. "You shall be bastinadoed! You shall have the stick!"

"Avast there!" thundered Tom, as he dashed towards him. "Threaten a British captain with the stick, will you?

"Take that, you rat-eating son of a gun."

And raising his knee, Tom caught the young Celestial at the bottom of his back, and pitched him headfirst into the pit of Whang-Sing's stomach.

Whang-Sing gave a screech, and doubled up.

"Threaten a British tar with the stick eh?" roared Tom, as again his knee was raised, and planted on the body of Bang-Wan.

And the sailor, in his delight at the other's yells, waved his hat wildly above his head.

Dick drew the girl from the window.

"Quick, quick!" he said.

"Make sail, captain!" cried Tom. "I and Sam will keep these craft from following. Here, Sam, drop that old gal and sail in here, and we'll give the pirates something to lay them up in port with."

"Tom, prevent them following us as long as you can. Come, darling; come, Sam."

"Stop, stop!" shrieked Whang-Sing.

"Stop, stop!" echoed Bang-Wan.

But their shouts were of no avail.

Dick dashed out of the courtyard, bearing Gustee-Ge in his arms.

After him sped Sam, carrying Chock-law on his back, and rocking from side to side like a ship in a storm.

In vain the two Celestials tried to pursue them.

Tom seized one by one hand, and the other by the other, and dragging them to the window, out of which Gustee-Ge and the nurse had come, he hoisted Whang-Sing, corpulent as he was, through it with his knee, and then, seizing the younger Celestial, he pitched him over on top of the elder man.

The squeal that Whang-Sing gave as Bang-Wan fell upon his chest fairly made Tom start.

"Shiver my timbers!" cried Tom, "if that old fellow's voice couldn't be heard further at sea than a fog-horn! Now look here, my hearties, if you try to get out of that for an hour I'll pour in such a broadside as will lay you up for repairs for a month. Don't you think I'm going away, acos I ain't; I'm only going to sit down under the window, and if you only get up off that floor, you'll think a bale of cotton was going down your throats, you will."

And shaking his fist at the really terrified men, he dropped to the earth, and crawling away past the window reached the screen.

He looked back.

He saw nothing of the two Celestials.

"The captain and Sam are bound to make all sail for the boat," he muttered ; "and as I don't fancy those fellows will get over this fear for a little while, I'll just steer my course after them."

He gave another look at the window and then darted outside the screen.

"Shiver my timbers!" he muttered as he ran on. "Here's Sam run off with that old gal; can't make that out. Sam was always fond of the gals; but that yaller-skinned old hag, that beats me. Though, by Jingo, t'other one is a beauty and no mistake."

He caught sight of Dick and Sam.

They were both leading the females who on account of their small feet could not go very quickly.

"I thought Sam would soon drop her," muttered Tom. "Ahoy there, messmate!"

"Ahoy!" cried Sam, looking back.

"Heave ahead, my hearty!" cried Tom. "But there how can he make sail with craft in tow? Why, she's as lumbering as a billy-boy. But that other one, she's as neat as a yacht; look at her lines and curves, and her figure-head. Douse my toplights, but the captain's got an eye for the pretty, or my name's not Tom Halyard!"

Thus muttering, the sailor reached the side of his messmates.

"I say, mate, you ain't going to keep her in tow much longer, are you?" asked Tom.

"Captain's orders," replied Sam.

"What?" cried Tom.

"Captain's orders," returned Sam, "or I'd soon cut her adrift, my hearty."

At this moment there were loud shouts behind them.

All instinctively turned to learn their cause, though they guessed them.

Puffing and blowing, and his fat sides shaking as he ran, came Whang-Sing.

A little distance behind him was Bang-Wan.

"Shake out another reef, captain," cried Tom; "we're pursued."

"Confound it!" said Dick. "Hurry, my darling—hurry!"

"Here, captain. You take this old hag in tow as well," said Sam, "and leave me and Tom to stop the chase."

"Do not hurtee my father," cried the girl.

"Bless your little heart," cried Sam, "we wouldn't feed him on sugar-plums."

But he prepared to fight if need be.

The girl smiled, for she took what Sam said to mean that no harm should come to her father.

Dick took the old woman's arm and hurried them both forward.

"Halloa, mate! that hullabaloo is fetching the rat-eaters out," cried Sam.

The cries of Whang-Sing and his companion had aroused the immediate neighbourhood.

The Chinese came out of their houses and surrounded the two panting men.

All asked questions at once.

But all the reply they got was—

"The barbarians—the barbarians!"

And as they both pointed towards Sam and Tom, the people thought of course they meant them.

"The captain will reach the boat in two minutes," said Tom, "and I fancy we can keep the pigtails back that long."

"Rather," said Sam.

On rushed Whang-Sing, and after him came a dozen or more of his neighbours.

"Look here, mate," said Tom, "let's floor half-a-dozen of 'em, and then run for the boat, acos yer know it won't be healthy if they leave us ashore."

"Thats the talk, mate. Just land 'em amidships. These fellows can't stand much punching, and I'll knock the wind out of 'em, and they can't sail without wind."

Whang-Sing suddenly stopped dead short.

His wind at least was gone, and he could go no further.

The others stopped also, not caring to go on by themselves, especially when they saw that Sam and Tom were evidently ready to give them a reception.

"Now's our time, mate," said Sam.

"To sail in," said Tom.

"No, to sail off, you lubber; so haul up your slacks and let's make tracks for the boat."

The two men turned and dashed towards the spot where they had left the boat in charge of her crew.

They reached it just as Dick, assisted by the men, placed the girl and her nurse in it.

"In you go, captain," cried Sam. "There's not a moment to lose."

Dick sprang into the boat, and Sam and Tom followed him.

"Push off," cried Dick.

The men obeyed, and the boat glided from the land as several howling and gesticulating Celestials came tearing down to the water's edge

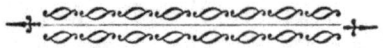

CHAPTER XIII.

IN WHICH MORE THAN ONE ARE PLACED IN TERRIBLE DANGER.

IN a lower apartment of the Purple Pagoda sat, at a table covered with papers, a stout Chinese in the robes that denoted his rank as a governor.

This was Mandarin Fum-Fum.

He was a man of keen perception and great learning, and but for his urgent solicitations to be allowed to remain at home he would have been chosen as a member of the embassy to one or other of the continental nations.

People wondered that a governor who took every opportunity of accepting bribes from those who had offended against the laws should decline to accept a post which would be so well paid for.

But then they did not know that Governor Fum-Fum was in the habit of making very large sums of money, and was accumulating great wealth from his proceeds as a sharer in more than one of the piratical junks that infested the seas around China.

The wily mandarin had pleaded his advanced age, his terrors at crossing the seas, and his belief that he could better serve his sovereign in his present position; and so the Brother of the Sun and the Moon had scratched off his name with the vermilion pencil, and Fum-Fum was left to pursue his villainies in his post of governor.

So Fum-Fum winked his little almond-shaped eyes, laid his yellow finger against his small nose, and shook his sides with laughter and pleasure combined.

But that was months before he sat in the pagoda, looking over a sheet of Chinese characters which represented the articles stowed away in the huge junk that rode at anchor opposite the Purple Pagoda.

"Good," he said, "very good!"

And he leaned back in his chair and rubbed his yellow hands together.

"Five captures, all their stores removed to the junk, and the vessels sunk and their crews slain. What a pity the ships cannot be brought into port! Then we could sell them and put more money in our pockets. Heigho! I wish I was the emperor; I'd have many things altered. How many dollars gone to the bottom? By Confucius! it's too bad to destroy that which would bring us more wealth."

"I hold there with you, sir governor, it is too bad," said a deep voice, and a stalwart and deeply-bronzed Celestial strode into the apartment.

The mandarin sprang to his feet with a look of terror on his face.

But it vanished in an instant and gave place to a smile.

"Welcome, Chow-Fow," he said, grasping the other's hand; "as welcome as water to the rice. I have been reading the list you sent me. You have had a prosperous cruise."

"Better than many," replied the pirate captain; "and glad am I that your excellency is pleased with our success."

"I should be worse than a barbarian were I not," was the reply. "When will you land your stores?"

"As there will be no moon I propose commencing to-night."

"Good again," said the mandarin. "The vaults will hold them, though the whole of your last cargo has not been disposed of."

"True; there's room enough in them for more even, than my junk will hold, and few larger ever spread her matting sails to the breeze when a prize was sighted."

"And plenty then left for captives or prisoners," said Fum-Fum, with a laugh.

"Talking of captives," said the pirate captain, "as I am desirous of making some, I know I shall not ask your excellency's aid in vain."

"Be sure of that, for I well know you would make no captive unless he would put money in our pockets to obtain his release."

The pirate looked slightly uneasy at this.

"I am afraid there is little to be made out of them," he said, "but much to be lost by their remaining at liberty."

"To be lost; How?"

"If what I have heard is correct, and I have no reason to doubt it, they, or at least one of them, have learned that my junk is not a honest trader, and that you have not only the same knowledge but are sharing in our piracy."

"By the bones of my father, you terrify me," cried the mandarin.

"And more—that it is their intention to communicate with the emperor through the British ambassador."

"Then we are lost," cried Fum-Fum. "We shall be beheaded, pressed between boards, or bastinadoed to death."

"Not if you secure their persons before they can reach the ambassador, who is now in Pekin; and I have discovered a means by which to bring at least one of them here, and as his companions will doubtless know to where he's come, they will seek him, when, they, too, can be made prisoners."

"Yes, yes, tell me your plan," cried Fum-Fum, excitedly.

The pirate then told the governor how he had learned that for the present Ned and his friends were detained in the vicinity of Canton by their belief that a young Englishman who had run off with the sweetheart or wife of Ned was in hiding near by.

But he did not tell the governor from whom he had got the information, nor uttered one word about the wealth Ned and his friends were supposed to possess.

Then he explained how, in order to place Ned in their power, he had obtained the services of one of his crew, a countryman of Ned's, to write a letter to that youth, asserting that those whom he sought were at the Purple Pagoda.

The mandarin slapped the pirate on the shoulder.

"By Confucius! you have saved our lives," he said, "but they must not live. Our safety demands that they die."

"True," replied the pirate. "They must share the fate of the crews of our prizes. You are never safe from the living, but the dead are powerless to do harm.

"True; dead men speak not, hear not, point not; and if the waters give up the bodies, are they not barbarians, and who will ask how they died?"

"None!" cried the pirate captain.

"And when may we expect him?" asked the mandarin.

"I have just dispatched the letter, and if he comes directly he has read it, he may be here in an hour."

"So soon?"

"Yes, if he suspects no treachery, for you know how impulsive these barbarians are. Why if I had not known that, they had boarded my junk many a time before I had been prepared to receive them. Hardly have the echoes of your first shot died away than they are alongside and ready to spring upon your decks. They are indeed what we call white devils."

"We'll not fail to be ready for these white devils," said Fum-Fum.

"Then I will take my leave of your excellency, for I have business on board as we shall commence landing our cargo to-night."

"Fear not he will escape me. He knows too much to suffer me to let him get out of the pagoda after once he is within it, only when we put him out, powerless to do us harm."

"Then for the present, farewell," said the pirate, bowing low.

"Farewell!"

The pirate captain strode from the apartment and out of the pagoda.

But he did not go on board his ship.

He made off in the direction where the house of Ching-Fow was situated.

Ever and anon he'd glance up at the gilded fronts of the shops and smile grimly as he read on their facias "No cheating here."

"But like the English and Americans, for whose benefit that text was supplied by the owner of the shop, he knew too well that he would be a shrewd man indeed who escaped being cheated by their proprietors.

He continued his walk, holding his head as high as though he were a honest man, when suddenly he paused and grasped the arm of a man who at that moment reached his side.

The fellow was a rough-looking sailor with a huge black beard and whiskers that disguised half his features, and gave him anything but a pleasant appearance.

As the captain grasped the man's arm his wrist became bare, and on it could be seen deep scars, which had evidently been cauterised, but would never be obliterated.

"Captain," cried the man in surprise.

"Ay," replied the other in English. "What do you here when I ordered no man should leave the junk till all the cargo had been taken on shore?"

"I'll tell you, captain," said the man. "I had reasons for coming ashore, and I got the permission of Zamra, your Malay lieutenant."

"But what reasons have you for coming ashore—you whom we always suffer to remain below when in port, lest you should be recognised—a prison-breaker and a murderer, for whose capture a large reward has been offered by the American government?"

"What is the fear of detection to a man who has panted for years to obtain his revenge," cried the other fiercely. "If Tom Stocton could but grip the villain he seeks by the throat, and squeeze the life out of him, they might drag me to a scaffold, and I should go content."

"What do you mean?" asked the pirate captain.

"This. You got me to write a decoy letter for you this morning."

"Well, if I did?"

"When I wrote it I did not think that two of the persons named therein were known to me, but when you had gone ashore, I was certain that the Bill Boaster spoken of is none other than the wretch to whom we gave the command of a vessel in our line of business, who betrayed us to the American authorities, and bolted with all he could carry away, as well as a girl he had on board, and whom he had stolen from her sweetheart. I followed on his track and run him down, but as I would have shot him dead, an accursed dog seized my pistol arm and ruined my aim, and left these scars you see here upon my wrist."

The captain let go the man's arm.

"Yes, that dog foiled my revenge, but I hung on his track till I was seized by the police and sent to gaol. How I escaped you know, but my longing for revenge has never slumbered; and now that I know the accursed traitor is here in this place, I will never rest till I find him and stain my hands in his cowardly and treacherous blood!"

"And meet your reward by swinging at the yardarm of an American cruiser."

"Were I lashed to death with a cat-o'-nine tails," cried Stockton fiercely, "I care not. Through that man I have suffered, and come what will I'll never rest till I have his blood."

And he turned fiercely away and strode on before the captain with a quick and excited gait.

Suddenly a man wearing the costume of a British petty officer issued from the gilded doorway of an elaborately tinselled shop.

A moment Tom Stockton gazed at him, then with the bound of a tiger he sprang upon him, and clutched his throat.

"Bill Boaster!" he yelled. "Pirate, traitor, and coward, I have got you at last—I have got you at last!"

CHAPTER XIV.

IN WHICH JUMBO HAS A SUSPICION AND NED NIMBLE DISCOVERS A REALITY.

NED dashed into the adjoining apartment, and seizing his hat, returned to where the surprised Jumbo and Tilda were looking first at each other and then at the young Celestial who had brought the letter in inquiring astonishment.

"Jumbo," he said, "I have information of where Minnie is to be found! I cannot stop to answer questions now. Even a minute's delay may cause me to lose her."

Then turning to the Chinaman, and thrusting his hand in his pocket, he added—

"You have indeed brought me good news. Take these few dollars for your trouble."

"Tankee muchee," said the Celestial,

with a grin. "Goodee payee, muchee tankee, an' wishee luckee."

"Yes—yes. Now go."

"Goee quickee," said the Chinaman, and hurried from the room.

"You can tell the others if they come in that I have news of Minnie's being in the Purple Pagoda, and have gone in search of her. Good-bye."

And before Jumbo or Tilda could speak, Ned dashed out of the apartment.

Another moment, and he was in the street, and hurrying in the direction of the Purple Pagoda, which could be seen from some distance, towering over the low houses of rich and poor.

When Jumbo had somewhat recovered his surprise, he turned to Tilda, who stood fanning herself with her gorgeously-painted fan, and remarked—

"Tilda Tompkins!"

"Dat's dis lady, for suah," was the reply.

"Tilda, does yer know what it am dat strikes dis yer 'specerble cullered gen'lam?" said Jumbo.

"Guess I'se got a bery good ijea," replied the negress.

"Den p'raps yer'll 'splain what dat ijea am," said Jumbo.

"Dis yer fist ob mine," replied Tilda.

"Git out. What's dat ar fist got ter do wid de fing what's struck me?"

"'Cos when yer wexes me, I allus lets yer hab dese fingers ober dat ar mouf ob your'n," said Tilda.

"Guess dat's trufe," said Jumbo. "But dat isn't the striker what's struck me now."

"What am it, den? I didn't see nuffin' hit yer."

"Oh, what iggerence!" said Jumbo. "Doesn't a sort ob kind ob feeling strike yer sometimes?"

"I know yer habs de feeling when yer gets structed, ob course."

"Well den, de feeling I'se got now I'se been strucked am dis."

"What?"

"Dat Massa Ned's been fooled."

"What wid?"

"Why, dat ar Chinaman," said Jumbo.

"How yer make dat out?" said Tilda. "How he fool him when he bringed him dat letter?"

"Why dat's where it am, yer see. It's dat ar letter what's fooled him."

"Den how could it be de Chinaman?" asked Tilda.

"Well, dey's bofe done it."

"Bofe?"

"Dat's it, I sees it, or de eddercation what I'se receibed ain't done dis yer nigger much good." said Jumbo. "I allus was cleber at working out ob tings, and dis is how I works out dis."

"Yer's a precious long while about it," said Tilda.

"Dat's acos ob yer iggerence an' 'patience, yer know. But dar, a woman neber did hab no sense."

"Oh, ob course not," said Tilda, fanning herself violently.

"Now yer look here, an' I'll 'splain what yer can't unnerstand," said Jumbo. "Dat ar letter couldn't do it all by itself, and so de Chinaman had to help it do it. Don't yer see de letter tells de lie, and de Chinaman helps it acos he brings it. When I seed dat fellow's face when Ned gibs him de money, den says I to myself, dat's a trap for Massa Ned."

"What he want wid a trap, eh?"

"He don't want it, ob course, but I reckon dis yer nigger don't know not nuffin if dat letter ain't been wroted to get Ned into a mess somehow. It was sent to wriggle him away, or perhaps ter kill him!"

"Oh golly! yer don't mean dat?" cried Tilda, aghast.

"I does; and dis 'sperior geniwus ob mine tells dis chile it am so," said Jumbo emphatically. "I tell you Tilda Tompkins, dat I smells a rat."

"Oh, where?" cried Tilda, jumping aside. "Oh, I can't a-bear 'em. I isn't got ober dose rats in dat ar pie, I isn't."

"Tilda, yer's a fool," cried Jumbo; "de rat I smells isn't a rat at all."

"What am it den?"

"What am it? Why it's a rat ob anoder sort. It's er—it's er—yer knows what it am. It's a rat what ain't a rat, but what we calls a rat. It am bery difficult to 'scribe, but yer know what it means."

"It's a rat, an' it 'tain't a rat, and yet it am a rat," said Tilda. "Well I 'fess my eddercation neber taught me to 'lucerdate dat ar 'sterious mystery. I neber was good at riddles, neber, unless it was riddling holes in de bottom ob an old sarspan to make a cullender ob it."

"Tilda Tompkins," said Jumbo severely,

"if I wasn't de best tempered cullered pusson in dis yer bressed worle, I know we'd quarrel sometimes. But dar I forgibs yer, acos I know how yer's been brought up. I tells yer dat I'se certain dat Massa Ned's been lured away—dat he's in some sort ob danger."

"What! from de rat what yer smelled?"

"Git out. Dar's two-legged rats as well as four-legged ones, and its de two-legged ones what means him harm."

"I unnerstands yer now," said Tilda.

"Den why didn't yer do so afore?" cried Jumbo. "Look here; I'se going arter Ned, acos if dar's any mischief I'll hab a hand in it."

"De mischief—what, you?" cried Tilda.

"Guess it won't be in de mischief as is meant for Massa Ned, but agin dem what's made it. Didn't he say dat Minnie was in de Purple Pagoda, dat ar place ober dar wid all dem bells a-hanging on it?"

"Guess he said somefing ob dat sort," said Tilda.

"Den dat's whar he's off ter, an' dat's whar I'se going arter him," said Jumbo.

"Yer is."

"Yes."

"When?"

"Now, dis minit. So I'se jus' going ter git dem ar 'wolvers ob mine, a'cos I might want 'em, yer know."

And Jumbo walked into the next apartment.

As Tilda walked in after him she heard him exclaim—

"Gor-a-mighty! What a fool dat ar Ned am!"

"What's yer say?"

"Why, Massa Ned's gone off wilout taking his 'wolver wid him," replied Jumbo. "Dar's no 'counting for de 'steaks fellers makes when dar in lub, brest if der am."

"Dey's generally bery great fools," said Tilda, pointedly.

"Guess dat's trufe," said Jumbo, as he concealed his revolvers under his robe. "Dar, I guess Massa Ned 'ull hear dese bark if any one tries ter hurt him. Jumbo de Onety-onth ain't de chile ter hang back when dat ar boy's in danger. Guess he knows dat."

"I'se coming wid yer," said Tilda,

"Yer sure ter want somebody ter take care ob yer, yer is."

"Dat's trufe," said Jumbo.

"So I guess I'll hab dis ar pistal ob Massa Ned's."

And taking Ned's revolver from the table, she hid it in her bosom.

In another minute Jumbo and Tilda issued into the street, and took their way towards the pagoda.

As they passed round the screen two men drew hurriedly back into the shop of Ching-Fow, before the door of which they had stood conversing.

They were young Ching-Fow and the pirate captain, Chow-Woo.

But neither Jumbo nor Tilda observed them, even if they had they would have no suspicion of any evil being plotted towards either themselves or their friends.

Together they hurried on, exciting passing comments from the pedestrians, but unmolested by any one.

Meanwhile, Ned had hurried with all the speed he could to the Purple Pagoda.

So excited was he by the hopes of finding Minnie there that no thought of suspicion of treachery entered his mind.

Neither did he remember that he was unarmed, although he expected to encounter his old enemy, Bill Boaster.

On his way he overtook the messenger who had brought him the letter, and he would have passed him without a word, but the man said hurriedly—

"If no lettee go in, askee for Mandarin Fum-Fum, de governor. He muchee big manee. He likee Englishmanee and makee letee go."

"Thanks, thanks!" cried Ned, and hurried on.

He reached the pagoda and knocked loudly at its door.

It was opened by a soldier, bearing in one hand a fan, and with a helmet of tinselled paper on his head.

"I must see the governor," said Ned.

The soldier closed the door and motioned him to follow him.

It was but a few steps however before they reached a screen, round which the soldier motioned Ned to go.

He did so, and stood is a large apartment, in which were two open windows, the sashes of which were glazed by

OR, THE SECRETS OF THE PURPLE PAGODA.

muslin, for no glass is used in China.

Near one of the windows, seated cross-legged on a kind of throne, and with a canopy over its head, was an idol; a lamp hung from the ceiling, and vases of great beauty and worth were scattered about on ornamental stands and over the matted floor.

The pagoda had originally been used as a place of worship by the Chinese, but for many years had been the palace of the governor.

At a table at the opposite end of the apartment sat the mandarin, pretending to be eagerly deciphering a sheet of Chinese characters.

"An Englishman," said Fum-Fum, looking up and speaking in English. "What want—what complaint have you to make?"

"Your excellency," cried Ned, "I have been informed that a young English girl and her abductor, a young Englishman, are at this moment in this pagoda. She is my promised wife, and was stolen from me by that villain, and I have come hither to take her from him, and if possible, punish him for the wrongs he has done us both."

"And I will aid you," said Fum-Fum. "Wait here and I will bring her to you."

Ned felt his heart beat with joy as the mandarin rose and passed through a door just behind him.

On this door Ned kept his gaze eagerly riveted, momentarily expecting the entrance of Minnie, when suddenly he felt himself seized from behind and his arms pinioned so firmly behind his back that he was powerless to offer the faintest resistance; but he felt that he had been trapped, and believed it to be the work of his arch enemy, Bill Boaster.

CHAPTER XV.

IN WHICH NED MAKES HIS ESCAPE AND BILL BOASTER FINDS THAT HE CANNOT.

Back through the doorway into the apartment strode the governor.

But he was alone.

In his hand he grasped a drawn sword and on his face there sat a look of devilish triumph.

"What means this outrage? Why am I held by these men?" cried Ned, indignantly.

"Because they obey my orders," returned the mandarin.

"Your orders or that villain Bill Boaster's?" cried Ned.

"I know nothing of him you call Bill Boaster," returned the governor; "I only know that you have managed to learn more than is good for you, and that to prevent you doing harm to me and others it is necessary to arrest you."

"Arrest me! for what? I have done no harm," cried Ned.

"That is because we have been in time to prevent you," replied the governor.

"I don't know what you mean. I came here on the receipt of a letter—"

"Sent to entrap you and a party you have with you," said the mandarin.

At this moment a black face appeared at each of the windows, and then quickly disappeared behind the muslin.

"Why, why should you seek to harm either me or my friends?" cried Ned. "We have never done you wrong—never known even of your existence. Either there is villainy in this or some terrible mistake."

"Neither the one nor the other, my young barbarian. You are dangerous to me and others, and my own safety demands that you be rendered powerless. Away with him to the vaults; securely chain him, that he be powerless even to make an effort to escape."

"Wretch!" cried Ned; "you shall suffer for this outrage on a British subject; the English ambassador shall learn of your villainy, and you will rue the day you ever offered insult or outrage to an Englishman."

"Away with him!" thundered Fum-Fum, whom the words of Ned only the more convinced that he had meditated betraying his connection with the pirates, "away with him to the darkest vault, and in chains let him writhe till night, then sever his head from his body and when the water gate is opened hurl his carcase from it into the river. Hence with him, away!"

The governor pointed with his sword towards the screen.

The men tried to bear Ned backwards, but so desperately did he struggle that they were unable to do so.

The governor took a step forward, and grasping Ned by the collar, was about to plunge his sword into the youth's heart, when he paused as a loud voice yelled out—

"Gor-a-mighty, I swar I'se de def ob de ole biling lot ob yer if yer don't let dat boy go!"

And Jumbo levelled a revolver through the window, fair at the governor's head.

"An' I'll kill yer ober agin for suah," cried Tilda Tompkins at the other window, shaking her parasol fiercely above her head.

Whether it was the fear of the deadly weapon presented at them, or a momentary terror of the black faces framed in the openings it is impossible to say, but the two men who held Ned relaxed their grasp, while the governor stood utterly dumbfounded.

In a moment Ned had twisted himself from his captors' hold.

The next he dashed his fist into the governor's face with such force as to fell him to the floor as if shot.

Then with a bound like that of an angry panther, he sprang through the opening at which Jumbo stood, knocking that worthy clean off his feet and laying him prostrate under the window.

"Gor-a-mighty," yelled Jumbo; "I'se busted up!"

Ned tore the revolver from his hand and rose to meet his expected pursuers.

But as his face appeared at the window the two Celestials, who had not moved from where he had left them standing, gave a wild howl and dashed behind the screen.

"Yah, yah, yah!" laughed Tilda in derision; "dar's cowards!"

"Up, Jumbo, quick!" cried Ned, seizing the black's arm to assist him to his feet.

"Yer's knocked all de quick out ob me." replied Jumbo; "if I'd on'y had my mouf open yer'd a-gone slick down dis froat ob mine, for suah."

"Never mind, Jumbo, let's away before they can obtain help and secure us. Come, Tilda, follow me."

Ned dashed round towards the door pistol in hand.

Jumbo, gasping for breath, for Ned had nearly knocked it all out of his body, drew the other revolver from beneath his robe and side by side with Tilda dashed after Ned.

The door opened and half-a-dozen soldiers appeared.

Up went Ned's revolver, and up went Jumbo's and Tilda's.

But the valiant soldiers did not wait for their fire.

With a howl they banged the door to, and their footsteps could be heard as they scudded away from it.

"Let's fire frue de door," said Jumbo.

"No, no," cried Ned; "better not; let's get away quickly. The reports may bring hundreds upon us, and there is some terrible mystery here which I am resolved to fathom."

"Guess we's got de best ob it, anyhow," said Jumbo, as he and Tilda followed in Ned's hurried footsteps.

"We knows how to do it," said Tilda. "Dat's trufe."

Ned waited for them to reach his side.

"You saved my life," he cried. "But for you what might have been my fate?"

"Guess dat ar goose ob yours had been cooked." replied Jumbo.

"But what do it all mean?" said Tilda.

"Heaven only knows," replied Ned, as they hurried along. "It is a mystery."

"An' yer didn't see Minnie?" asked Jumbo.

"No," said Ned bitterly. "If she indeed be there, then is Bill Boaster answerable for this outrage. But I do not believe, from the governor's words, that she is. He suspects me of a desire to do him harm, and by that letter sought to entrap and prevent me; but then, how knew he of Minnie and Boaster? for I'll swear both are mentioned in the letter which caused me to visit the pagoda. But I can't think, now, my brain is on fire!"

Jumbo rubbed his back ruefully.

"Guess I'se a-fire. Dat ar bump jus' shook de whole ob me into a heap."

"I'm sorry, Jumbo, but I thought you'd see me coming," said Ned.

"I reckons I felt yer, an' I'll feel yer for a month ter come, I knows," replied the negro. "Why de debil didn't yer go frue de winder where Tilda was?"

"Because I am sure you would rather I knocked you down than Tilda."

"Dat's trufe," said Jumbo; "though I'd rader Tilda felt de 'ffects ob it dan dis chile."

"Hear dat, now?" said Tilda. "Yer waggerbone——"

"For Heaven's sake, do not stop here to quarrel!" cried Ned, looking anxiously round to see if they were pursued.

But no.

The door of the pagoda was still closed.

Ned knew how heavy had been the blow he had struck the governor in his desperate excitement, and he attributed their not being followed by the soldiers to Fum-Fum not having yet recovered from his insensibility.

But every moment there might be a hue and cry after them.

So he continued to hurry Jumbo and Tilda on at their utmost speed, telling them to conceal their weapons, as he did his own, but in such a manner as to have them ready at a moment's notice.

"You must tell me how you came to my rescue just at the nick of time when we get home," said Ned; "and then I must sit down and think over what has happened, and all I have heard, and take counsel with Harry and the rest, for that there is some strange mystery attached to this adventure I am sure; but what that mystery is, time alone will solve."

Jumbo and Tilda saw that it would be useless to speak further till they reached their lodgings, so together the trio went on in silence.

But that silence was suddenly broken by the report of a pistol, and looking up they saw a man, dashing towards them with a smoking pistol in his hand, while behind him at some short distance was another man, with a long and open knife in his grasp.

The foremost man was evidently an Englishman or an American, but the pursuer, though evidently a European by his dress, could not be recognised as to nationality, so deeply was he bearded.

"Help, help!" cried the foremost man, as he dashed some blood from his eyes which trickled from a wound in his forehead. "Help! Keep him back! Ha!"

He had slackened his speed to implore the assistance of Ned and Jumbo, but on catching sight of Ned's features, he uttered the exclamation, and dashed on at redoubled speed.

For a moment Ned stood as though thunderstruck, and then he cried out—

"Bill Boaster! by Heaven!"

"Ay, Bill Boaster!" yelled the man with the knife; "but I'll have his blood if I drink it!"

Ned only heard the words Bill Boaster had uttered, for he, too, had started in pursuit of his long time foe.

Fleeter of foot than Tom Stockton, for he it was who held the knife, Ned soon passed him, and as he ran, he shouted—

"Coward and villain, turn and face me!"

And he drew his pistol.

Tom Stockton saw the weapon, and heard Ned's words, and in tones that were hoarse with rage, he shouted—

"Back, boy! If you rob me of one drop of that traitor's blood, I'll bury my knife in your heart!"

"Back you!" shouted Ned, without turning his head. "He is my prey, and he who robs me of him dies by my hand! Stop, Bill; or by the Heaven above me, I'll shoot you through the back!"

As Ned raised the weapon, Bill caught his foot against a stone and pitched heavily to the earth.

Both Ned and Tom Stockton sprang forward with a yell of triumph.

But Ned gained the prostrate man a few yards in advance of the other.

"Back!" yelled Tom Stockton. "Leave him to me! He is my prize, and woe to him who stands between us!"

Ned planted his foot firmly in the centre of Boaster's back, and with levelled revolver and flashing eyes, confronted Tom Stockton.

"Think not I fear you or your knife," he cried, in husky tones. "What wrong this wretch may have done you, I know not, but it cannot be a thousandth part the injury he has done to me and mine. I have followed him for thousands of miles to wrest a treasure from him, and make him suffer for his infamies. No man shall rob me of my revenge—by Heaven, I swear it!"

"Then curse you! Your blood be upon your own head!" yelled Stockton, raising his knife.

"But another step," cried Ned, "and I fire! But one movement of foot or hand, and I'll scatter your brains as surely as there is a Heaven above us!"

CHAPTER XVI.

IN WHICH NED NIMBLE IS MADE A PRISONER, AND ALL IS BLACK WITHIN AND WITHOUT.

WITH a yell that would not have disgraced a Comanche Indian, Jumbo, revolver in hand, bounded to the assistance of Ned, and with a shriek that would have shamed a wild cat, so shrill was it, Tilda ran on by the negro's side wildly flourishing her fan.

For a moment, desperate as he was, Tom Stockton recoiled before that gleaming muzzle.

But for a moment only.

Uttering a fearful imprecation, he again dashed forward.

Ned, true to his word, fired.

But the bullet, instead of penetrating the brain of the maddened pirate, slit his left ear, and passed on into space.

Ere Ned could again pull the trigger, the maddened Tom had closed with him, and gripping Ned's wrist, gave it so fierce a twist that he dropped his weapon to the earth.

Then he in turn seized the wrist of Tom, so as to prevent him using his knife.

Locked in a deadly grip, they swayed hither and thither, trampling upon the prostrate form of Bill Boaster.

But the young man cared not for the wounds he received from the feet of the combatants.

He rolled himself from beneath them, and just as Jumbo came up, he sprang to his feet and dashed madly away towards the pagoda.

So desperately were Ned and Tom engaged, that for a few moments they did not observe the flight of Bill, but when Ned saw him hurrying off, he cried—

"After him, Jumbo! Shoot him down; Don't let him escape! On your life, don't let him escape!"

A yell of ungovernable rage broke from Tom Stockton's lips.

"Furies seize you!" he cried. "I'll have your blood for his!"

He wrested his hand free, and raised his gleaming blade to bury it in Ned's body.

But at that instant Jumbo struck Tom fiercely on the temple with the butt of his pistol, and dropping the upraised knife, he staggered and fell upon its blade driving it some inches into his shoulder.

Stooping quickly and securing his revolver, Ned rose, and shouted—

"After him! He must not escape me!"

And he bounded after Bill.

Jumbo and Tilda followed, but he ran so swiftly that the blacks were left behind in a few moments.

On towards the pagoda ran Bill, and on his trail hung Ned, determined that if he could not overtake the villain to fire at him and seek to bring him down.

But the thought that if his shot proved fatal he might never learn where to find Minnie made him hesitate each time that he raised his weapon.

Not once did he look behind, or he would have seen that a small crowd of Chinese had gathered around the wounded Tom, and were pointing Ned and his friends out as those who had inflicted the injury upon the pirate.

Panting, despairing, Bill Boaster ran on, looking for some means of escaping his pursuers.

But none presented themselves.

On one side lay the wharves.

To attempt to find shelter there he knew would be in vain.

But one hope presented itself.

He might find safety in the pagoda.

He knew it was the residence of the governor, and that for one like him to seek protection of a magistrate was like running into a trap, but then he knew that Chinese officials, no matter what their standing, were open to bribery, and he could well afford to bribe even so high a personage as the Mandarin Fum-Fum, thanks to the wealth he had stolen from Dost Mahomed.

He was not ten yards from the door of the pagoda.

He cast one quick glance over his shoulder, and saw that Ned was scarcely as far behind him.

"Oh that my pistol was loaded!" he gasped. "I could kill him now!"

He saw that the door of the pagoda was closed, and a cold sweat broke over his body.

He felt that Ned would be upon him ere he could summon it to be opened.

But even as the thought flashed through his mind, the door of the pagoda was flung open, and through it poured some ten or a dozen tinted helmeted soldiers.

With a cry of joy, Bill flung himself amongst them, shrieking loudly—

"Save me! save me!"

"Foiled!" cried Ned bitterly. "No; come what will, he shall not escape me!"

And in his rage, Ned fired.

It was an unfortunate shot.

Ned's usual coolness had deserted him, and the bullet found a resting-place in the fleshy part of one of the soldier's arm.

With a howl the man dropped his musket, and his companions raising their guns fired a volley at Ned.

But the Chinese were execrable marksmen.

The only damage done by their fire was that one of the bullets struck Tilda's fan, knocking it out of her hand and breaking it's handle.

Then, having exhausted their powder and shot, the soldiers, seeing the revolvers of Ned, Jumbo and Tilda raised, turned and fled into the pagoda, driving Bill before them.

"Follow me, Jumbo," cried Ned. "Though five hundred oppose me, he shall not escape;"

And ere the terrified Celestials could close the door, Ned had bounded over the threshold.

Jumbo would have followed him, but the door was closed in his face.

At the same moment the governor who had recovered from the effects of the blow Ned had dealt him, appeared in the hall or vestibule.

"Seize him!" he cried, on seeing Ned. "If you let him escape, your heads shall pay the penalty!"

Bill crouched behind the soldiers in terror.

"Villain," shouted Ned. "Coward, you shall not escape me!"

And he fired again.

The ball could not reach the cringing wretch for the body of the soldier behind whom he crouched received the ball in his breast.

Ned had sprung forward as he fired, and this presented the opportunity for others to get behind him.

Fearful of the governor's threat, they were not slow to do this.

Flinging themselves upon Ned from behind, they pinioned his arm.

One of the men dashed his revolver to the floor by a blow from his musket stock.

There was a short, sharp struggle, and then Ned was hurled to the floor.

His arms were forced behind him and bound together, and Ned Nimble was a prisoner in the Purple Pagoda.

They raised him to his feet, and stood him before the governor.

Fum-Fum gazed at him in triumph as well as he could through two swollen and blackened eyes.

"Barbarian!" he hissed, "you escaped me once, but you will not do so again. By the bones of my father, you shall die!"

Then turning to Bill, he cried angrily—

"Who is this? Another of them? Let him share the fate. Away with them both to the vaults!"

Bill flung himself on his knees before the governor.

"Hear me, most illustrious governor," he cried. "That man sought my life, and I fled hither to seek your protection."

"Are you not a friend of this barbarian?" asked the governor—"one of his party, who by falsehood seeks to do me an injury in the sight of our emperor?"

"I swear I am not," said Bill.

"My friend?" cried Ned, indignantly. "He is a villain, a coward, and a traitor! One whom I have sought far and near for months. He is the villain whom I came here to seek, and who you in your letter said I should find together with his victim in this pagoda. He is Bill Boaster, the pirate, robber, and assassin; the abductor of the girl I love, and the monster whom I have sworn to slay."

The governor's face, contorted though it was, wore a strange expression.

"You will have to wait for your revenge in the other world, if there be one," he said. "Away with him, and I will decide what torture shall be inflicted before he dies. Barbarian for that blow you shall receive a hundred. Away with him, and your heads shall fall if he escapes me!"

He raised his hand.

"Wretch!" cried Ned, "you shall suffer for this."

The soldiers motioned to Bill.

But the mandarin simply remarked—

"Not now."

Ned was borne along the vestibule by four soldiers.

He could make no resistance with his arms tied behind his back.

But his tongue was free, and he shouted—

"Bill Boaster, though you escape me, you will not long triumph in your villainy. I may fall, but there are those who will avenge me. Coward and villain, your hour of punishment will yet come."

"But not before I shall know that you are no more!" hissed Bill.

Ned was borne down a long flight of stone steps, one of the soldiers preceding those who forced him onwards, carrying a lantern.

Down till a huge iron door was reached across which was a stout wooden bar.

This the man who carried the lantern raised from its socket, and suffered its end to drop heavily on the floor.

Then the door was flung open, revealing a dungeon into which no ray of light could penetrate save that brought thither by human hands.

Into this dungeon Ned was forced by his captors.

From iron rings rivetted in the stone wall depended chains, at the end of which were iron collars and waist belts, which opened with a hinge and closed with a clasp that needed the use of a key to open them.

The man set his lantern on the stone floor, and taking one of the chains in his hand, opened the collar at its end.

Muttering some words to his companions, the soldiers forced Ned back against the wall, and while they held him there, the fellow clasped the iron collar round Ned's neck, and the sound it made as he snapped it together, struck upon Ned's heart like the knell of doom.

Then the man took another chain from which depended a larger hoop of iron.

This hoop he clasped round Ned's waist, and snapped it as he had done the collar.

"Dat makee fastee," said the fellow, retreating a pace, and looking admiringly at his work. "No shootee Chinee mancc; gotee tightee, an' soon beatee, killee— beree goodee."

The others laughed, as if greatly pleased.

Ned said nothing.

He knew that words would avail him naught with these men.

Had not the governor said that their own heads should fall if he escaped?

Of what avail then would be threats, prayers, or entreaties—even bribes?

His heart sank within him.

But oh, bitterest feeling of all, Bill Boaster had escaped him!

The villain might live to triumph in his fall, and persecute the girl he loved, and for whom he had endured so much.

This was the most agonising thought.

Were Bill punished, and Minnie restored to freedom and home, how willingly would he have died, but to feel that he must die and she still live on to be persecuted by that villain Boaster was more than he could bear, and he feared that if he was not soon deprived of life he must go mad.

With jeers and laughter the soldiers picked up the lantern, and filed out of the dungeon.

The door was closed upon him.

He heard the heavy bar drop into the iron socket.

Around him was a darkness so black that it appeared to be solid.

A darkness deeper even than that of the horrible Kanah-khaneh of Bokhara.

And chained as he was, how could he hope to escape?

That cruel iron band round his throat, that hoop around his waist precluded all hope.

And how long would he be suffered to live?

CAN TAKE YERSELF OFF, AND DIS WID YER AS WELL,' CRIED JUMBO."

What tortures would be inflicted upon him before the cruel blade severed his head from his trunk, and his body was floated out to sea?

These thoughts ran wildly through his brain, chased each other through his mind as he tried to penetrate the blackness around him.

"Oh, Heaven!" he cried at last, "in Thee and Thee alone can I hope for succour. If Thou desert me, all is lost— lost!"

CHAPTER XVII.

IN WHICH FUM-FUM AND BILL BOASTER ENTER INTO A FEARFUL COMPACT.

BILL BOASTER was handed over to the charge of the rest of the soldiers by the governor.

"Guard him well till my return," he said.

Then turning to Bill he remarked—

"Barbarian, before I decide how I shall treat you, I will hear your story; but first I must see my doctor, for the blow given me by the white devil was a heavy one, and I fear me it will be long ere I shall recover from its effects. You cannot leave here till I return, and any attempt to do so will consign you to the same fate as the other."

Bill was too shrewd not to see that he must comply with the mandarin's orders, so he replied—

"Most illustrious governor, I am your slave. I will make no attempt to leave the pagoda until I have your permission to do so."

"It is well," replied Fum-Fum. "I know how to punish those who disobey."

So saying he passed behind the screen into the apartment of the idol, crossed the room, and issued through the door at the farther end.

Bill breathed a sigh of relief.

He had feared lest he should share the fate of Ned.

He acknowledged to himself that he had indeed had a narrow escape.

He was certain that Ned would never rest while he lived to seek to punish him and rescue Minnie from his power, but he never dreamed of meeting with another enemy, and that one Tom Stockton.

Bill imagined that he at least was powerless to do him harm.

His surprise was only equalled by his terror when he found himself in the grasp of that desperate ruffian, whom he believed either in durance vile or dead.

Too well he knew the bloodthirsty nature of the sailor, who, with his companions, he had robbed and betrayed to the American authorities, and when he found himself in his hands, for the moment he had given himself up as lost.

Then fear had given him strength, and he had wrested himself free as Stockton's knife glanced along his forehead, inflicted a superficial wound, and covered his eyes with blood.

Then he had bounded away, to be pursued by his relentless enemy, and turning, fired at the man in hopes to stay his pursuit.

But his aim was unsteady, and the bullet had gone wide of its mark, and again he dashed on, calling for help, only to find that he had appealed to one, if not a villain like Stockton, was one to whom that appeal must fall dead.

For his villainies had steeled the heart of Ned against him—nay, more, had excited all the desperate passions of his nature, and made him an enemy as relentless as the sanguinary-minded pirate himself.

Mean, despicable, and dishonourable himself, he expected always to find the same trait in others, and anxious to gain favour, even in the eyes of his gaolers, he thrust his hand into his pocket and drew forth several gold coins.

"Here, good fellows," he said, "share these amongst you. But for your timely aid, that villain who has been taken hence would have slain me. All barbarians are not like him. I, at least, know how to be grateful and reward my friends."

The almond-shaped eyes of the Celestials sparkled as he placed the coins into the outstretched hand of one of the soldiers.

"Goodee, tankee—muchee tankee,"

cried the soldier, as he closed his fingers over the gold as though he feared it would vanish. "Bellee goodee English manee."

And then he opened his hands and showed the coins to his companions.

Bill saw in an instant that he had made them his friends.

He was about to question them as to the probable intentions of the governor towards him, when the sound of a gong boomed through the place.

The soldier hastily thrust the coins into his pocket and sprang round the screen.

In a few moments he returned.

"The governor bids me takee you before him," he said addressing Bill.

"I am ready to attend him," replied Bill.

But his face went pale with mingled feelings of doubt and fear.

Evidently the soldier observed this, for he bent his head to Bill's ear and whispered—

"Gibee governor muchee monnee, and no fear. He likee monnee."

And he placed his finger on the side of his nose, and gave Bill a look he could not misunderstand.

Then he drew him round the screen, and placed him before the mandarin, who, with a cloth bound round his temples, and with his drawn sword lying on the table before him, presented anything but a comfortable appearance.

"Leave us, Ti-Sing," said the governor. "When you hear me strike the gong, come at once."

The soldier bowed almost to the floor and disappeared.

Bill felt far from reassured as the governor fixed his swollen and bloodshot eyes upon him.

"Barbarian," he said, "how came you to be pursued by the youth who now rests in one of our dungeons? What wrong have you done him that he should seek your life?"

"Your excellency," replied Bill, "it would be too long a story to tell you why that desperate man seeks my life. Suffice it to say that he imagines I have wronged him, and that in the wickedness of his nature he would slay me."

"Hark, you, Englishman," said the governor, "though you would throw dust in my eyes, and seek to persuade me that you are the injured and persecuted, know that I have information that stamp you the villain and he the true man."

Bill started.

"And yet you consign him to a dungeon," said Bill.

The words slipped out before he could prevent them, and he bit his lips with vexation.

"Disguise and deceit are useless with me," said Fum-Fum. "You have stolen from him a girl whom he loves. Is it not so?"

Bill was silent.

The mandarin watched him narrowly for some moments, and then in a pointed tone, said—

"Bill Boastsr—for such I know your name to be—you will find it better to make me your friend than your foe."

"As an honest man," began Bill, "I protest——"

"Hold!" cried the mandarin. "Do English pirates call themselves honest men?"

Bill started and became deathly pale.

Fum-Fum smiled.

He had marked well the words of Ned when he had called Bill a pirate and a traitor, and now he felt sure that the young Englishman before him had indeed been a pirate.

Leaning across the table, he seized Bill's wrist.

"Where lost you the fingers of this hand?" he asked.

"In Bokhara," replied Bill.

"How?" asked the governor, keeping his gaze fixed intently on Bill's face.

"I was travelling in the mountains, when I was seized by the soldiers of a rebel prince, and forced to fight for him against the Amir of Bokhara, and in that battle I lost those fingers."

"What prince?"

"Dost Mahomed, the amir's brother."

"And you were not then maimed at sea? Lie not to me. They were severed from your hand when boarding a rich merchantman."

"I swear they were not," cried Bill. "In every fight on the ocean I escaped without a wound."

"And yet you boarded many vessels in search of plunder," said the mandarin.

"True," replied Bill, thrown off his

guard, "but, I was never—ah, confusion!"

The mandarin laughed aloud.

"Englishman," he cried, "those who lie should be careful not to betray themselves. You admit you have been a pirate as that countryman of yours asserted."

"I admit nothing," said Bill, looking round in hopes of finding a means of escape.

When he turned again to the mandarin Fum-Fum had a pistol in his hand, and his finger rested on the trigger.

Bill grew paler and paler.

Not for a moment did Fum-Fum take his eyes off him.

He seemed to enjoy Bill's confusion, for his half-closed eyes twinkled, and a smile wreathed his swollen features.

"Hark you, barbarian," said the governor, "there are few things unknown to me. My spies are everywhere, and I know who and what you are. How I obtained that information is my business. My duty, as governor of these parts is to consign you to death."

"Mercy!" cried Bill, falling on his knees.

"Rise. I have not said that I shall do so," said Fum-Fum. "I merely say as governor it is my duty; but my heart is soft, and mercy can be purchased, for there are others who know as well as myself what you have been, and their silence would have to be secured."

"Only say what you require," cried Bill, "and I will give it."

"Bah!" cried the mandarin, "it is impossible."

"Not so; I am rich," cried Bill. "Name your price, and I will pay it without a murmur."

"Then you must be rich indeed," said Fum-Fum, with difficulty suppressing the joy he felt.

"I am," said Bill; "at least I have——"

"Enough, enough," said Fum-Fum. "I did but try you. You deserve death, and would like me to forget my duty—me the representative of the Brother of the Sun and Moon. A sum equal to ten thousand English pounds would not make me forget that I am here to deal out justice, punish the wrongdoer, and avenge the majesty of outraged laws."

"I will give that sum, your excellency—I swear it—if you suffer me to go hence, and give me your promise that none shall molest or harm me."

Fum-Fum shook his head.

"I dare not," he said. "What, place my own existence in your power? No, no. Is Fum-Fum a fool, that a barbarian thinks to make him his tool?"

"I swear I will never betray you!" cried Bill.

"Who can believe a liar and a traitor? Did you not betray your own friends?"

Bill could not reply.

He believed that Fum-Fum was well informed as to his antecedents, when indeed the wily governor only guessed a part of them from Ned's words, and was playing upon the other's fears to extract a goodly sum from him.

But Bill had placed himself further in his power, and the mandarin's greed rose accordingly.

An idea struck him by which he could increase the sum it was evident Bill was willing to give to be permitted to go free, and at the same time secure his silence.

"Hark you, barbarian," he said. "You hold in your power a girl whom you have torn away from her friends. You love her?"

"I do."

"Then for her sake I will be merciful, but on certain conditions."

"Name them."

"A sum equal to twelve thousand English pounds shall be paid to me, and to secure your silence, the girl to be placed with me till you sail for England. Start not; I mean her no harm. By the bones of my ancestors, I swear it. On this condition only will I spare your life. Reject my offer, and you share the dungeon and the fate of your enemy who pursued you hither."

"On one condition, excellency, I consent," said Bill, huskily. "I will hand you over the gold, I will place the girl in your keeping as hostage till I can obtain a passage to England, on condition that I gaze upon the corpse of Ned Nimble."

"Agreed," cried Fum-Fum. "Over his dead body your ransom shall be paid. At noon to-morrow you shall gaze upon your foe and mine—dead!"

CHAPTER XVIII.

IN WHICH JUMBO AND TILDA COME TO GRIEF.

JUMBO and Tilda stood looking at the closed door, undecided how to act; but when the sound of the shots which Ned had fired in the vestibule broke upon their ears, the negro roused himself.

"I'se bound to hab dat ar door down," he cried; "I'se boun' to, I tells yer, or Massa Ned'll get it hot."

And Jumbo made a kick at the door.

"Why don't yer help me kick dis yer door down?" cried the black, again raising his foot.

Tilda was not slow to assist him.

Jumbo dealt another heavy kick on the door; but, losing his balance on one leg, he received Tilda's kick in the centre of his back.

"Gor-a-mighty!" yelled Jumbo, "what's dat?"

"Dat's dis foot," said Tilda. "What for yer chuck yerself agin it? Yer ain't a door am yer?"

"I'se a dead un, I is, I know!" cried Jumbo; "an' yer's been an' kicked me jus' where I falled down when Ned knocked me ober under dat ar winder?"

"Oh, de winder—dat's it! Let's get in at the winder," cried Tilda.

"I'se boun' to hab dat ar Ned out ob dis yer place, I is," said Jumbo, "so foller dis yer walliant warrior ter de winder."

And Jumbo turned and dashed round the pagoda towards the windows.

Tilda followed Jumbo round the pagoda.

"Dis yer fan ob mine am quite spiled," she moaned.

"Oh, blow de fan! What's de fan ter Massa Ned?"

"How's I ter blow de fan? Yer knows it ought ter blow me, an' it won't," said Tilda.

"Den chuck it away. Golly, look dar!" cried Jumbo.

"What's dat?" cried Tilda.

"Dey's been and fastened de winders up!" said Jumbo.

"Den we'll hab to knock 'em down dat's all," said Tilda.

Shutters had been placed before the openings.

"I reckons dat won't take dis yer chile long," said Jumbo.

And he dealt the woodwork a blow with his fist.

"Gor-a-mighty!" he yelled, jumping about, and shaking his hand.

"What's de matter?"

"I'se been and knocked dis yer hand ob mine," he cried.

"What for yer try to hit dat ar wood wid yer hand?" said Tilda. "Yer ought ter know better nor that, yer ought."

"What I do den to get in dar?"

"Yer calls yerself a cleber nigger, doesn't yer?" said Tilda.

"Guess dar arn't a cleberer."

"Yer's a fool, dat's what yer are."

"How's yer mean?" said Jumbo.

"As if a nigger would go for to knock anyfing down with his fistes," said Tilda, "unless him lost his skull; den, ob course, he couldn't help it."

"I'se been an' gone an' hurt my footses, an' now I'se hurt my fistes; so jes' yer stan' aside, Tilda, or you'se bound to go frue dat winder as well as dis yer head ob mine."

Tilda drew aside, and Jumbo, retreating some paces lowered his head, and ran full butt at the shutters.

But Jumbo had forgotten one thing, and that was, that as the bottom of the opening was as high as his shoulders as he stood upright, it was considerably higher than his head in his crouching position.

Instead of striking the shutter with his head, he struck the stonework several inches below it and rebounding he sat down at Tilda's feet, seeing one of the finest pyrotechnic displays he had ever witnessed in his life, and with the sounds of a dozen kettledrums ringing in his ears.

"Oh, I'm brest," cried Tilda, "you'se been an' gone an' done it!"

"Am it broke?" moaned Jumbo.

"What, yer skull?" cried Tilda. "Yer iggerent fool! did yer fink yer could get through a stone wall?"

"Am dis yer dis worle or de toder one?" said Jumbo, vacantly.

"I reckons yer's a-trying ter go to de toder one, ain't yer?" said Tilda. "If dat ar skull ob yours hadn't been as fick as dat ar wall, yer'd a-knocked dem ar brains ob yours out, yer would."

"I hasn't got any brains," said Jumbo, "dey's all turned into fireworks."

And he rubbed the top of his head vacantly.

"Git up wid yer, do," cried Tilda; "dar's a lot ob people a-coming."

She aided Jumbo to rise, but so heavy had been the self-inflicted blow on his skull that he felt quite dazed.

Passing his hand across his eyes, he cried—

"I'se boun' to hab it dis time."

Again he retreated, again he ran forward with lowered head, and bounding up, struck the shutter fair in the middle of the panel.

There was a crash, a splintering sound and Jumbo's head went through the panel.

Then down dropped his legs, and he hung by his neck on the splintered timbers, his head inside the apartment, and his body out.

The yell he gave as the splinters fixed themselves in his neck was enough to rouse the neighbourhood; but strange to say, those assembled in the vestibule of the pagoda heard nothing of it.

Tilda echoed the cry as she saw the dangerous position in which he was placed, and flinging down her mutilated fan, with great presence of mind she forced away the splintered wood from around Jumbo's neck till he could withdraw his head from the jagged orifice.

Then down he dropped to the earth suffering considerable pain from the wounds and splinters in his neck and cheeks.

"I reckons dar's somefing wrong 'bout dis chile!" he moaned. "Am dar been an earfquake in dese yer parts? Oh, golly!"

He had driven a small splinter of wood that adhered to his neck further into the flesh as he passed his hand over it.

"I feels as if dis yer worle was a-coming ter an end," he added. "Tilda, am I a-libe?"

"Guess yer wanted ter kill yerself," said Tilda; "why yer's got erough wood a-sticking 'bout yer ter make yer coffin,

yer hab. Here get up; I don't like de look ob de fellers what's a-coming; dey's a-pointing to us, dey is. D'ye hear?—dey's a-pointing."

"I feels de points if I doesn't see um," said Jumbo. "I'se got 'bout a hunnered skewers in dis neck ob mine, I'll swar."

"An' I'll 'swar dese yer fellers don't mean not no good," said Tilda. "Dey's arter us, for suah."

Jumbo struggled to his feet.

Sparks still floated before his eyes, sounds still rang in his ears, and the splinters still pricked into his flesh at every movement of his head.

In fact the blow he had struck his head against the stones had half stunned him, thick skulled as he was, and he felt dazed.

He could, however, make out a crowd of Celestials approaching.

Nor could he mistake from their gesticulations that they meant mischief to him or Tilda.

He passed his hands several times across his eyes as if to clear the cobwebs from his brain, and then said—

"Tilda, we's in for it."

"I reckons we is," said Tilda.

"Whar's my 'wolver?"

"Dar it am."

"Den I reckons I'll hab ter use it."

He made an attempt to pick it up from the ground on to which it had fallen when jerked from its resting-place beneath his coat, when, with a loud yell, the Celestials dashed forward, and flung themselves upon him and Tilda.

"Gotee, gotee!" they cried.

Two of them, who had pounced upon Jumbo in his stooping position, had made sure of an easy victory; but as the black threw up his body, he flung them both on to their heads with a force that threatened to break their skulls.

"Gor-a-mighty! what's yer arter?" he yelled, standing on the defensive.

Tilda made her nails cut little grooves in more than one cheek ere she was held powerless by a couple of the Chinese.

For a moment the Celestials fell back before the stalwart black, but a voice in the rear called upon them to secure him, and in a body they again rushed forward.

Jumbo had not possessed himself of his revolver.

It lay still at his feet, and though his

temples throbbed as if they would burst, he showed a bold front; and, as they dashed forward, he struck out, knocking one after the other over as though they were ninepins.

Had the negro kept his back to the wall of the pagoda, his capture would not have been an easy matter, for the Celestials feared to come within reach of those black fists, which every time Jumbo shot them out dropped a yellow-skinned Chinaman to the earth.

But in the excitement of the struggle Jumbo forgot caution.

He was not content to stand only on the defensive, especially as he saw Tilda being borne away by two men.

He resolved to attack despite the numbers opposed to him.

" I reckons as how dis chile can smash de ole biling ob yer!" he shouted.

And dashing forward, he toppled his assailants over, one after another, as if they had been trusses of straw.

"Come on!" he cried; "I're Jumbo de Onety-onth, and de chile ter do it. Come and smell dese yer fistes, and if I don't put a stopper in dem ar scent bottles ob yours, say as I isn't a true-born nigger, what can wallop a hunnered Chinamen afore breakfast. What yer arter? Get out ob dat ar, or I'll bust yer!"

Three or four Celestials had worked their way behind him and secured his arms.

Jumbo tried to fling them off, but in vain; so, giving a leap, he flung himself backwards, hurling his captors off their feet, and falling back with all his weight on the top of them.

They squealed like a lot of rats and let go their hold, but before Jumbo could rise to his feet to renew the battle, half-a-dozen others flung themselves upon him and held him down.

This increased the weight on those beneath him, and the yells and shrieks of the undermost were enough to curdle the blood of those who heard them.

Jumbo plunged and kicked, but all to no avail.

His arms were secured to his sides, his legs were tied together, and with an exultant shout, he was raised on to the shoulders of six or eight men.

Then a superbly-attired Celestial approached, and exclaimed—

" To the chokee with him! We must teach these dogs of barbarians how to behave themselves in China!"

CHAPTER XIX.

IN WHICH JUMBO AND TILDA ARE PUT TO THE TORTURE, AND JACK, CHARLEY AND SALLY COME TO THEIR RESCUE.

RESISTANCE on the part of Jumbo was in vain.

His head ached, his arms ached, and his back pained him considerably.

With his arms and his legs tied, what could he do?

Only vow vengeance on his captors, and this he did in no measured tones.

"Wait till dis chile gets him arms and legs free, an' I guess dat Jumbo de Onety-onth ull hab a somefing ter say ter yer, yer pig-eyed waggerbones. I'll be de def ob all ob yer, I will."

The Chinese took no notice of his ravings, unless it was to pinch him maliciously.

" Put blackee manee in chokee," was the reply.

" Gor-a-mighty! if dese yer fistes ob mine was free, I reckons dey'd gib yer chokee, an' smashee too, yer yaller wampires! What's yer going ter do ter dat ar Tilda?"

" Puttee in chokee too," was the reply.

" If yer only lays a finger on dat ar lubly cretur, dere won't be a Chinaman left in dese yer parts when I gets free," said Jumbo. " Yer better mind what yer about now, for yer's boun' ter get it hot, yer is, so I tells yer!"

The Celestials laughed and jeered at his threats, and the sumptuously attired one who had ordered him and Tilda to be conveyed to punishment, struck Jumbo across the thigh with the flat of his sword, saying—

" Silence, or you shall have it worse than I intended!"

"Who de debil's yer?" cried Jumbo.

"I'm the head of the police," was the reply. "So beware!"

"Go ter de debil! Who cares for yer, yer rat-eating son of a gun? Yer de head ob de police, am yer? I guess I'd make a better fing nor you out ob a bundle ob ole rags! Why, in de States dey wouldn't hang such a ting up at de door ob a rag shop, let alone put yer in a grocery winder ter nod ter de people outside. Get out wid yer! Gor-a-mighty, de head ob de perlice! I guess dis yer chile ud make a better one out ob a ha'porth ob putty."

"You shall suffer for this," said that functionary, who though he did not understand every word that Jumbo said yet guessed enough to know that they were far from complimentary to him.

"Den yer'll hab ter look out for yer eye," said Jumbo. "I'se good at putting a mouse on a cheek bone, and one yer can't eat eider."

"Silence!" cried the officer, again striking Jumbo with the flat of his sword.

"Look here, yer waggerbones!" cried Jumbo. "I'll gib a dollar to any one what hits dat cowardly whelp a smack on de side ob his nose, or I'll gib yer one back for it when I gets my hands free."

But no one accepted the offer, so the head of the police did not become the recipient of the blow which Jumbo hoped some one would deal him.

In a short time they reached a kind of square surrounded by houses of the better class of Chinese, principally merchants engaged in the tea trade.

By this time a goodly crowd had assembled, and amid hooting and jeers, Tilda and Jumbo were placed in the centre of the square, supported on either side by a couple of Chinese.

The head of the police then gave some rapid orders, and about a dozen men dashed towards one of the buildings on the left of the square.

The bystanders now began to evince great interest and to talk loudly and gesticulate wildly.

In a few minutes the men were seen returning, bearing with them a couple of strange objects.

As they came through the crowd, Jumbo saw that they were rough trunks of trees, with stout boards attached to one end, in which were large holes.

"What de debil's dey arter?" muttered Jumbo.

But Tilda did not hear him, as they were kept apart, at a distance of some eight or ten yards.

Jumbo, however, soon saw what was meant to be done with the timbers, for the men, reaching the centre of the square, lowered the instruments from their shoulders, and standing them upright with the planks with the holes at the top, waited till their companions raised a kind of plug in the ground, and then they dropped one of the trunks into the hole to about one third its length.

Another plug was raised, and the second instrument dropped into its place.

They now stood at about ten yards apart.

"What de debil's dey for?—ter stick bills on ter tell de people dar's some ob de houses ter let, I wonner? But what's dem ar holes for? Can't make it out, brest if I can."

While he looked Jumbo saw half the board at the top open about a foot, as a man wound it up by a kind of winch in the post.

"Bring him along!" cried the chief.

Jumbo was carried to the post and stood against it.

"What's yer arter?" he yelled.

"Force his head down."

A couple of Celestials forced Jumbo's neck down into the half-circle of the largest centre hole, and held it there, assisted by another Celestial who had drawn Jumbo's false plait through the hole and hung on to it tightly.

Then the bonds that secured his arms were cut, and his arms forced up, and his hands drawn over the boards, till his wrists rested one in each of the smaller holes.

And then, while held in this position by the Chinese, a man set the winch to work, and down came the top board, the holes in which closed over Jumbo's neck and wrists.

"Gor-a-mighty! I'se chocking," gasped Jumbo.

The fellow at the winch gave it another turn, and Jumbo thought his head was coming off, and his hands as well.

His mouth opened wide, his eyes seemed to start from his head.

He was unable to move one way or the other.

I'se a gone un, for suah !" he thought. "Oh, golly ! am dis de end ob Jumbo de Onety-onth ?"

Having secured him to this torture post, the chief of the police cut the bonds of his legs.

"You may kickee now, if likee," he said, "but if do kickee, pullee head off, see if don'tee !"

Jumbo only moaned and tried to get a sight of Tilda.

That lady seeing Jumbo placed in the instrument, gave utterance to such a series of howls ard fought so desperately with her gaolers, that they had to force her down to the ground, and hold her there till her time came to be placed in the diabolical instrument reserved for her reception.

As soon as Jumbo was thoroughly secured, the police officer gave orders for Tilda to be placed at the post, and kicking, biting, screaming and squealing, she was half-dragged, half-carried up to the instrument of torture.

She gave her captors plenty of trouble before they could secure her as they had done Jumbo, and not a few faces would smart for some days to come from the long red seams Tilda carved on the yellow-shinned Celestials with her long sharp nails.

But at length she too was secured.

The posts faced each other, and the two victims of Chinese cruelty could each watch the other's sufferings.

But they could not talk.

The boards were screwed down too tightly to admit of that.

They could only look at the contorted face and drooping hands that protruded through the holes in the boards.

To increase their agonies, they were compelled to stand on tip-toe, or run the risk of dislocating their necks.

The whole affair was something like the old pillory long since done away with in England.

Now commenced volleys of abuse from the crowd, jeers, insults, and even showers of missiles.

More than once Jumbo and Tilda were struck on the face and hands by the refuse thrown at them by the delighted mob.

Louder and louder became the noise,

Fiercer and fiercer the onslaught of refuse, and nearer and nearer crowded the Celestials to get better aim at their victims.

One of the Chinese police had procured a whip with which he lashed away at the legs of Jumbo, while a comrade eager to make the negro's sufferings the greater, pulled fiercely at the false pigtail, never thinking that the plait was only fastened to the woolly pate of its wearer by a strap.

Jumbo and Tilda gave themselves up for lost, when there was a shout in a true English voice, and the crowd were scattered right and left as if a bombshell had fallen in their midst.

"Let 'em have it straight from the shoulder. Down with the rat-eating whelps. Strike home, Charley. Shoulder to shoulder, lad. Down with 'em !"

It was Jack's voice that rose above the noise of the crowd.

And it was Jack's fist that rolled Celestial after Celestial on to the earth with bleeding faces and sorely bruised eyes.

"Give 'em their gruel. Wire in, Sally. We'll have old Jumbo out of that, or my name ain't Charley."

"Go it, my boys ! I'll show 'em what sort of a woman I am," cried the shrill tones of Sally Jones. "I'll teach 'em to put Tilda and Jumbo in them ar things. Down you go. There's one from the gal brought up in the Dials. That's the sort of woman I am."

And Jack, Charley, and Sally, the two former fighting with their fists, and Sally striking right and left with a short thick bamboo, forced their way through the crowd and up to the instruments of torture, where stood the chief officer of the police and those who had assisted him to carry out his decree of punishment on Jumbo and Tilda.

One of these men had forced a fan into Tilda's hand, telling her she'd want it to keep her face cool, and had just turned to hear the cause of the disturbance, when Charley flung one arm round his neck, and getting his head into chancery punched furiously at the fellow's face.

He had heard his jeering remarks to the negress, and in his indignation, he severely pummelled that startled and terrified Chinee,

The police officer called upon his assistants and made a cut at Jack with his sword.

But Jack avoided the blow, grasped the fellow's arm, gave it a twist, causing him to drop his weapon, an 1, planting a blow under his ear, knocked him amongst his companions all of a heap.

Then he turned upon the fellow with the whip, and hitting out with all the force of his strong arms, he knocked him down by a blow under the chin as if he had been a ninepin.

Sally had caught one of the Celestials, and belaboured him heavily.

The fellow howled, and tried to escape and in so doing fell.

But Sally's temper was up.

She seized him by the legs, and pulling them up under her left arm, she belaboured his back so heavily that the fellow shrieked for mercy.

"I'll give you mercy!" cried Sally. "There! how d'ye like it? There's mercy for you! There! there! there!"

The Chinese around stood terrified.

They could only look on with staring eyes and open mouths.

In vain did the officer and his satellites call upon them to protect them.

In vain did he threaten that they should all share the punishment if they did not seize the white devils.

Not one of the bystanders stirred unless when Jack make a dash after some one in their direction, and then they scattered like mice on the appearance of a cat.

The threats and exhortations of the chief officer were soon silenced.

Charley, having flung the fellow away from him whose face he had been pummelling, he made a dash at the officer, and giving him one straight from the shoulder, fair between his little eyes, he dropped him to the earth as neatly as Jack had done a few moments before.

It was not long before Jack, Charley, and Sally had disposed of the police, and then they made a rush upon the crowd.

Those who composed it did not stop to meet the onslaught.

With screams of terror and yells of dismay, they broke and ran in all directions.

In their eagerness to get away from the barbarians, many were thrown down and trampled under foot.

Though their number was large their courage was small.

They dared not face those who had so severely punished the police.

The desperate blows of the two men and the woman who had burst into their midst struck terror to their cowardly hearts and they fled precipitately.

"Now get the poor beggars out," cried Jack.

He sprang to the post where Jumbo was confined, while Charley went to the relief of Tilda.

But they did not understand how the thing was worked.

Jack saw the winch, and believing that he must turn it, he gave it a sharp twist.

A gurgling choking sound made him look up, and the sight that Jumbo's face presented startled him.

He had tightened the boards instead of loosening them, and saw that so far from easing he was increasing the torture.

Quickly he reversed the screw, and the boards opened.

The next minute he had lifted Jumbo in his arms, and laid him on the earth.

Charley released Tilda, and supported her on his knee, and Sally, drawing a scent-bottle from her pocket, held it to her nose.

"Is I dead?" asked Jumbo.

"No, old man, you are all right," said Jack; "or at least you will be soon."

"Deu," said Jumbo, "if I'se alibe I means ter hab wengeance for dis yer 'digernity to Jumbo de Onety-onth."

And rising to his feet, he looked round, and then dashing upon the officer as he was slinking away, he seized him by the shoulder in a firm and powerful grasp.

CHAPTER XX.

IN WHICH JUMBO HAS HIS REVENGE AND THE OFFICER GETS A TASTE OF THE PUNISHMENT HE HAD INFLICTED ON THE NEGRO.

THE officer turned his bruised and blackened face to the negro.

"If you hurtee, you get muchee stickee," he cried.

"You givee dis chile chokee, did yer?" cried Jumbo. "Jewellikins, but I reckons yer'll get chokee yerself. I'se boun' to let yer hab it, so jus' yer come along."

"Letee go!" cried the man.

"Jack, jus' yer haul dis yer willing up to dat ar ting. Dis yer han' ob mine hurts, an' I can't give him de proper twist."

"All right, old man. Now then, puppy scruncher, you've got to take your physic."

And Jack, gripping the Celestial's shoulder, dragged him to the instrument in which Jumbo had been placed.

"Jus' poke de willing's head in dat ar 'ole," said Jumbo, "an' I'll gib him de screw up, I'se boun' I knows how ter do it."

Jack forced the fellow's head into the orifice.

"Neber mind his hands," said Jumbo, "dey'll do to scratch him back wid, a'cos I'se going ter larrup him when I'se made him tight, I is. Ole him down Jack—dat's it."

And Jumbo put his hand to the winch. Down came the board.

"Mercee—hab mercee on poor Chinaman!" cried the fellow.

"Guess I'll hab all dat," said Jumbo. "How's yer like dat?"

And Jumbo gave the winch another turn.

"Oh you killee! I no breathee! Have mercee!"

"Course I will. Dar, dat's it. Golly! look at dem ar little eyes ob his'n. Ain't dey grown big? Ha, ha!"

Jumbo had put on more pressure, and the Celestial's eyes fairly started from his head.

He would have cried out, but was powerless to articulate.

"How's yer like dat?" asked Jumbo. "Guess yer tinks it prime, doesn't yer? Neber tasted it afore, didn't yer? Guess

yer does now den. Shall I gib yer anoder turn?"

"No, no," said Jack, laying his hand on Jumbo's arm; "another turn would kill him."

"Guess dat's trufe," said Jumbo. "But den, yer see, dere'd be an end of him, and he wouldn't be able to put anoder fellow into chokee."

"He won't be in a hurry to do so, I'll wager," said Jack.

"Tilda," cried Jumbo.

"Dat's me," said Tilda, who, under the care of Charley and Sally, had come round a bit.

"Yer see dis yer willing?"

"Ob course I does, dough dese yer eyes ob mine do ache, dey does."

"I'se a-going ter teach him the danger ob putting such extinguished inderwiderels as our magernanermous majesties into dat ar ting."

"How's yer going to do it?"

"I'se going to borrow dat ar stick ob Sally, and den I'se going to wire into dese yer legs an' back of his'n, I is."

Sally threw him the stick.

"Don't spare the beast," she said; "for if you do, I'll show him what sort of a woman I am."

"Now den," said Jumbo, flourishing the bamboo, "dis yer's to teach yer how to 'spect the mighty mighterness ob 'zalted pussonages what honours dis yer rat-eating country wid de splendifferous splenderosity ob dar presence. How yer like dat?"

And Jumbo gave the fellow a cut across the bottom of his back with the stout cane.

The Celestial did not answer in words, but began to rub away at the injured part with both hands.

"Yer'd better take dem ar fistses ob yourn away, or I'se boun' ter hit ye across de knuckles, I is," cried Jumbo.

Down came the stick again, and the Celestial failed to remove his hands; his knuckles suffered.

"Here, let's hab a go at dat ar," said

Tilda, "I'se dat full ob wengeance, I is, dat I could eat him, de cruel beast."

"Guess I wouldn't," said Jumbo, as he surrendered the stick to Tilda.

"Don't spare him!" said Sally. "If it had been me he'd served as he did you, I wouldn't have left enough of him to make a bunch of dog's meat."

"How cruel," said Charley. "But there Sally, you always was, you know."

"What was I?" cried Sally.

"A vixen," said Charley, dodging out of reach of her hand.

Tilda took Sally's advice, and did not spare the officer.

Smarting from what she had undergone, she thrashed away at the lower extremities of the Celestial with all her force, nor did she cease till her aching arms were too powerless to inflict further punishment.

Meantime the others stood on their guard lest a dash should be made at them by those under the command of the man whom they had placed in the pillory, or any of the crowd who stood looking on at a respectful distance.

But no attempt was made to interfere with the punishment they were inflicting.

Perhaps because the Celestials dreaded to encounter the heavy blows of Jack and Charley, and perhaps because they were not ill-pleased to see the police officer made to suffer the same torture as he was only too fond of inflicting upon others,

"Now," said Jack, as Tilda let fall her arm, "let's get away from here before assistance arrives. Some one will perhaps give note to the authorities, and we may find it difficult to escape."

"Dat's trufe," said Jumbo. "But what's ter be did wid dis yer willing?"

"Leave him where he is," said Charley.

"And let his fellows get him out of it," added Sally.

"It's time to scarper," said Charley; "but look out for squalls as you go."

"I'se dat sore I could squall till I busted," said Jumbo.

"And so is I," said Tilda. "Dis yer neck ob mine's broked, it is, I knows for suah."

"Never mind, Tilda; Jumbo will mend it when we get home," said Charley.

"I'd like ter gib him anoler twist afore I went," said Jumbo, looking at the poor wretch.

"Let him alone," said Jack; "he's got it bad enough."

"Come on, you fool!" said Charley. "We've got you out of one mess; you don't want to get into another, do you?"

"Guess I didn't say I did, did I?" retorted Jumbo. "Yer cheeky wagger-bone——"

"There's gratitude!" said Charley.

"Dat's trufe!" said Jumbo.

"Look here," said Jack; "I'll go first, the women follow next, and Charley and Jumbo bring up the rear, and if any attempt is made to stop us, we'll have to fight."

"I'se ready," said Jumbo.

"And so's I," said Tilda. "Dar's a lot ob fought in me, dar is! and I'se full ob wengeance agin dese yer people!"

"It's only a way they've got, Tilda," said Charley.

"Den, it's a bery bad way. Why dis neck ob mine——"

"Oh, blow your neck!" said Charley.

"How's I blow my neck?—tell me dat ar," cried Tilda.

But Charley did not answer.

He placed himself beside Jumbo, and Jack leading the way, they crossed the square.

The Celestials gave way before them, and opened a line through which they passed.

But from the threatening looks of the mob, they feared that they would not escape without a desperate struggle.

Having passed through the crowd, Jack said—

"Mind you are not attacked from behind."

"All serene," said Charley; "I've got one eye at the back of my head."

"I hasn't got no eyes dar, but I'se got a lot ob bumps, I has," said Jumbo.

"Don't be bumptious," said Charley.

"What's dat?"

"What's the use of explaining? you don't understand Greek."

"Am it Greek?"

"Of course it is. Halloa, look at the beggars!"

All turned to see a half-a-dozen hands releasing the police officer from his painful position.

"Wonder how he liked it?" said Sally.

"Guess about as much as I an' Tilda did," said Jumbo.

"I reckons I didn't like it at all," said Tilda. "I fought my head was off, I did."

"An' I knowed mine was," said Jumbo. "When dey gib dis yer winepipe dat ar twist, I fought I was a gone coon for sartin suah."

"Don't stop to jaw," said Jack, "let's dive down this street, I know where it leads to."

They dived down a narrow street, and hurried along it till they came to another up which they went at a good speed.

Jack expected that, as soon as the officer had recovered sufficently to order a pursuit, a hue and cry would be raised after them.

But such was not the case.

Up one street and down another they went, till finally they came out into the one in which they lodged without meeting with any molestation.

If, indeed, any pursuit had been attempted, they had completely baffled their foes.

They reached their lodgings in safety, but fairly tied out.

Tilda flung herself in a bamboo chair.

"I 'clare to goodness," she cried, "if dis ain't de wustest part ob de worle I eber seed."

"Dat's trufe," said Jumbo. "I'se dat ar disgustered wid it dat I wows ter goodness if eber I gets out ob it I'll neber come into it agin. Dem ar suberjects ob mine was bad enough, but dese yer Chinamens am wuster nor dem. Hullo, dar! what de debil yer do in dat ar room?"

And Jumbo sprang to his feet as he caught sight of a couple of figures through the half-closed doorway that shut out the inner apartment.

Following his gaze Jack and Charley sprang to the door.

Ching-Fow the younger stood close to the window, but he was alone.

"What are you doing here?" asked Jack.

"Begee pardon," said Ching-Fow. "Me come seekee Massa Nedee. No findee, so lookee here for him."

"What do you want with him?" asked Jack, eyeing the young Celestial suspiciously.

"He tellee me come to him. He wantee speakee me," replied Ching-Fow.

"Dat's a lie!" said Jumbo.

"How do you know?" asked Jack.

"'Cos Massa Ned went out afore me an' Tilda," replied Jumbo.

"He may have returned," said Charley.

"Guess he habn't, though," said Jumbo.

"How do you know?"

"'Cos we know where we left him, don't we, Tilda?"

"I reckons we does; poor Massa Ned."

Jack and Charley were struck by the tones of Tilda's voice.

"I forgot ter tell yer all 'bout it," said Jumbo. "Dis yer pain put it out ob my head."

"About what?" asked Jack.

"I'll tell yer derectly," replied Jumbo. "But fust I'se got suffing ter say to dis yer chopstick. Now, yer better be bery careful how yer tells me lies. What's yer doing here?"

"I comee to lookee for Massa Nedee. He tellee me comee when he wentee outee widee mannee what broughtee him lettee."

"Well, p'raps dat's trufe," said Jumbo. "But whar's dat oder chopstick what was here wid yer just now?"

"Blackee manee try makee foolee ob Chinamanee. Don't know what he meanee; no manee here at allee."

"You lying waggerbone," cried Jumbo; "I see him wid dese yer eyes ob mine. Yer better tell whar's he's gone, or I'll break ebery bone in yer body, I will. Whar am he? Speak de trufe, or I'll bust yer!"

CHAPTER XXI.

IN WHICH HARRY RESOLVES UPON A DESPERATE AND DANGEROUS UNDERTAKING.

CHING-Fow fell upon his knees.

"Oh, goodee blackee manee," he cried, "Have mercee upon poor Chinamanee."

"Whar's de oder one? Yer better tell de trufe, or yer's as good as a corpus, yer am," cried Jumbo.

"Blackee manee much mistakee. No other manee here."

"What! when I seed him? Is yer going ter tell me as I'se a liar?" cried Jumbo.

"No tellee dat; but tellee muchee mistake. Lookee, no manee here, only poor Ching-Fow."

"You saw double, old man," said Charley. "There's nobody else here, and I've looked everywhere, even under the beds."

"Den I sees double, dat's all," said Jumbo. "Why, I swears ter goodness dat dese yer eyes ob mine——"

"Oh, blow your eyes!" said Charley. "You know you squint, and that made you fancy you saw two men instead of one."

"Beree goodee. Dat's de truthee," said Ching-Fow.

"Yer say I squints, does yer?" cried Jumbo. "Say dat agin, and I'll make yer squint till yer can see roun' free corners at once, I will."

"Let the fellow go," said Jack. "You must have fancied you saw some one else and evidently he only came here expecting to find Ned."

"Look here," said Sally, "I ain't so sure of that. Just hold him while I take a look round to see if he has been up to anything. I know he's bad enough for any dirty work."

Sally took a survey of the apartment. Evidently nothing had been disturbed.

"All right," she said. "Let him go."

"Yer can take yerself off," said Jumbo, "and dis wid yer as well."

And he gave the young Celestial a kick that facilitated his movements considerably.

When they were again alone, Jack turned to Jumbo.

"What about Ned Nimble?" he asked.

Jumbo and Tilda both speaking at once told him about the letter Ned had received; how he had dashed off to the Purple Pagoda in expectation of finding Minnie there; of Ned's capture and rescue by himself and Tilda; of their meeting with Bill Boaster, and Ned's recapture by the governor; the second attempt to rescue him, and their own capture by the police.

Of their punishment they knew.

As Jumbo and Tilda finished their story, Harry Honour and 'Dolf returned.

The story was repeated, this time by Jumbo alone, and Harry's face grew hard and rigid as he listened to the recital.

"Poor Ned!" said Harry. "But at the sacrifice of my own life will I rescue him."

"And I," said 'Dolf.

"And I," repeated the others.

"This letter was a trap to get him into their power, whoever they may be," said Harry, "and Bill is at the bottom of it."

"Dat's de mysterious mystery ob it," said Jumbo. "Dat meandering swor dat he didn't know Bill Boaster, an' Tilda heard him say so, didn't yer?"

"Guess I did dat," replied Tilda.

"Tell us every word you heard, Jumbo. Don't omit a sentence, there's a good fellow," said Harry.

"I guess as my memoratic memory isn't so bad but as I can reccerlect all what dey said."

"Then out with it, for Heaven's sake!" said 'Dolf.

Thus pressed, Jumbo repeated word for word the conversation he had listened to outside the window of the pagoda.

Long did Harry think over what he had heard, and at length springing to his feet, he cried—

"By Heaven! I believe I've hit it!"

"What's yer hit?" asked Jumbo.

"The truth—the whole truth!"

"I didn't see yer hit nuffin," said Tilda. "Did yer, Mrs. Jones?"

"Get out!" said Sally. "What yer driving at now?"

"Ma'am," said Tilda, freezingly. "I'd hab yer ter know as how I's not dribing at anyfing."

"Hold your tongue," said Sally. "Do you want to drive it out of Master Harry's head?"

"I didn't know as he'd got anyfing in his head," said Tilda. "I'se quite sure dat such a bery decent young man——"

"Oh, you fool!" interrupted Sally.

"I returns de complerment, ma'am," said Tilda. "Fool! Oh, dear, how bery wise we is, Mrs. Jones. I'se boun' ter make a cursey to yer. I'm sure yer bery 'sperior wisdom ob course entitles yer to the dispect ob de iggerent Tilda Tompkins."

And Tilda rose and made a curtsey, pressing her lips together and turning up her nose with the most supreme contempt as she did so.

This raised Sally's ire to such a degree that she sprang up to slap the face of Tilda, but Jack's restraining hand fell on her arm.

She turned fiercely upon him.

" Sally," he said, and his voice was low but severe, "none of that. There is too great a danger threatening Ned for any of us to think of aught but saving him. Do not cause me annoyance by these stupid quarrels. Sit down."

" Who are you ordering to sit down, sir ? " said Sally. " You forget what sort of a woman I am."

" It is you who forget yourself," said Jack. " When the life of one who has so greatly befriended me is in danger it is no time for my wife to cause me pain and annoyance by making a fool of herself."

Sally would have retorted but the look Jack gave her warned her not to go too far.

She sat down and sulked.

Never before had Jack spoken to her so firmly.

She was surprised and annoyed, and yet she could not but admit to herself that it was foolish of her to get out of temper with Tilda.

She sat sulking at one end of the room, while Tilda took a seat at the other.

The five men grouped themselves in the centre of the apartment, and discussed Ned's danger, and what had led to his visiting the pagoda.

That Bill after all was at the bottom of it they believed, especially as he had taken refuge in the pagoda from Ned and the sailor ; but the threat which Jumbo had overheard the governor utter about floating out Ned's body when the water-gate was opened, brought about many surmises.

Why should the water-gate be opened at night ? for what purpose, and where was the gate situated ?

Then again, what could the governor have meant when he asserted that Ned and his friends had learned too much, and if suffered to live, might betray him to his master, the emperor ?

What could they possibly have learned that if revealed could bring about Fum-Fum's ruin ?

If he were an honest man, and honestly fulfilling his duty, how could he be injured ?

But was he what he pretended to be?

The universal answer was No, or he would have nothing to fear.

And if he had reasons to fear, what were the causes?

The water-gate suggested itself strongly to Harry's mind.

Why need it be opened at night to float out Ned's body unless it was also opened for another cause ?

And these thoughts suggested another.

Was Fum-Fum, the governor, in league with the pirates who infested the Chinese waters ? and was the pagoda used as a store-house for the booty of these robbers of the seas ?

Argue which way they would, Harry, 'Dolf and Jack came to the conclusion that they had hit upon the truth.

Furthermore, the suspicions of Harry and 'Dolf had been excited towards the junk anchored opposite the pagoda.

She did not look like an honest trader.

There was that in the looks of her crew that bespoke them villains.

And again their numbers seemed out of all proportion to that required to work an ordinary trading-junk.

By associating the pagoda, the junk, the water-gate, and its being opened at night, together with the fact that there was no moon, a very fair conclusion was arrived at.

And that was that Fum-Fum was in league with the pirates, that the cellars of the pagoda formed the store-house for their booty, which would be landed during the night.

Having come to this conclusion, Harry said——

" Our only hope of saving Ned is by getting into that pagoda, not by the way which Ned entered but by the water-gate; and to do so it will be necessary to get in the moment it is opened. Heaven only knows whether then we may be in time."

" But where is this water-gate ? " said Jack. " The pagoda stands some distance from the shore."

" It must be at the end of a tunnel running from the river under the ground on which the pagoda is built.

"'BEHOLD THE TORTURE OF HIM YOU LOVE—THE REVENGE OF THE MAN YOU SCORN' CRIED BILL BOASTER.'"

"We will obtain a boat, and seek for the water-gate," continued Harry.

"And be detected by the pirates," said Jack.

"True," said Harry; "we will wait till it is dusk. I am a good swimmer, and when it is too dark to attract notice, either from the vessels at anchor or from the shore, I will plunge into the water, and seek to discover the entrance to the gate. If Dick Darewell were here we might get the aid of his boats and crew, but unfortunately the ' Lord Warden ' set sail this afternoon."

"I can swim well," said Jack, "and I will accompany you."

"Two may excite notice where one would escape it," said Harry. "No I will go alone ; and if I can find any inlet likely to lead to the pagoda, I will return, and then we will get a boat, even if we have to borrow it without leave ; and, provided with lights and well armed, we'll have Ned, if alive, out of the pagoda, and if dead terribly avenge him."

"We will," said 'Dolf huskily.

"Then since we can do nothing till dark, strike the gong and bid them bring up dinner," said Harry.

Charley struck the gong, and when an attendant entered, ordered the dinner to be brought.

The meal was soon placed on the table.

It was consumed in silence, for each was engaged with his own thoughts.

And these were not of a cheering nature.

Even if they should be able to find the water-gate, and effect an entrance to the pagoda, would they be able to rescue Ned ?

Their hopes said Yes, but their hearts whispered No.

No wonder that they ate sparingly, that they had no relish for their food !

The meal was soon ended and cleared away.

Then Harry rose and went into the inner apartment; and going to a box, took therefrom a six-chambered revolver which he wrapped carefully in an oilskin case.

In another piece of oilskin he wrapped several wax tapers, and secured both in a belt around his waist.

He threw off his coat and waistcoat, and put on a blue guernsey over his shirt, took off his boots, and substituted a pair of thin, light slippers belonging to Sally.

By this time it was quite dark.

He returned to the others.

Jack and 'Dolf begged to accompany him, but Harry was firm.

"No ; better that I go alone," he said. " Whether success or failure attend me, I will land about fifty yards this side of the junk, where I shall expect to meet you in an hour. Come well armed, for we know not what we may have to encounter."

"You will not attempt to enter the pagoda alone, even if you find the entrance ? " said Jack.

"No, I will return for you, unless something which cannot be foreseen occurs to prevent me I need not enjoin caution, I know. In an hour we meet again, unless Heaven wills it otherwise."

They wished him God-speed, and Harry started on his desperate errand.

He reached the wharves, passed along them for some distance, then, seeing that the coast was clear, he uttered a prayer for success, and boldly plunged from the shore into the dark waters.

CHAPTER XXII.

IN WHICH NED IS SLUNG UP AND BILL BOASTER ENJOYS HIS MISERY.

But for the wish of Bill Boaster to gaze upon the corpse of Ned Nimble, there is little doubt but that our hero, would have been put to death that night, as the governor had vowed he should be, and that long ere daylight his lifeless body would have been floating out to sea.

But Bill's promise of paying Fum-Fum twelve thousand pounds, and placing Minnie in his hands as a hostage for himself on condition that he should look upon his lifeless enemy, gave poor Ned a longer lease of life.

So the order for his execution was countermanded, and a barbarous torture to be inflicted on the poor lad in his dark dungeon under the Purple Pagoda.

Ned had given himself up for lost, and yet there was one ray of hope in his heart—the hope that Jumbo and Tilda might be able to befriend him.

But how?

That was a question he asked himself, but one to which he was unable to reply.

Still the hope forced itself upon his mind, and would not be wholly banished.

As he grew calmer and more accustomed to the terrible blackness of his dungeon he tried to think what probabilities there were of escape, even if Jumbo should seek out their friends and tell them of his captivity in the pagoda.

But think as he would he saw none.

Then he wondered whether he could bribe his gaolers.

He knew that bribery was an institution in that part of the world—that every man was to be bought at a price—and he was well able to pay even the most exorbitant demand.

In this direction there appeared brighter hopes than even in the assistance of his friends, willing as he knew all of them would be to aid him.

He tried his chains, but they were too firmly fixed in the wall and around his neck and waist to give even the faintest prospect of being able to force them away.

The hours sped on, when he heard footsteps without, and then the bar dropped from before the door.

The next moment the door was opened and the light of the lantern streaming into the blackness, caused Ned to close his eyes.

Faint as was the light, yet it dazzled Ned's vision.

It was some moments before he could face the glare.

Then he made out two men, one of them bearing the lantern, the other with a stout rope coiled around his arm.

As Ned's gaze fell upon the rope, his heart sank within him.

Had they come to do the murderous work so soon?

Brave as he was, Ned trembled.

"How English manee likee Chinee prison?" asked the fellow, holding up the lantern. "No fightee Chinee manee here. Muchee darkee, and chainee holdee tightee."

And the fellows laughed.

"Why have you come here?" asked Ned. "What do you want with me?"

"Governor bidee us comee see English manee all safee."

"He could have spared you the trouble," said Ned. "How could I get out of this fearful place?"

"No chancee. No getee outee. Chinee hold him tightee. No escapee now we gotee."

"I know it is impossible for me to escape unless you help me," said Ned.

"Harkee what he sayee," cried the man with the lantern. "Chinee manee helpee! He, he!"

And the fellow laughed as if tickled at the idea of such a thing.

"And why not?" said Ned. "I have done you no harm. If you kill me, you will be no better off, while if you aided me to escape from here I could make you rich—give you more gold than ever you could possess."

The men looked at each other meaningly.

Ned saw that the mention of gold had touched them, so went on quickly—

"I have done no wrong that I should be thus incarcerated in a dungeon. I only sought to punish one who has wronged me, and I swear I never meditated ill towards the governor or any of your countrymen. I have plenty of money, and you must know that what an Englishman promises to do, he will perform. Unfasten these chains and point me out the way to escape from the pagoda, and I will give you more gold than you can ever hope to obtain by serving your master."

"English manee talkee talkee."

"I will do more than talk if you will aid me to escape. I will do all I say."

"No catchee, not suchee foolee," said the man with the rope.

"Why not believe me?"

"Because no foolee," was the reply. "Letee gotee outee, then laughee at Chinee manee, and say gotee no monee. No catchee Chinee manee."

"I swear I will give you the money. You shall go with me to get it. I am no Chinese to lie and cheat and rob, but an Englishman whose word is his bond whose promise is as sacred as his oath."

The Chinese whispered together for some moments, then turned to Ned.

"How muchee gibee ? " asked he with the lantern.

"A thousand dollars to each of you," replied Ned.

And he watched the countenances of the two men eagerly.

But he could learn nothing from their looks or features.

Again the men conversed together in whispers.

Ned's heart again grew hopeful.

Would they aid him to escape for the promised reward ?

Yes; he felt sure that they would.

He had excited their cupidity.

"Well," he said at last, " you will earn the gold by setting me free. You will make yourselves rich by doing an act of justice and kindness ; you——"

The man with the rope sprang forward and laying his hand over Ned's mouth, cried loudly—

"Silence ! The torture must be applied. It is the governor's orders, and we, his slaves, must obey."

The other dropped the lantern on the floor, and seized Ned by the shoulders, and forced him back against the wall.

Ned tried to speak, but the hand pressed tighter over his mouth.

Then he heard voices and footsteps on the stone staircase, and guessed the reason of the sudden alteration in the men's manner.

He could distinguish the tones of Fum-Fum the governor.

Then, as he listened, a cold perspiration broke out over his face and body.

Other tones fell upon his ears.

Tones more hateful to him than those of the man who had doomed him to death.

They were those of his bitter and malignant enemy, Bill Boaster.

Too well he knew them to be mistaken.

They fell upon his ears like the knell of doom.

The hopes that had sprang to his bosom fell instantly, and blank despair took possession of his heart.

Oh, were he but free for one minute —one, that he might wreak a terrible vengeance on the head of Bill !

But he was powerless, and must submit to the taunts and jeers of his foe.

Then one desperate effort he made to hurl the men from him and snap his cruel chains.

As well might he have sought to lift the nine-storied pagoda as burst his bonds.

Then Fum-Fum and Bill Boaster entered the dungeon.

The governor turned furiously on the two men.

"Why have my commands been disobeyed ? " he cried. "Why have you not inflicted the torture of the sling ? "

The men bowed to the earth.

"Excellency, the barbarian is strong and desperate," one replied. "He has struggled so hard that we could not fix the rope."

"See to it quickly, or you shall have the stick," cried the governor.

Then he turned to Bill.

"But for you," he said, "his head would be lying there now."

And he pointed to the floor.

Ned had not yet spoken.

He had been glaring at Bill Boaster as a caged tiger might glare at the hunter who had entrapped it, but now he cried in a husky tone—

"But for that villain ! If it is to him I owe a moment's life, then it is that he might gloat in my tortures and my sufferings. Oh Heaven ! give me power to burst these bonds, that I may tear his accursed and coward heart from out his body ! Villain, wretch, assassin, this is your work ! "

"There you are wrong," said Bill. "You have me to thank that you are now living. But for me, you would have lost your head an hour ago. But I prevailed upon his excellency, the governor, to suffer you to live till to-morrow."

"Liar ! " cried Ned.

Bill's pale face flushed, and he took a step forward.

But suddenly recollecting himself, he stopped short, and turned his gaze on to the swollen and blackened face of the mandarin.

"You hear him ? " he said.

"I do. 'Tis he who lies, for it was at your desire that I suffered him to live till now."

"And if so, for what purpose, villain ? " cried Ned. "Not from pity for me, but to gratify some fiendish malice of your own."

"There you lie not," said Bill. "I implored the governor to suffer you to live that I might avenge, at least, some of my sufferings, some of the insults and indignities that I have endured at your hands."

"I knew it, cowardly, despicable hound that you are!" cried Ned.

"Hard names do not hurt me," said Bill. "I am used to them—at least from you."

"Despicable viper and contemptible coward, brave only when your foe is powerless, I loathe and despise you. Do your worst; Heaven will yet avenge me!"

"Ha, ha, ha!" laughed Bill, "I am content to wait for that. But now I have come to see you writhe and hear your groans—come to feast my eyes upon your sufferings, and glory in your pangs. Ned Nimble, it was a bad day's work for you when you made me your enemy. I swore I'd hunt you to your death, and at last I shall keep my word."

"Up with him!" cried the governor.

In spite of Ned's struggles, one of the men fastened one end of the rope into the iron collar, while the other secured the other end round the ankles of the prisoner.

Then one end of a long chain was thrown off a staple in the wall, and the links running through a pulley in the rafters above, descended till it was caught by one of the men.

The centre of the rope with which Ned was secured was fastened to the chain, and then the governor cried—

"Up with the young barbarian!"

The man who had unhooked the chain from the staple now commenced to pull upon it, and his companion assisting him the rope was drawn taut, and Ned's legs being dragged from under him, he hung suspended, face and chest downward.

"Here," cried Bill, "I will give you a hand."

And the monster, placing his hand on the chain, aided the men to draw the body up higher and higher, till Ned hung, his form curved like a bow, within three feet of the roof of the dungeon.

The weight of his body resting upon his neck and ankles, the torture that Ned now endured was fearful.

The strain upon the two extremities seemed to threaten to tear his head and feet off.

His eyes seemed to fill with blood.

Confused sounds rang in his ears.

His temples throbbed as though they were being beaten with heavy hammers.

The whole place seemed to float in blood, and through the ensanguined mist he saw, as in a haze, the face of Bill Boaster wearing an expression of most fiendish triumph.

Ned tried to speak.

He could not.

The pressure on the throat was so fearful that he could not articulate.

His hands were still free, and with these he beat the air wildly, and made frantic—but, of course, impossible—attempts to seize Bill Boaster by the throat.

Oh, if he could but get him within his grasp—if he could but strangle the life out of the villain with his dying clutch!

But his hands only grasped the air, while mingling with the sounds in his ears, came the laugh of Boaster, and the words he uttered—

"Ned Nimble, it is my turn now. But I will not endure my triumph and your misery alone."

Ned tried to answer, but only a gurgle escaped his now foaming and bleeding lips.

Denser and more dense grew the red haze around him, louder and louder the sounds in his ears, fiercer and fiercer the throbbings in his temples.

But he saw Bill Boaster glide away through the mist towards the door of his dungeon.

He felt insensibility stealing over him, a weakness which he believed to be death and then all became blank.

Fum-Fum made a gesture to the gaolers.

The men lowered the body of Ned to within four feet of the floor; then taking hold of another chain, fastened it to his ankles and drew his legs out straight.

"Good," said the governor; "that will do."

A deep sigh broke from Ned's lips.

Suddenly he was awoke as if from death by a loud and piercing shriek.

He opened his bloodshot eyes.

There again was Boaster before him, holding back a female form, whose head and arms were extended towards him.

Ned gazed upon the white horrified face.

A shiver ran through the whole length of his frame, and he tried to gasp out the one word "Minnie!"

Then in his ears rang the voice of Bill Boaster, in tones of thunder, as he again relapsed into insensibility—

"Behold the torture of him you love—the vengeance of the man you scorn. Now is there none to stand between us. You are mine—mine at last!"

CHAPTER XXIII.

IN WHICH HARRY HONOUR LEARNS ONE OF THE SECRETS OF THE PURPLE PAGODA

SLOWLY and silently Harry Honour made his way through the dark waters in the direction of the Purple Pagoda.

He kept as close in shore as possible in order to avoid being seen and questioned by the crews of any of the vessels laying out waiting their turns to get alongside the wharves.

The blackness of the night favoured him in this respect, but increased the difficulties of his discovery of the water-way to the pagoda.

His eyes soon became accustomed to the darkness, and he saw the tall pagoda, with its purple tiles and gilt corners, standing out amid the blackness of the night.

Every stroke brought him nearer and nearer to it, and ere long he had swam within the shadow of the hull of the huge pirate junk.

Now, if ever, caution was necessary.

There were no lights on deck, but through the openings in her sides he could see the glimmer of lanterns, as men, bearing them, passed to and fro among the various compartments in the huge black hull.

He could hear the men at work, or trampling on deck, the rattle of a chain, and the whiz of ropes as they glided through well-oiled blocks, and ever and anon the thud and bump of some heavy substance as it fell upon the deck or was swung over the side of the junk into lighters on the far off side of the vessel.

Softly but swiftly Harry glided through the water and past the huge vessel, and gradually neared the shore.

The tide was high, and when he touched the rocky bank he tried in vain to feel the bottom with his feet.

High above him and at some distance inland he knew stood the pagoda.

But he could not see the tall structure now, for the high bank shut it out.

If there was indeed a channel to the pagoda he felt sure that he must be near it now.

Swimming with one hand, he felt along the rocks for an opening.

But in vain.

On, on he went, but still no opening presented itself to his strained sight or touch.

He must have swam some distance beyond the pagoda, and he turned over on to his back and floated while he tried to think.

"I must have missed the channel," he muttered to himself, "if indeed there really be one. I am a long way past the pagoda now, and to go on would be useless. No, I must go back and examine every foot of the rocky bank. I must have passed it in the darkness."

Harry turned over again on to his chest, and bringing himself round with a few strokes, swam close to the rocks, and while he kept himself above the surface with one hand examined the bank carefully with the other.

On, on, till again he was abreast of the junk, and still success had not crowned his efforts.

Was it possible that after all there was no waterway to the pagoda, and that they were all mistaken in their surmises?

He had began to think they were so when the sounds on board the junk satisfied him that they were not.

The wharves were closed; there was silence on board all the other ships. Why should there be sounds of loading on board the junk, and that these sounds should be rendered as subdued as possible?

No, they had not suspected wrongly that the junk was a pirate, and that the governor was in league with the sea robbers ; and all that he heard pointed to the fact that those on board the junk were desirous of every secrecy in their work.

Had they been honest traders why were not the usual sounds of men hauling up cargoes heard ringing over the water ? Why were there no lights on deck for the men to work by, and why did they work when the wharves were closed ?

Again Harry glided past the huge hull, but in the opposite direction to which he had gone before.

And again did he examine every foot of the shore.

And again did disappointment reward his search.

Once more he could see the outline of the pagoda rising out of the surrounding darkness.

And as he gazed towards it he saw a light flash across one of its topmost windows.

He saw it but for a moment, the next it was gone.

Instinctively Harry kept his eyes rivetted upon the spot where the light had appeared.

But all was blackness for some minutes.

Then again the light flitted across the window and disappeared.

Still Harry watched.

Another long pause, and the light again passed near the casement as if carried by some one across the apartment.

When darkness again ensued Harry turned his gaze upon the junk.

A lantern was run up to its masthead, glided down, run up again, and once more glided to the deck and disappeared.

"If they were not signals I never saw any," thought Harry. "Now if I go ashore and wait for the others I may lose the chance of discovering this secret waterway, for I believe the pirates are about to put off their boats for land, and if I attempt to follow them I may be seen and captured. What's best to be done ?"

While Harry tried to decide, he without heeding what he was doing, propelled his body towards the junk, and just as he came abreast of the stern of the monster vessel he saw a large boat glide round its bows.

But the faintest splash met his ears.

Indeed so faint was the dip of the muffled oars that the wash of the waters against the rocky bank almost drowned the sound.

"I must trust to luck and prudence," muttered Harry, "and follow that boat; and, when I have learned the secret of this hidden waterway, I will turn back and join the others."

So deciding, Harry struck out and followed in the wake of the boat.

The wash of the rising waters upon the rocks deadened the sound as he cleaved a passage for his body through them, and so rapidly did he swim, lest the boat should suddenly disappear and leave him without his being able to solve the mystery, that he got dangerously near the craft as the rowers raised their oars out of the water, and suffered the vessel to drift on at the will of the wind and wave.

Low as was the tone as a voice said "Ship oars," yet Harry heard it, and so close to the boat was he now that he saw the flash of the blades as the men nearest the shore brought their oars aboard.

Then the boat drifted against the rocks and was held stationary.

Harry held his breath in suspense while he just kept himself from sinking by treading the water and moving his hands by his sides.

Suddenly across the dark water shot a ray of light, and as Harry gazed the rocks seemed to open.

Into the ray of light the boat was pushed ; then its bows disappeared, and its stern swerved round, and the next moment was gone.

And with it went the light, but not before a few rapid strokes brought Harry Honour opposite the entrance to the channel into which it had gone.

The boat was shut out from his gaze, but there was a black rift in the rock, which as Harry strained his eyes to penetrate, gradually grew narrower and narrower.

He had discovered one of the secrets of the Purple Pagoda.

But should he avail himself of it, or return to his friends ?

Quick as lightening thoughts flashed through his brain.

Should he, ere it was too late, pass through that black opening alone ? or should he return to where he had promised to meet the others, and trust to the gate being again opened?

If the former he might be in time to aid Ned.

If the latter he might be too late.

Nearer and nearer the rocks came together.

Another moment and the opening would be closed.

His mind was made up.

He would risk all for Ned's sake—even life itself.

He gave a sweeping stroke.

He passed through the narrow crevice into the stygian blackness beyond.

And then, with a grating sound, the opening closed behind him.

It had been dark enough in the river without, but in the tunnel the blackness was that of the grave.

Harry, just keeping his head above water, listened.

All was silent as the tomb.

A feeling of awe stole over his heart.

What if his presence had become known?—what if he had rushed upon his fate?

For a moment his feelings nearly overcame him; but he recovered his calmness and his courage, and, setting his teeth firmly together, he softly propelled himself along through the blackness.

In a few moments his hands came in contact with a wall.

He could go no further in that direction.

He turned to the right, and a couple of strokes brought him to a stop.

He turned to the left and then some distance ahead he saw a gleam of light on the water.

He swam towards it, and saw an opening again on his left, and, as he neared it, heard voices, and the thud of tubs and bales as they were landed on the rocky side of the channel.

The turns in the channel prevented one single ray of light streaming towards the entrance.

That which Harry had seen from the river had been thrown from the roof above to show that the gates were open, and had only been suffered to flash for a moment to guide the boat in.

Up to now the stygian darkness had proved Harry's safety, but now came the moment of his danger.

Once within the light he might be seen.

And yet, to remain where he was till all again became dark was to perhaps prevent his discovering the whereabouts of Ned, and compel himself to find a grave in the black waters of the narrow channel.

"To hesitate is to be lost!" thought Harry. "I will trust in Heaven and my good right arm, and if I fall I shall at least fall in a good cause!"

With these thoughts flashing through his brain, Harry set to work again, and swam to the opening of the other channel which led back again towards the river.

It seemed to be about thirty yards long, and a sloping ledge of rock formed a pathway on either side, the highest part being at the further end, and in which was a large door, evidently an entrance to the basement of the pagoda.

On to those ledges the pirates were hoisting large bales, tubs, and boxes from the lighter which was moored to iron rings, rivetted just below the pathways, while several men were rolling, dragging, and carrying the merchandise through the large doorway.

Both those in the boat and those on the rocks used the greatest expedition, and so engaged were they in their work that they paid no heed to anything else.

Harry took all this in at a glance, and seizing the edge of the path where it was nearest the water, he drew himself quickly up on to it, and lay flat down on his chest where the shadows were blackest.

He could not be seen by the men in the boat now, and if he could escape the observations of those on the ledges or landing-stages, he might, when all the goods had been removed into the pagoda, himself effect an entrance into the building.

But though crouching in the shadow, his danger was great.

Should one of those men, now so hard at work, come along the pathway, his discovery was certain.

He must prepare for the worst.

He drew the oilskin from his belt, and unwrapped his revolver.

As he thrust the skin back he felt the piece containing the wax tapers.

In the darkness he had forgotten that he had provided himself with them.

He was not sorry for this now, as, had he struck one in the black channel, he might have betrayed his presence.

Hard as the men worked, yet to Harry it seemed as if the boat would never be unloaded; moments seemed minutes, and minutes hours, in his trepidation and desire to discover where Ned was a prisoner.

But at length the last box was lifted to the ledge, and the pirates began to unmoor the boat.

Then a loud gruff voice said—

"The other lighter will be loaded by time we return to the junk; look out for the light at the masthead, and be ready to open the gate."

A half-dozen voices replied, as the boat was pushed off to the centre of the channel.

"Tell the governor the captain will come in the next boat," said the same gruff voice.

The men dropped their oars over the sides, and the lighter passed along the channel, round the bend, and was lost to Harry's view.

The men carried their last load through the doorway, and then all was silent again.

"Now," mutterred Harry, rising to his feet; "now or never! but a few minutes and the pirates will return. Heaven grant that I may discover and rescue my more than brother—brave Ned Nimble!"

CHAPTER XXIV.

IN WHICH JACK, CHARLEY, JUMBO, AND 'DOLF SET OUT IN SEARCH OF NED NIMBLE.

"Now, lads," said Jack, as soon as Harry had departed on his dangerous but gallant errand, "after the events of to-day, and as we have no desire to run foul of the Chinese police, I think we had better disguise ourselves as much as possible before we set out to meet Harry, and learn whether he has discovered anything or not."

"What! take off ob dis yer magernifercent meandering gown," said Jumbo.

"Yes, and look like a man, and not like a woman," said Charley.

"I doesn't want not none ob yer insulting oberserwations," said Jumbo. "I'se been dat ar wexed to-day, dat if I gets wexeder I'se boun' ter do somebody a mischief, I is."

"What with?" asked Charley.

"Wid dese yer fistes ob mine, ter be sure," was the reply.

"Why, that ain't a fist," said Charley, pointing to Jumbo's wounded hand.

"What am it, den?"

"That's a leg of mutton, I should say. It's about as big as your head, and as soft as putty. It would be about as much use in a fight as a feather pillow."

"Say yer dunno. Dar's a lot ob fight in dat ar hand, I tell yer."

"Why it couldn't bruise a fly," said Charley.

"Guess dat's a lie!" said Jumbo "So don't yer go poking ob yer fun at dis chile, or I'se bery likely to put dat ar fist in dat ar mouf ob your'n."

"What, that?" said Charley.

"Guess I said so."

"Why you half-bred cannibal, do you think I was like you, fed with a dustman's shovel instead of a spoon when I was a kid?" said Charley, "or that I was weaned upon the thigh bones of a poor nigger instead of nice tops and bottoms!"

"Look yer," cried Jumbo, "don't yer go fur to carry it on too far, or I gibs yer tops and bottoms, one in de eye, and de oder in de wind dat'll knock all de cheek out ob yer. Heah dat, now?"

"I've heard a pig squeak before," said Charley.

"Get out ob dis, or I gibs yer pig!" yelled Jumbo.

And he made a dash at Charley.

Charley threw up his arm, and caught the blow on it.

"Gor-a-mighty!" yelled Jumbo, "I'se hit yer wid de wrong fist. Yer wagger-bone willing, I'se boun' ter be de def ob yer!"

"Try next time with your head, old man," said Charley laughing, and dashing into the inner room where Jack and 'Dolf already were.

"If eber I gets to a cibilised nation again, yer may call me a nigger if I doesn't cut dat ar Charley," said Jumbo, nursing his hand. "I reckons dat I 'graced de ole ob my race when I conperscended ter notice dat ar waggerbone, I does."

"You're a pair of fools, both of you!" said Sally, who had not yet got over her bad temper.

"Dat's trufe," said Jumbo.

"Mrs. Jones," said Tilda, "I wonner how yer'd like ter me ter call your husband a fool? Yes, ma'am, answer dat ar question."

"You may call him what you like, for all I care," said Sally.

"Oh, indeed, ma'am, may I? Then, ma'am, since I'se got yer admission, I ain't a-going ter be so unperlite as ter call such a nice, kind gen'leman an ole fool. Oh no, not me; I shall 'dress him as my dear Jack, and——"

"What?" cried Sally. "Now, look here, Tilda Tompkins, you know what sort of a woman I am."

"Oh, ob course, I does. I'd like to be 'formed ob who doesn't. Dar's no mistaking what sort ob a woman yer is. Yer's allus a-telling and a-showing ob us what's yer quality, ma'am."

"Dat's trufe," said Jumbo. "But I hasn't got not no time to argy de p'int, so I leebs yer to yer 'fectionate jaw, I does, and hopes as how yer'll enjoy it."

And Jumbo left the apartment.

"Ignorant nigger!" said Sally.

"Did yer 'dress dat ar obserwation ter me, ma'am?" asked Tilda.

"You, indeed!" said Sally. "You are beneath my notice."

"I'se bery glad to hear dat, ma'am," retorted Tilda. "I'se no desire ter be 'oticed by my 'feriors."

"You're what?" cried Sally.

"'Feriors, ma'am, dat's what I said. Perhaps yer don't know de meaning ob dat word. If yer doesn't, den I 'fers yer ter de 'rectory what ob course I was edicated in, when I went ter boarding-school."

"What!" cried Sally; "you—you go to boarding-school?"

"Yes, ma'am, me," said Tilda.

"I don't believe it. What did you do at boarding-school?"

"Don't beliebe it?" said Tilda.

"No, you never was at a boarding-school in your life," cried Sally.

"Why, I swars to gracious I was. Why, I cleaned more nor forty pairs ob boots ebery morning for de gals, and I washed up all de——"

Tilda stopped suddenly, and looked confused.

Sally laughed loudly.

"Oh, oh, the cat's out of the bag!" she cried. "You was rubber, scrubber, and general washer up, was you? The lowest menial in the worst berth a girl can have. Educated in a boarding-school, and cleaned all the boots! Well, I do think I'm a cut above that, though I was brought up in the Dials."

"Mrs. Jones," said Tilda, "it's a pity as yer doesn't do as de Dials does, den."

"Indeed, and what may that be, pray?" asked Sally sarcastically.

"Why, put yer hands ober yer face, ma'am, ter hide de blushes what yer 'licious notions puts dar. But p'r'aps yer too bad ter blush, ma'am. Dar are such fings as women being so wulgar dat when dey tries ter blush dey finds it's so hard dat dey's in danger ob bursting a blood-vessel."

"Well, there's no fear of you blushing," said Sally.

"No, ma'am, I scorns ter do it."

"What's dat yer scorns ter does?" asked Jumbo, entering the room.

"Tell the truth," said Sally.

"Dat's trufe," said Jumbo.

"Golly! what's yer been and gone and did?" cried Tilda, jumping up.

"How yer like de look ob me?" asked Jumbo.

Tilda did not reply.

She simply shook her head and sat down again.

Jumbo had got rid of his Chinese costume, and attired himself in a pair of blue serge trousers, a blue guernsey, and a peak cap.

"Well, you look what you are fit for," said Sally.

"An' what am dat ar?"

"A cook's mate. Well, you're Slush to a T," said Sally.

"Fought I looked like de captain ob a man-ob-war," said Jumbo.

"Captain of a bone barge perhaps; or better still, you are just the cut of one of those rascals who meet little boys in the street, and pretend that they have got some smuggled cigars, and will sell them cheap ; and when the little idiots part with their halfpence, palm on to them some brown paper stuffed with hay. Yes, you're the very cut of those fellows."

"Dat's trufe," said Jumbo. "I knowed dar was somefing bery s'perior in dis chile."

Jack, Charley, and 'Dolf now came from the next room.

They had all rigged themselves out in blue serge trousers and blue guernseys.

"What cheer, my hearty!" cried Charley, hitching up his trousers, and giving Jumbo a slap on the shoulder ; " run down the main-mast and chuck the jolly-boat over board."

"I'll chuck yer oberboard if yer don't keep dat ar fist off ob my shoulder," said Jumbo.

"Look out for squalls, you lubber," said Charley, "or I'll clap you under hatches in a brace of shakes. Now then, messmates, what's the course ? "

"Why, yer is," said Tilda ; "yer's about de coaress feller as eber I seed."

"Clap a stopper on your jawing-tackle," said Charley, "and hand over the brandy-bottle. I'm going to splice the mainbrace before I set sail, shiver my timbers if I ain't ! "

"Jus' yer look yer," said Jumbo, "dar's two female womans a-sitting in dis room, so if yer's busted dem ar' braces ob your'n an' wants to mend 'em, yer'll hab ter be decent ard go in ter toder room ter splice de brace."

"A nip of brandy won't do us any harm," said Jack. "But hark you, lads, have you all got your popguns and knives ? "

Each replied in the affirmative.

"Then drink and let's be going. Time's nearly up."

"Den I guess I'll get my hat on," said Tilda.

"No women with us to-night," said Jack. "You will both stay here till we return ? "

"What ? " said Sally.

"You must remain at home, my dear. We may have to encounter considerable danger," said Jack.

"Then I will share it," said Sally.

"And I'll ditter," said Tilda.

"No, no," said Jack. "We may all have to take to the water for what we know."

"I guess I'se used ter de water," said Tilda. "I'se a berry good sailor, I is."

"I know that, Tilda, but we may have to swim for it. So pray stay at home with Sally. And besides, I think it unwise, after finding that fellow Ching-Fow here, to leave the place with no one in it. I half suspect that young Celestial; and remember, we have got a good deal to lose."

"Then I'll stop," said Sally.

"And so will I," added Tilda.

"You'll be very happy and comfortable together, I know," said Jack.

"As happy as two cats with their tails tied together, and slung across a line," said Charley. "Meow-wow-mow."

"Stow it," said Jack.

"Right you are, mate," said Charley. "How do you feel, 'Dolf, in that rig ? "

"All right," replied 'Dolf, " but I shall feel happier when I know that Master Ned is safe."

"Then let's be off," said Jack.

And he stooped and kissed his wife.

"I hope we shall soon be back, Sally, and bring Ned with us," he said.

"We're boun' ter do dat," said Jumbo.

"Avast, messmate," said Charley, " we mean to try."

"Dat's trufe," said Jumbo, "though dis yer neck ob mine——"

"Hang yer neck," said Charley.

"Guess it's been hung enough to-day, so I reckons dat I won't be taking ob no adwice from yer, Massa Charley."

"Then take it from me, Jumbo," said Jack. "Don't you and Charley get quarrelling, and so attract notice to ourselves. The mission we are bent on is a dangerous one, and if we would rescue Ned, we must be guarded in all our words and movements."

"Dat's trufe," said Jumbo, "so I moves de fust rebelution, and dat is——"

"Shut up ! " said Charley.

"And a good resolution too," said 'Dolf.

They all shook hands with Sally and Tilda, and then, Jack leading the way, they left the house and emerged into the street.

Then Jack took hold of Jumbo's arm.

"Bress yer sole, I'se strong enuff ter walk by myself," said Jumbo.

"I know that, old man," whispered Jack; "but you're not strong enough to eep from quarrelling with Charley if ou two get together, so leave him with olf, and come along with me."

"Dat's trufe," said Jumbo. "I'se boun' er hab a row wid dat ar waggerbone."

"There must be no row to-night," said Jack, "for even on so simple a thing as a word may depend the safety, the liberty, even the life of our best and dearest friend, Ned Nimble."

CHAPTER XXV.

IN WHICH THE DOVE BECOMES AN EAGLE, AND HELP ARRIVES IN THE NICK OF TIME.

WITH a heartrending shriek Minnie Sash ore herself from the hold of Bill Boas-er, and sprang towards the again insen-ble form of her suspended lover.

But ere she could fling her arms round the quivering frame of Ned, the governor seized her and drew her back.

"Oh, wretches, monsters, inhuman ends!" shrieked Minnie; "have you no ity, no mercy?"

"None," hissed Bill in her ear. "Why hould I have mercy when you have none n me? Look upon him and see your wn work; blame your own self for his ufferings, for you are the cause."

"Oh Heaven, why dost thou not strike he wretch dumb?" cried Minnie. "I be cause—I, who would gladly give cy life to save him one single pang."

Then she fell upon her knees at the eet of the governor.

"Oh, man, you have power, be merci-ul. On my knees I implore your mercy or him—for the victim of this human end's malice. Spare him! oh, spare him in mercy!"

"You plead in vain," cried Bill, "not one pang shall he feel the less. I have paid twelve thousand pounds to see him suffer and punish your obstinacy, and by heaven I will have my revenge to the full on you both."

"Devil!" gasped Minnie.

"Thanks to you," he replied; "you might have made me a man, you forced me to become a fiend. You have raised a devil that will not be laid; like Fran-kenstein, you have made a monster, and like him you suffer from your own creation."

"Oh, why are there no lightnings in heaven to strike this monster dead?" cried Minnie.

"Ha, ha, ha!" laughed Bill, "'tis my hour of triumph now, my hour of revenge."

"Oh, man, man," cried Minnie, appeal-ingly to Fum-Fum, "you at least are human. You never had cause to do him harm; on my knees I implore you have mercy. Have mercy, and my prayers shall rise day and night for mercy on your head."

Fum-Fum jerked her to her feet.

"You appeal to me in vain," he said.

"Then to you I pray," cried Minnie, turning to the gaolers; "your hearts are not, cannot be dead to every feeling of humanity; release him and Heaven will reward you."

"And the governor will have your heads struck from your bodies if you dare raise a hand to baulk me of one mo-ment's revenge," cried Bill.

The men shook their heads.

"Wretch," cried Minnie, "if I cannot save I can at least avenge him!"

As she spoke she grasped the hilt of Fum-Fum's sword, and by a quick jerk drew it from its scabbard.

The governor and Bill both made a grasp at the weapon.

But Minnie drew back and, drawing herself up to her full height, and her features assuming a look of the utmost desperation, she swept the weapon around her head, causing them to fall back pre-cipitately.

No longer was she the weak, trem-bling, weeping girl.

Fire flashed from her eyes, her nostrils distended, and her taper fingers closed round the hilt of the sword with a grip of iron.

In the space of one moment she seemed changed from an angel into a demon.

No longer did her tones come in quivering accents, no longer was her voice choked with sobs.

But standing in such a position that none could get behind her, she cried in a loud, steady tone of concentrated determination—

"Release that victim of your malice, or by the Heaven above me you die!"

"Seize her!" cried Fum-Fum.

"Disarm her!" cried Bill.

But the gaolers were terror-stricken.

Neither advanced a step.

All were unarmed.

The only weapon in the cell was that wielded by Minnie.

"You are master here," cried Minnie fiercely, levelling the sword at the governor's breast, "release that poor wretch from his bonds or you die!"

"There he shall hang till he dies," cried Bill. "Fool, drop that sword! Take it away from her, cowards—are you afraid of a woman?"

As he spoke Bill sprang forward.

Like a flash of lightning the weapon cleaved the air, and with a howl of agony Bill retreated with the loss of part of one of his ears.

The governor now sprang upon her to disarm her, but again the sword flashed and was buried half way to its hilt in Fum-Fum's bosom.

Throwing up his arms and falling back, he unsheathed the weapon from its fleshy scabbard.

Then with a deep groan he sank to the earth.

For a moment Minnie stood horrified, as it were, at her work, gazing down upon the dying man as he clutched at the ground on which he lay.

Taking advantage of this, Bill, smarting with pain and fury, sprang upon her, and throwing his arms around her, held her firmly in his grasp.

"Help! disarm her! take the sword away! she has killed the governor!"

At this the gaolers advanced and seized her.

But despite their strength they could not wrest the weapon from Minnie's grasp.

"She has slain the governor. Kill her, kill her!" cried one.

"No, no," cried Bill, "harm her not. Tear the sword from her grasp, but harm her at your peril!"

Again they essayed to possess themselves of the gory steel.

But as if she had become possessed of superhuman strength, Minnie resisted their attempts and even wounded one of the men in the leg.

But this fictitious strength Minnie felt was fast deserting her, and from her lips issued a loud and piercing cry for help.

"You may scream your heart out," replied Bill, "there's none here to help you."

"Heaven will help me," cried Minnie, clutching at the villain's throat, "and in that I trust."

"Fool, drop that weapon. I'd kill you but that death would be too poor a revenge. I'll torture you till death would be a mercy. Again I say drop that sword, or I'll break your arm."

And he gave her arm a violent twist.

The pain he caused her made her shriek aloud, but she still kept firm hold of the sword.

"Help, help!" she shrieked. "Oh, Heaven, have you, too, deserted me?"

"Help there is none," cried Bill. "You are powerless. There is none here to aid you—none, none."

"Liar! there is one!" thundered a voice behind him.

At the same moment there was a blinding flash, the ping of a bullet close to his ear, and the thud of the missile as it buried itself in the wall beyond.

Then came another flash, and another, and almost together the two gaolers flung up their arms and fell heavily to the ground.

Bill released his hold of Minnie, and sprang round.

The villain recoiled with an oath.

Then an arm was flung round Minnie's waist, and the well-known voice of Harry Honour exclaimed—

"I will save you, or die!"

Bill realised in a moment who the new arrival was.

His hand went to his bosom, and a curse escaped him when he found he had no weapon.

As through the smoke he saw the two gaolers writhing on the earth, and knew that the next moment he might share their fate, he turned and dashed through the open doorway towards the staircase.

Harry caught sight of his retreating form, as he felt Minnie sinking heavily on his arm.

He raised his revolver, and fired after Bill.

There was a howl of pain—a stumble on the stairs.

Harry would have dashed after him.

But at that moment a hysterical sob broke from Minnie's lips, the sword fell from her hand to the earth, and she fainted on his shoulder.

Harry suffered her form to slide gently to the floor of the vault, and the smoke clearing off, he saw the suspended figure of a man beside him.

One look, a start, and a cry!

"Ned, Ned!" he gasped.

There was no reply.

He seized the lantern from the floor, and held it up.

"Merciful powers! it is too late—too late!" he gasped.

His hand dropped to his side ; but a sigh, soft as an infant's, broke upon his ears.

Up he swung the lantern, and gazed eagerly into the face of Ned.

Again a sigh broke from the lips of the suspended youth.

With a glad cry, Harry placed the lantern on the floor, and seized the mandarin's sword.

"He lives, he lives, thank Heaven!" cried Harry. "Oh, Heaven be praised! I may yet be in time to save him."

In a moment he had severed the cords with the bloodstained sword, but still Ned hung suspended by the chains.

Eagerly Harry's eyes followed the iron links till he had mastered the mystery of their fastenings.

To throw off the chains from his ankles, and suffer Ned's feet to touch the ground, was the work of a moment.

But in vain he tried to release the poor fellow's neck and waist from the iron bands.

He dared not remove the arm which supported the fainting form of Ned, or the poor fellow's legs would have given way, and he would have hung by his neck and waist.

"Minnie, Minnie!" he cried.

But there was no answer.

The poor girl was insensible.

Her overstrained nerves had relaxed, and she was in a dead faint.

"Oh, Heaven!" gasped Harry, "have I found him only to leave him to perish? If that wretch has escaped my bullet he will soon return with the others, and all will be lost!"

Then he began chafing Ned's temples with his hands.

"Ned, dear Ned," he cried. "Rouse up, dear boy. Try and rouse up. It is I, Harry, who speaks. Ned, Ned!"

A sigh was the only reply he got.

Wildly he cast his eyes around the floor, then turned them again upon the iron bands.

A small hole in the centre of each gave him a clue to their fastenings, and a bunch of keys hanging to the girdle of one of the dead gaolers satisfied him that they were locked.

He reached out his hand towards the keys.

But the man lay too far off.

He feared to let go of Ned, lest the even momentary pressure on his neck should finish the work his inhuman torturers had began.

Oh that Minnie would come to.

Again and again he called upon her by name.

But in vain!

"Every moment's delay is fraught with danger," thought Harry. "Heaven help me, I must be cruel to be kind."

He let go his hold of Ned, and sprang for the keys.

As he expected, Ned's legs sank under him, and he hung by the neck and waist with his hands touching the cold floor of the dungeon.

To tear away the keys from the man's girdle was the work of a moment.

To lift Ned and insert one of them in the neck band was that of another.

Fortunately the key fitted, the lock snapped and the band opened.

In an instant it was thrown off by Harry, and the waistband unlocked.

Then Ned's form sank heavily on his arm, and kneeling on the ground, Harry supported his senseless friend's head on his knee.

"Thank Heaven I have released you from that infernal machine," muttered Harry. "But oh, can it be too late to save him?"

He fancied he heard a shuffling sound without the dungeon.

In an instant he remembered that three out of the six chambers of his revolver were empty.

He drew the sword to his side, and grasping his revolver in his hand, turned his face to the door and waited in breathless anxiety.

Was it Bill Boaster returning with others to aid him?

He felt it must be.

Even though he had released Ned from the torture, he might be powerless to save his life.

But he had still three bullets left in his revolver, and if he could not save he could at least avenge him.

"Yes," he muttered, as he levelled the weapon at the opening, "Ned may die, I and Minnie may perish, but Bill Boaster shall not live to triumph in his villainy, and gloat over the destruction of Ned Nimble."

CHAPTER XXVI.

IN WHICH AN ATTEMPT TO ESCAPE IS SUDDENLY FRUSTRATED.

THE scuffling noise still continued at intervals, yet Harry, glaring out into the darkness, could see no one approaching.

He listened intently, and after awhile discovered that it came from the other side of the vault, and that it sounded like the scraping of some object against the stone wall of the dungeon.

"It is the men unloading the second boat," thought Harry, "and from the position of this place the vault through which I passed must be next to this."

Nor was he wrong in his surmise.

It was indeed the vault through which he had ventured from the landing-stage of the channel, and the staircase up which he had stolen after the men had deserted it ran parallel with the one down which he had made his way to Ned's prison.

This thought set his mind greatly at rest for the moment, and he again essayed to bring Ned round to sensibility.

He chafed his hands and forehead, and called on his name.

Only inarticulate sounds rewarded his endeavours.

Suddenly one of the gaolers flung out his arms, and gasped in a faint voice—

"Water, water!"

"He still lives," said Harry. "Perhaps his desire for water may allow me to procure it for Ned and Minnie."

He laid Ned gently back on the floor of the dungeon, and leant over the wounded Celestial.

"Where can water be procured?" he asked. "Speak quickly and I will get it for you."

"Water, there!" gasped the poor wretch, with difficulty extending his hand towards the doorway.

Harry turned to the opening.

Eagerly he looked around.

Just outside the door was a small wooden vessel half filled with water.

It had been placed there by the man who now asked for it ere he entered the vault, and but for Minnie's heroism and Harry's arrival would have been used for bringing Ned to his senses and prolonging his tortures.

"Thank Heaven!" cried Harry, seizing the pail, and returning to the vault.

He flung some of the liquid in Ned's face and forced a drop down his throat, well soaking the poor lad's bosom as he did so.

"Water, water!" still moaned the wounded man.

But Harry stooped down beside Minnie, bathed her temples, and taking some of the fluid in the hollow of his hand, held it to her fluttering lips.

Then and not before did he attempt to relieve the sufferings of the Celestial.

He held up the man's head and gave him a drink from the pail.

The water evidently greatly revived him.

He tried to rise on his elbow, but the effort was too great, and, with a groan he sank back on the damp floor.

Again Harry hurried to the side of Ned.

The eyes of the youth were open, and there was a convulsive twitching of his lips.

"Ned, Ned, speak to me, old boy. Don't you know me? It's Harry Honour."

And while he spoke Harry dashed the water into Ned's face.

"Come, rouse up, dear boy," said Harry. "Come, come, old fellow, try and pull yourself together. Don't stare like that at me as if you didn't know your old chum Harry?"

"'DEATH TO THE ASSASSINS OF FUM FUM!' CRIED BILL BOASTER.'"

"Harry, Harry?" muttered Ned, as if he had somewhere heard that name before and was trying to recollect where.

"Yes, dear boy, Harry Honour, your old chum, who has come to get you out of this pirates' nest. Ah, that's it, old boy. You're better now. Exert yourself a bit, and you'll be all right in a minute."

Ned made an effort to sit upright, and Harry aided him to gain a sitting position on the floor.

For some moments Ned gazed wildly into Harry's face, and then reason seemed to dawn upon him, and, clutching Harry's arm, he gasped—

"Yes, yes! it's Harry! dear old Harry."

"To be sure it is," said his friend.

"Then it was not real. It was only a dream after all," muttered Ned.

But as he turned his gaze from Harry's face round the place, he gave a start and cried—

"Oh, Heaven! it was all too true."

"Don't agitate yourself, dear boy," cried Harry. "You are safe, and I am here."

"Minnie, Minnie!" cried Ned. "Was she here? Did I see her, or——"

"Be calm, old man. Minnie is here, and in safety."

A wild hysterical mingled sob and laugh broke from Ned's lips.

And then, clutching Harry again, he cried—

"Bill, the monster! Bill Boaster, where is he? I will kill him."

He sprang to his feet, swayed to and fro, and would have fallen had not Harry caught and supported him.

"Steady, dear boy, steady. You are too weak to stand at present. Bill cannot harm you now, if ever he is able to do so, for I think I winged him as he tried to escape from here."

Ned passed his hand several times over his forehead as if to clear his brain.

"What's that?" he cried suddenly, as a sigh fell upon his ears.

"Sit down, old boy," said Harry. "Your limbs are cramped with the torture they have inflicted upon you. You will be allright in a few minutes. There, that's it."

And Harry gently forced Ned to sit upon the ground with his head proped up against the wall.

"Here, Ned, take a good swig at this, it will revive you."

"Heaven bless you, Harry," returned Ned, as he bent his lips to the pail Harry tilted on his knee that his friend might drink therefrom.

Ned imbibed a quantity of the cooling liquid, and lay back with a sigh of relief.

"Now don't move, don't stir," said Harry. "Keep quite still a few moments and you'll be yourself again."

Harry now went over to where Minnie lay.

As he leant over her the poor girl opened her eyes.

By the light of the lantern which Harry held over her she recognised him.

Recollection returned to her in a flash and she looked quickly and fearfully around.

"Have no fear, Minnie," whispered Harry. "He is gone."

"Boaster!" she gasped.

"Yes, and you are safe with friends. Can you sit up?"

"Oh, yes, yes."

"Hush! don't speak—at least, not now," said Harry, in a whisper.

"But Ned, dear Ned?" she asked in a low, quivering voice.

"Only needs a few quiet moments to be all right again. I have got him down and he is fast recovering from those villains' cruel work."

He still kept himself between her and Ned as he helped her to sit up.

"Minnie," he said, "we are all three of us still in great danger, and we must be careful what we do. For Ned's sake, my sake, and your own be calm, and be guided by me."

"I will, I will!" she said.

"Can you rise?"

"Oh, I am strong again," she said.

He helped her to her feet.

"Come to Ned, then," he whispered; "but for Heaven's sake do not cry out or faint or do or say aught that may bring any one here, for there are those in the next vault who would slay us without mercy did they but know what was transpiring here."

He led her over to where Ned sat with closed eyes and head resting against the wall.

Minnie dropped on her knees by his side.

For a moment she gazed into his pale

pain-convulsed face, and then throwing her arms about his shoulders, she cried in sobbing tones—

"Oh, my darling—my darling!"

Ned unclosed his eyes, and despite the warning gesture of Harry, clasped Minnie to his bosom, exclaiming—

"Minnie—! Oh, Heaven be praised!"

Then his face dropped upon her shoulder, and he burst into sobs.

Harry was about to rebuke this show of feeling, but he thought that perhaps he had better not.

"It may do them both good," he muttered. "They will perhaps be the stronger and calmer for it."

He turned away therefore, and examined the forms of the governor and his subordinates.

Fum-Fum was dead.

Minnie's hand had stretched him a corpse in the presence of the victim he had tortured and the villain who had bought his cruelty.

One of the gaolors was also bereft of life, and the spot of blood on the front of his blouse told where the bullet had found a resting place in the fellow's bosom.

The other still breathed, but around his lips was blood and foam, and Harry shook his head as he saw that the man was bleeding internally, and knew that his lease of life was nearly run out.

Satisfied that no harm could come to Ned or Minnie from either of these, he strode to the doorway, and advancing to the foot of the steps listened intently.

He heard no sound above.

"Where is Bill Boaster?" he muttered to himself. "I fancied I heard him fall on the stairs. I'll get the lantern and look."

He was about to return to the vault when he bethought himself of the wax tapers in his belt.

To extract one and light it was the work of but a few moments.

By its light he examined the stairs.

There was no one there.

"Confusion!" muttered Harry. "I must have missed him, and the wretch will soon return with assistance. A moment's further delay may be ruin or death."

He turned to re-enter the vault, when his eyes rested on a black spot on the stone steps.

He held the taper down to examine it.

It was blood—fresh wet blood.

He looked at the other steps.

Some were clear, but on three of the were spots of blood

"He did not escape me scot free," said Harry to himself. "I thought I hit him and now I'm sure I did, for this must his blood, the infernal villain!"

He went back to the vault.

Ned had risen to his feet and still he Minnie in his arms.

"Do you think you can walk, de boy?" he asked.

"Yes," replied Ned; "my legs a still terribly benumbed, but I am othe wise all right now."

But as he spoke he laid his hand his neck and gave a painful gulp.

"How you must have suffered," sa Harry; "but thank Heaven it was worse, bad as it must have been."

"Thanks to you, Harry—thanks you."

"Don't say any more, Ned, there no time for words. If you think ye are able to walk actions must take the place for the time being."

"I am growing stronger every moment said Ned. "Here, old friend is the elix that has brought back life and streng to me."

And he pressed Minnie to his hea and kissed her passionately.

"Pray Heaven you may never agai be parted," said Harry. "But, Ned, w are not out of danger. Though tl governor of this place lies cold in deat yonder, Bill Boaster has escaped m He has left a trail of blood on the stej without and may be even now returnin with assistance."

"Oh, that I could strangle him!" cried Ned, "for what he has made poo Minnie endure."

"Take this sword, Ned. Come wha may we will sell our lives dearly. Bu I pray Heaven we may yet escape from this fearful place."

"We will escape or die together, said Ned.

"Come then," said Harry, taking up the lantern and leading the way fron the cell, pistol in his hand.

Minnie clung to Ned's arm, a praye on her lips, but with fear in her heart.

Harry placed his foot on the foremos

step and paused as voices from above reached their ears.

"Hush! some one comes," cried Harry, drawing back and blowing out the light.

"Stand close to the wall. Let not a breath betray our whereabouts, and leave all to me, come what may."

CHAPTER XXVII.

IN WHICH THE LAMB AGAIN FALLS INTO THE CLAWS OF THE TIGER.

CROUCHING back close against the wall, Harry on one side of the steps, and Ned and Minnie on the other, and holding their breath lest their respiration even might betray them, the three waited in agonised suspense.

Suddenly a gleam of light fell half down the steps, but did not penetrate to the bottom.

Then a loud and clear voice exclaimed —

"That will do, Cheeko. If the governor is in the torture-chamber I can find him. Did the first boat's crew say I should be here to-night?"

"Yes; and we informed the governor."

"And how about the prisoner? Was he thrown into the water-channel?"

"No, for the governor had decided that he should live till to-morrow."

"Why?"

"I do not know, captain, but I heard that the barbarian who went down with him had induced him to let the prisoner live till to-morrow so that he might see him tortured in the sling to-night."

"What barbarian?"

"I know not, captain."

"No matter. You need come no further. I've been down here times enough to know my way."

"Will you take the lantern, captain?"

"No, for there will be one in the vault. Tell my fellows I shall not be long, and give them a drink, for they have worked hard to load and unload."

"Your commands shall be obeyed, captain," was the reply.

Then the light vanished off the top steps, and footsteps sounded on them.

Nearer and nearer they came to where the three scarcely-breathing friends stood.

At length they knew the figure stood between them.

"Halloa!" muttered a voice, "where's the door? Ho! within there, 'tis I, excellency, I—Captain Choo-Woo. Open the door. It's as dark as the bottom of the sea here. Where can the door be?"

"There!" cried Harry, springing forward.

And with a thrust into which he threw all his strength, he hurled the captain through the open doorway, into the torture-vault.

The unexpected push hurled the pirate captain off his feet, and sent him floundering across the dead body of the governor.

Then Harry seized the door, drew it close, and lifting the heavy bar, dropped it into its socket before the startled pirate could realise what had happened.

"He's trapped," said Harry.

Ned breathed a deep sigh of relief, and so did Minnie, whose feelings during the last few minutes could be better imagined than described.

Harry lit one of his tapers.

"Never mind the lantern," he said. "Come on. Quick, while the coast is clear."

Harry mounted the steps, Ned following close behind, his right hand grasping the sword, his left round Minnie's waist.

On reaching the top of the stairs, and seeing no one about, Harry dropped the taper, before the flame touched his fingers, and turned to Ned.

"Dear boy," he said, "we must try to get out of this infernal place, somehow, but I tell you, our chances are fifty to one against it. The steps to our left lead to a large vault where the pirates store their booty—for this governor was nothing else than a pirate himself—at the opposite end of the vault is a doorway opening into a channel, natural or artificial, that leads to the river, the entrance to which is by gates made to appear but a portion of the rocky bank. It was by taking advantage of the moment when those gates were opened to admit the pirates' boat, that I succeeded in getting into the pagoda."

"Through the channel?" said Ned.

"Yes, dear boy. I swam through it in pitch darkness, and secreted myself till the pirates had gone, and their assistants in the pagoda had taken their departure to some other part of the building. What guided me to you I don't know, unless it was Providence; but whatever it was, thanks be to it, for it enabled me to save you and Minnie, at least, for a time, and punish those who so cruelly used you."

"Heaven bless you, Harry. I shall never forget your noble work."

"Stop there, Ned," said Harry. "Now the pirates are still in the outer cave. Should we be discovered we are lost. We must seek some place to hide, or some other means to leave this infernal pagoda."

Ned placed his hand on Harry's arm.

"There are other ways than that by which you entered, Harry," he said.

"Of course there are," returned Harry, "but in trying to find them we must be careful not to run into a hornets' nest, for you may be certain there are plenty of the governor's attendants in the place, to encounter whom is to run the risk of recapture, perhaps torture—perhaps death."

"Oh, Heaven forbid!" said Minnie. "If they tear me from you again I shall die."

"Cheer up, dear Minnie," whispered Ned. "Let's place our trust in Heaven and our good right arms. I hear no one near us. Strike a light, Harry, if you possess one, and perhaps I may be able to find out some means to leave this fearful place. I escaped from it once, and may do so again."

"Grant we all may," said Minnie.

Having lit another taper, Ned looked round.

"Yes, I remember where we are. This way."

He passed along the vestibule, and drawing Minnie round a tall screen, entered the room in which he had first seen the governor.

As Minnie's eyes caught sight of the idol at the further end of the apartment she started, and clinging to Ned, pointed towards it.

"There is someone there!" she gasped.

In the gloom in which the farther end of the apartment was bathed, she had mistaken the wooden figure for one of flesh and blood.

"Fear not, darling; it is but a Chinese image of worship. This is one of the governor's apartments, and I do not believe any dare enter it without his permission. Ha!"

With this exclamation, Ned struck the taper from Harry's hand, placed his foot on it, and extinguished it.

"Hark!" he whispered.

All listened in breathless suspense.

They were in pitch darkness.

The shutters were up before the openings on either side of the idol.

For a moment each believed there was some one in the apartment.

Clutching their weapons, they waited, trying to strain their eyes through the surrounding blackness.

Were they deceived? or did they really hear a faint groan?

The moments passed, during which Ned felt the form of Minnie trembling like an aspen leaf, but no further sound reached their ears.

"It must have been fancy," said Ned, in a whisper, "or some noise from the apartment beyond. Place your hand on my shoulder, Harry, and follow me."

Harry did as he was requested, and together they crossed the apartment to the opposite wall.

"It was from one of these windows I escaped, after being lured here by that letter," whispered Ned. "The opening is near the ground; if we can remove the shutters we can escape with ease."

The night was so dark without that no ray of light penetrated through the hole which Jumbo's head made in the panelling of the window-shutter.

"Do not tremble so, darling!" said Ned, in a whisper, to Minnie. "The attendants are in another part of the place, and the governor, we know cannot enter the room himself. Courage, dear one, and liberty will soon greet us."

"But Boaster," gasped Minnie, "'tis he I fear."

"Fear naught," said Ned. "Are not I and Harry with you? and will we not sacrifice our lives to defend you from harm?"

"Oh, I am sure of that, dear Ned,"

"KIL-LI UTTERED ONE CRY, SPREAD OUT HIS ARMS, AND FELL DEAD."

she replied, in a whisper; "but I cannot shake off the fears that assail my soul."

Ned tried to cheer her, but even he felt that Boaster might prevent their escape yet.

And so did Harry.

He felt certain that he had wounded the villain, for the blood-marks on the stairs proclaimed that fact.

But that he had slain him he dared not hope, and living, he knew that Bill would do all in his power to prevent their escape, ay, even to encompass his and Ned's death.

But he kept his fears to himself, and turned to comfort and console Minnie.

Ned passed his fingers down the sides of the shutter in search of the fastening but failed to discover anything that might loosen it.

Again and again he tried, but all in vain.

"Have you got another light, Harry?" said Ned, speaking with difficulty from the pain in his throat.

"Yes, dear boy."

"Strike it, then, for I cannot discover how this shutter is secured."

Harry was about to comply, when again a sound that apppeared to be close beside them, reached their ears.

Instead of lighting the match, Harry held his pistol in the direction whence he fancied the noise came.

"Hist! did you hear anything?" he asked in a whisper.

"I thought so," said Ned.

"And I," replied Minnie, clinging more closely to her lover.

Again they listened, but the sound was not repeated.

"It must have been fancy," said Harry, at last. "I would have fired in the direction but that the report might bring a lot of these Chinese devils upon us."

"No, no, don't fire; the shot would be heard by the soldiers in the guard-room near the door," said Ned. "But if I hear it again I'll thrust with my sword, and Heaven help whoever may be in concealment here?"

"Shall I get a light?"

"Yes; there is no help for it if we are to get out of this terrible place," said Ned.

"Look round quickly when I strike it," said Harry, in a whisper.

"I will," was the low reply.

Harry struck the match on the butt of his revolver.

The instant it flared up Ned looked round the apartment.

He saw no one.

"It's all right, dear boy," he said.

"Thank Heaven," fervently muttered Minnie.

Harry breathed a sigh of relief, and held up the light for Ned to discover how the shutter was secured.

This he soon found, and drawing the bolts, Ned thrust it open.

"Put out the light, Harry. We must not be seen by any one outside."

Harry blew out the taper.

The cool night air came through the opening and fanned their cheeks.

"Out you go, Ned, and I will lift Minnie through the window to you," said Harry.

"Do, dear boy! Fear not, dear Minnie, the distance to the ground is so short."

He paused only to press a kiss on her lips, and mounting to the sill, passed through the opening, and dropped on the other side.

The next moment his head and arms appeared at the opening.

"Come, dear one," he cried. "To liberty and happiness."

Harry thrust the revolver into his belt, and placed his hand on Minnie's waist to assist her to mount to the window-sill.

As he raised her from the floor, a heavy blow fell on the back of his head, and Minnie torn from his grasp, was hurled shrieking back.

"Help, help—Ned, Ned!" she shrieked.

A loud derisive laugh broke on their ears, and the voice of Bill Boaster pealed through the darkness.

"You shriek in vain. Sooner than Ned Nimble should tear you from me, I'll blow your brains out, as I now do his!"

Ned had sprung back into the apartment, and Harry by a mighty effort, was trying to keep his feet, when there came a flash, and a report, and the ping of a bullet sounded in Ned's ears.

In that momentary flash, he caught sight of Minnie struggling in the hold of Boaster, and he dashed forward to her rescue.

But he had not taken three steps when there was a blaze of light, and a dozen soldiers with levelled muskets stood between him and his merciless foe.

CHAPTER XXVIII.

IN WHICH NED AND HARRY RECEIVE HELP, 'DOLF IS SURPRISED, AND JUMBO GETS A SHOCK.

As Ned and Harry recoiled before that grim array of shining barrels, the shrieks of Minnie and the coarse and triumphant laughter of Bill Boaster rang in their ears and goaded them almost to madness.

Harry levelled his revolver, and Ned gripped his bloodstained sword.

" Seize the murderers of the governor," cried Bill. "Death to the assassins of Fum-Fum ! "

" Fire ! " cried a voice.

Quick as lightning, Ned seized Harry by the arm, and falling to the floor, dragged him with him.

There was a lurid flash, a loud rattle, and amid the thud of bullets rang out once again the piercing cries of Minnie Sash, and the loud laughter of the man who held her in his arms.

But as the smoke curled upwards towards the ceiling, Ned and Harry sprang to their feet.

Not a word was spoken, but simultaneously they dashed forward.

Bang, bang, bang ! went Harry's revolver, and then he turned the weapon in his hand and sprang upon the soldiers, smashing at them right and left with its heavy stock.

Hither and thither flashed Ned's sword, dealing fearful cuts, and bringing many a cry from those who felt its keen edge.

" Beat out their brains with the stocks of your guns ! " cried Boaster. "Death to the assassins of Fum-Fum ! "

Then as the soldiers grasped their guns by the barrels, he drew Minnie, shrieking, beyond the screen, and her cries could be heard growing fainter and fainter in the distance.

Three of the soldiers had fallen beneath the weapons of Ned and Harry, but now, with their clubbed guns, the others kept the desperate youths at bay.

Ned forgot all his weakness, all his pain.

He raged like a baffled lion from side to side, striking blows fast and furious.

But the unequal contest was made more unequal still by a blow from the butt of one of the Chinese muskets, which shivered his sword nearly to the hilt.

But with its stump Ned made a rush to break through the line of soldiers and pursue Boaster.

In vain.

He was hurled back.

The next moment he and Harry were beaten to their knees, and another threatened to see them a shapeless and lifeless mass on the floor.

But as, with a cry of triumph, the soldiers raised their muskets to beat out their brains, a terrific volley was poured in upon them from the open window, spreading dismay and destruction through their ranks.

Then the voice of Jack Jones rang out like a clarion cry—

" To the rescue ! Down with the cowardly assassins ! "

Another volley, and then Jack sprang through the window into the room, and dashed upon the demoralised Chinese.

Behind him came 'Dolf, Charley, and Jumbo, and the terrified soldiers broke and fled, in their eagerness to escape, and the terror caused by these new arrivals, carrying away with them in their flight the screen before the opening.

" Follow ! follow ! " cried Ned struggling to his feet. "Save her—save her ! "

He staggered forward a few steps, and fell heavily upon the floor.

" Minnie, Boaster, after her ! Follow me," cried Harry, springing to his feet, and making for the door.

But ere he could reach it, another party of Chinese soldiers stood without.

" Down with the barbarians—death to the assassins ! " cried one, pointing with his sword.

" I guess dat stops yer jaw," cried Jumbo, firing his revolver.

And stop it it surely did, for the bullet

entered the officers mouth, and he fell dead in front of his men.

The next moment the others fired their revolvers, and the soldiers, seized with a panic, turned and fled, as did those who came before them, dragging their wounded and dead comrades with them.

"Follow, follow!" cried Harry, dashing through the opening.

Jack, Charley and Jumbo followed him.

But 'Dolf stopped beside Ned.

"My dear master," he said, "my place is at your side. Are you hurt much?"

"Go 'Dolf, go, dear fellow, and take Minnie away from him. Never mind me. Save her, and I care not what be my fate."

"Don't ask me to go and leave you, Master Ned," said 'Dolf. "I swore to my old master never to desert you, and I will not break my promise. Thank Heaven we came in time to save you."

He lifted Ned up and sat him on the chair which Fum-Fum had used in the morning.

"My place is here, Master Ned, and my body is your shield. If they return, they shall kill me before they can harm you. The others will save Minnie if it is possible, but I stay here, to save, or die with you!"

And placing himself before Ned, the faithful fellow kept his eyes fixed on the doorway, and his revolver levelled at the opening.

"Oh, Minnie, Minnie!" groaned Ned, "and I am powerless to aid her."

He made an effort to rise from his chair, and fell back into it.

The blow from the butt of the soldier's musket, added to what he had already suffered, had completely prostrated him, and he was weak as an infant.

'Dolf felt that both himself and his young master were in a desperate position.

At any moment the soldiers might appear and destroy them; a shot might be fired through the doorway, and Ned at the mercy of his foes.

Eagerly he listened for some sound to give note of the approach of foes or the return of friends.

But though he could hear voices, they appeared at some distance from the apartment.

True he could lift Ned through the open window, and by that means escape from the pagoda with his young master, but he knew that Ned would never agree to seek his own safety while his friends were in danger, and even his own soul rebelled at such a thought.

For himself he cared not, but Ned's safety was all in all to him.

At any moment they might be assailed and shot down.

If he could but conceal Ned till the others returned with Minnie, or failing in that, till they were certain that they had perished in the attempt.

Eagerly he looked around.

The lanterns that seemed to have been lit by magic on the appearance of the first body of soldiers still burned brightly.

Every portion of the huge apartment was visible.

But no place of concealment presented itself.

Only the open window pointed the way of escape, and this he knew Ned would never avail himself of while his friends were fighting for him and the girl he loved.

He saw the curtain across the shrine of the idol, but never thought of it concealing a doorway leading to another part of the pagoda.

But the thought flashed upon him that perhaps they could conceal themselves behind the idol, and from there be able to make a better stand, should they be assailed, than where they now were.

Keeping his gaze still fixed upon the door through which friends and foes had alike gone, 'Dolf walked backwards to where the idol crouched on its haunches, and lifting the curtain hanging at its side, saw behind the wooden figure an opening in the floor.

The trap which usually covered this opening was raised, and lay back against the pedestal on which the figure sat.

Taking a quick glance towards Ned and the door, 'Dolf thrust his leg down the hole, and discovered that his foot rested on a step.

That there were steps leading to some place beneath the room in which they stood he was not slow to determine on.

He hurried back to Ned's side.

"Master Ned," he said, "there is a trap-door behind that figure, and steps leading down from it. Here you are in fearful danger. Let me lead you there, and if our enemies return, they will fancy we have escaped by the window. There we can await the return of our friends. If the worst comes to the worst lie in concealment till all hope of Minnie's rescue or their return is gone."

"Oh Heaven! why am I so powerless," cried Ned. "Why am I forced to remain idle whilst others fight my battles, and do what I would myself do?"

"Don't talk like that, Ned," said 'Dolf. "You are weak and suffering. You have gone through much, but it is useless adding to your miseries. Let me help you to the trap, or out of that window, and then, if you will, when you are in safety, I will seek out Harry and the others, and do my best to kill that villain Boaster, and rescue poor little Minnie from his hands. But here you only present a mark to any coward who may fire through that opening at you."

"Oh, 'Dolf, it is hard—cruel hard to be thus," said Ned. "I am powerless to aid them, and I do but endanger your life. Do with me what you will. I cannot resist."

"'Tis for your own sake, dear Ned," said 'Dolf.

As he spoke he helped Ned from the chair, and half-drew, half-carried him to the side of the idol, and lifting the curtain, aided him to get behind it.

The blow from the butt of the musket had so benumbed Ned's right arm that it was utterly powerless, but he held on to the back of the idol with his left hand, felt with his foot for the first step of the ladder down the opening in the floor.

This he found, and going down a few steps, stood half-way down the trap.

Closing the curtain round the idol again, 'Dolf stood on the edge of the trap, his body hidden by the huge figure of the Chinese god.

"Can you hold on, Ned?"

"Yes."

"Without falling, do you think?"

"Yes; and you?" asked Ned.

"I'm all right. The idol completely hides me from any one who may enter the room, while through the opening between the arm and body I can see all that may transpire, and get a good shot at anybody without fear of being hit in return."

"But when your shots have all been fired, can we escape?"

"Well, we'll trust in Providence," replied 'Dolf.

"True; 'Dolf, you teach me my duty."

"Hist!"

And 'Dolf's hand was laid on Ned's lips to enjoin silence, while his eye was placed to the small opening in the carving between the arm and the body of the idol.

Ned was silent, but eager.

There was a rustling without, as if caused by silk sweeping against silk.

Then two forms came into view, and 'Dolf could hardly suppress the cry of admiration that rose to his lips.

Two young and beautiful women stood a short distance from the idol, but how they entered the apartment 'Dolf knew not.

They were attired in the most gorgeous coloured silks, and their bosoms fairly glittered with jewels, as did also their slippers.

As they stood there in full view of 'Dolf, they looked around the apartment in surprise.

"Not here," said one, in soft and silvery tones.

"Not here," added the other. "And those sounds of firing which we fancied we heard? What can it mean?"

"Surely no harm has befallen the governor?" said one.

"Or Chow-Woo," added the other.

"The gods forefend," was the reply. "Fum-Fum brought me word that the captain would come with the boat, and be here for me to welcome him on his return, and praise him for his bravery, and congratulate him on the success of his cruise. Oh, if ill has befallen my husband I shall die of grief and despair?"

"Oh, Loogee, banish such fears from your heart. Your husband is safe, be assured, safe as my own dear Fum-Fum."

"But my heart sinks within me, Fee-Woo-ta. Heard you not the sound of muskets, and the voices of men in anger? I must know the worst."

And then, throwing herself on her knees before the idol, Loogee clasped her hands together and cried—

"Oh, great god, have mercy on me, and bring my husband safe to these arms!"

Then, rising, she crossed the apartment towards the doorway, but stopped half-way, and uttered a wild and piercing shriek, while with distended eyes she pointed to the matted floor.

"See—see!" she cried, in tones of agony.

Fee-Woo-ta sprang to her companion's side.

A cry of horror escaped her lips, and she recoiled as if stung by a serpent.

"Blood—blood!" gasped Loogee.

"Blood!" echoed the other, as she stood aghast at the sight.

The dead and wounded had been dragged away by their companions in their flight.

But their blood had stained the matting where they had fallen.

And on this blood the two women gazed, their lovely features convulsed with horror, their bosoms filled with a terrible fear.

For some moments they stood gazing at the horrid spectacle, then gave utterance to loud shrieks, and fled towards the door.

As they reached it, they recoiled in terror and alarm, as through the opening sprang the stalwart form of Jumbo, holding in one hand a long blood-stained knife, and in the other a revolver, while his features worked with intense excitement and his eyes blazed in their sockets.

"Gor-a-mighty! what's dis?" cried the negro, startled at the vision before him.

A moment they stood confronting each other, Jumbo in surprise, the women in terror, then the latter turned, and uttering piercing shrieks, fled across the apartment, raised a curtain on the opposite side of the room, and disappeared behind it.

CHAPTER XXIX.

IN WHICH THE PIRATES DISCOVER THEIR CAPTAIN.

WHILE Jumbo stood glaring in the direction in which the two Chinese ladies had disappeared, Jack and Charley entered.

"What's the matter with you, you old fool," asked Charley. "that you stand like a stuck pig looking as if you was going to have a fit?"

"Am dar angels in dis yer land ob debils?" said Jumbo, without removing his gaze from the curtain.

"What do you mean, you idiot?"

"I'se seen 'em, I swar to goodness I hab, and dey wanished wid der wings all a glittering in yellow and blue and di'mon's"

"Where's Ned and 'Dolf?" asked Jack, looking round. "This is the place we left them in, ain't it?"

"I think so," said Charley. "Yes. See, there's the blood on the floor."

"Then where's Ned?"

"I reckons as how dem ar angels hab been an' flyed away wid him an 'Dolf," said Jumbo.

"Have you gone crazy?" said Charley.

"Guess I'se gone more nor dat," replied Jumbo. "Yer just should a-seen 'em a-glistening and a-glittering an' a-flying about dis yer room like de fairies at de pantermime at de featre."

"But Ned and 'Dolf? Hang the fairies!" said Jack impatiently.

"Guess I'd like ter, roun' dis yer neck ob mine," said Jumbo.

"Did you see Ned?" asked Charley.

"Guess I didn't see not nuffin but dem ar lubly angels."

"Oh go to the deuce!" said Charley.

"Ned and 'Dolf have escaped out of the window, I expect," said Jack.

'Dolf pulled aside the curtain and stepped forth.

Up went three revolvers and covered him.

"Don't fire," said 'Dolf; "it is I."

And he strode forward.

"Where's Ned?"

"Behind the curtain. Poor fellow! He's powerless and weak as a baby," said 'Dolf.

Ned staggered up the trap, and from behind the curtain.

"Minnie?" he asked eagerly.

"Can't be found, nor Bill either," said Jack. "The cowardly Chinese are all wounded, dead, or flown, but we can find nothing of Minnie or her persecutor."

"Where's Harry?" he asked. "Nothing has happened to him?"

"Nothing to speak of," said Jack. "He bade us wait him here. He knows how to find the vaults, and has gone to see if they are there."

"Alone?" said Ned.

"Yes; he thought it best that we should not go with him, as one was more likely to escape discovery than two or three, and should he find those we seek have made their way into them, he will return for our assistance."

Ned was about to reply, when Harry dashed into the room.

"Quick, quick!" he cried. "Out of the window with you! There are other and more desperate foes than the cowardly soldiers we shall have to meet else. The pirates have been alarmed, and are making their way here from the vaults, and they are doubly armed and used to fighting."

"Go, and without Minnie? Never!" cried Ned.

"Don't be foolish, Ned. There are at least twenty of these desperate fellows, and to remain here is to be slain to a man. Boaster has escaped with Minnie. To escape ere it is too late may enable us to rescue her from his hands, while to remain longer here is certain death."

"Hark!" cried Jack, stepping towards the door.

The footsteps of the ascending pirates could be heard.

"I will not go while there is yet a chance of Minnie being in the pagoda," said Ned.

"Ned, you will ruin all," said Harry. "Better that we escape now, and return by-and-bye than remain and perish at the hands of the desperate ruffians now advancing."

"Let's take to the trap behind the idol," said 'Dolf. "They will never dream to look for us there with that window open."

"Yes," cried Ned. "The trap, the trap!"

"Bring him this way, Jack," cried 'Dolf. "Quick, quick!"

At that moment the loud and angry voices of the pirates were heard in the passage outside.

Jack seized Ned in his strong arms, and followed 'Dolf as he bounded towards the curtain.

'Dolf flung up the curtain, and pointing to the opening beyond, said in a hurried whisper—

"Down there, Jack. Mind the steps. That's it. Now, Charley, Jumbo, follow him quick. I and Harry will keep watch here."

Without waiting to question him, Charley and Jumbo passed under the curtain behind the image, and down into the darkness of the hole.

'Dolf drew Harry behind the curtain, and suffered it to fall into its place.

Not a moment too soon.

While even yet the curtain closed around them, the pirates poured through the doorway into the apartment.

They were principally Chinese, but there were also Italians, Spaniards, and Malays, and all were armed with pistols, knives, and cutlasses.

A more terrible-looking set of ruffians could not well have been found in a body.

A howl of rage escaped them on seeing the open window, and with their cutlasses and pistols they pointed towards the opening.

With an oath one stepped forward.

He was the Malay lieutenant of the pirate junk.

"Gone!" he said in a rough, harsh voice. "But where's the captain? Where's the governor? They are not among those lying without there. Strike that gong!"

One of the pirates struck a gong that hung at the side of the doorway.

While they waited for some one to answer the summons the pirates examined the apartment, only the foreigners going close up to the idol.

On finding the blood on the floor they pointed it out and stood talking and gesticulating wildly, all speaking at once.

There was no response to the summons, and with an oath Zanara the Malay struck the gong a heavy blow with the butt of his pistol.

"Go, find some of those dogs that hide in holes while their master is in danger," he cried, "and drag them here."

Two or three of the pirates hurried to obey the order.

In about half a minute they returned, dragging a Celestial with them.

It was Cheeko, the man whom Ned and Harry had heard talking to the pirate captain at the head of the steps leading to the torture chamber.

"Why did you not come at the sound of the gong?" cried Zanara fiercely.

The fellow trembled.

"I feared it was the barbarians, who sought to murder me," he cried.

"Coward!" yelled the lieutenant, striking him with the flat of his cutlass.

"Mercy," whined the fellow. "I knew not it was you who required my presence. The soldiers who rushed to my room for safety told me the governor's apartment was filled with English devils with big swords and many-mouthed guns, and that to approach it would be death."

"Where is the governor?"

"I know not. He went to the torture chamber to see the barbarian put in the sling an hour since."

"And our captain—where is he?"

"The great Chow-Woo went after the governor. I saw him descend the stairs. I have not seen them since."

"And who are these barbarians that have cut up the soldiers and spread such havoc through the pagoda?"

"I know not," was the reply.

"Know not?" cried the Malay.

"No. I secured myself in my room when I heard the firing, and when the soldiers, compelled to fly from the English devils, forced the door, I dared not leave it lest I too fell by their arms."

"Take that as a reward for your courage," cried the Malay, striking him a severe blow across the cheek with the flat of his cutlass. "Now light us to this place where the governor and captain are so busy with their tortures that they cannot hear that the pagoda has been overrun by the English in their absence."

The man dashed out and returned with a lantern.

"I am ready," he said.

"Yes, to go where you know there is no danger," said the lieutenant. "Lead on. Some of you follow me; others remain here till I return."

So saying, he followed the attendant from the apartment.

About half the number went with him.

Harry and 'Dolf from their place of concealment saw and heard all.

But in the face of that well-armed mass they dared do nothing but remain silent where they were.

Even had their weapons not been empty they would have stood little chance against so desperate a band.

But they had now not a single shot amongst them, and to issue forth and trust only to their fists and knives would be worse than madness.

They could only await in silent anxiety the issue of events, thanking Heaven that no suspicion of their hiding-place had entered the minds of the bloodthirsty pirates.

Zanara and his men followed Cheko down the steps leading from the vestibule to the dungeon, on reaching the door of which the Celestial attendant gave a start and exclaimed—

"The door is fast; the bar is in its place. They must have left."

Zanara pressed forward.

"Yes, the door is fast, and on the outside," he said. "Where can the captain be?"

As if in answer to this query came a rap on the other side of the door.

"Open, open!" cried a voice, sounding low and hollow through the massive panels.

Cheko almost dropped the lantern in his fright.

But the Malay dashed him aside, and seizing the bar, flung it from its socket.

Kicking the door open, he looked in.

Before him stood the pirate captain.

"Captain!" he exclaimed.

"Oh! is it you, lieutenant? You are indeed welcome. I thought I was doomed to remain in this dungeon till death overtook me."

"What has happened?" asked the lieutenant, seeing the bodie lying on the ground of the dungeon.

"The governor has been stabbed to the heart, the two torturers are slain, and the prisoner has escaped," was the reply. "But what sounds were those above? Have you been attacked?"

"No, but the governor's guards have by several English, I hear, and the cowards suffered themselves to be cut and shot down without resistance. In their eagerness to escape, some of them entered the storehouse, and thus we learned what was going on, and fearing danger to yourself, sought you in the governor's apartment and failing to find you there, turned our footsteps hither."

"You did well, or I might have died here. What of the English barbarians who have had the temerity to attack the guard ? "

"They have evidently escaped from the pagoda. The shutter is down in the governor's room, and through that they must have fled."

"And the barbarian friend of the governor's and the girl—know you aught of them ? " asked the captain.

Zanara stared at him in surprise.

"Girl ? " he said.

"Yes. After I had been thrust into this dungeon I heard a moan, and having the means of obtaining a light I procured one and found one of the executioners alive, but the man was dying from his wound. Yet he lived long enough to tell me that while the governor and a young barbarian were torturing a prisoner and forcing an English girl to witness it another barbarian burst upon them and shot them down."

"I know nothing of this," said Zanara, "and have seen no English girl."

"There is yet some mystery to be explained," said Chow-Woo. "But first to break the terrible news to Fee-Woo-Ta, and assure myself of the safety of Loogee."

He passed out of the dungeon followed by Zanara.

"Bring the body of the governor up with you," he said addressing the pirates. "Oh, if any harm has befallen my beloved Loogee I will have an Englishman's life for every hair of her head. By the bones of my father I swear it! "

CHAPTER XXX.

IN WHICH MINNIE LEAPS FROM ONE DANGER INTO ANOTHER.

UNLIKE most men who delight in inflicting pain upon others, Bill Boaster was no coward.

His bravery was the only redeeming point in his character.

Given the same weapons and the same chances, Bill would fight to the last.

But he was also cautious.

He would not throw his life away, but bide his time.

With only his fists to oppose Harry Honour's pistol, and one of those hands minus three of its fingers, he felt it would be madness to dash back into the torture-chamber and seek to possess himself of Minnie.

He was over-matched, and so he made his way, despite a wound in the fleshy part of his leg, to the guard-room, and asserting that he was acting on Fum-Fum's orders, obtained the soldiers and laid his trap for securing the poor girl.

And he had succeeded admirably.

Leaving the soldiers to fight when he saw the arrival of Ned's friends, he dragged Minnie along a passage and up a narrow flight of stairs, to an apartment where she had been placed by the governor but a short time before, when Bill, in accordance with his promise, had brought her to the pagoda as a hostage for his own behaviour, and from which he had taken her to see the torture to which Ned was subjected.

This apartment was very small, and contained nothing but a bamboo bedstead and a couple of bamboo chairs, a window high up in the wall, and very narrow, and resembled more a prison than anything else.

To what use it was generally put Bill did not know, but he gave a shrewd guess that it was for the use of any one likely to pay for liberty, till their ransom arrived.

Closing the door behind him, Bill roughly thrust Minnie into one of the chairs, and stood before her.

All the poor girl's courage had deserted her.

She felt week as an infant, and powerless to resist in any way.

" You thought to give me the slip and be off with Ned, didn't you ? " he hissed.

She made no reply.

"You little thought that when you stood in the dark in that room that I was close to your side—that I could by holding out my arm, grip your shoulder. No, you knew not how I found it difficult to suppress my laughter when you thought your freedom so near, and how I waited for the moment you thought it was certain, to dash the cup of hope and happiness from your lips, as I did when I hurled you back from that open window.

Only a sigh and a sob answered him.

"I have often thought," continued Bill, "when I have watched a cat suffer a mouse to escape its claws, what happiness it felt when it pounced on it again. Yes, and that was what I felt when I saw you at that window, and I knew I had only to put forth my hand to prevent you escaping me."

"Fiend!" gasped Minnie.

"Oh, you have found your tongue at last," sneered Bill.

"Would it were the sting of a serpent and could strike you dead," said Minnie.

"That it cannot do," said Bill, "but it has often stung me to madness. It has goaded me to deeds that in days gone by I could never have believed I could have performed. It has poured venom into my heart till it has poisoned all my better nature."

"Your nature was ever that of the wolf," she cried, "the most treacherous, the most despicable, the most merciless of animals; but like the ravening wolf, you will be hunted down as sure as night follows day."

"Ay," he replied, "but between the then and now?"

He gave her such a look that she shuddered and turned cold.

"Coward," she said, "to torture a woman thus. Can the world produce another such monster?"

"Many of them," said Bill. "Hark! that shot may have laid your milksop lover low. There's another; perhaps it has found the heart of his friend Harry."

"Wretch, have you no mercy?" she cried, springing from her chair.

"Mercy, what is that?" cried Bill; "mercy! you and he killed it long ago."

"'Twas your own wicked will," she said, "your own base nature."

"Have it your own way," he said. "Ha, the firing alarms you, does it?"

"No, would one of the bullets reached my heart," she replied.

"No fear of that," he said; "but if they reach not Ned's, he will only escape till he is sawn in two for the killing the governor."

"Killing the governor?" cried Minnie. "You know that it was my hand that robbed that wretch of his existence —my hand that avenged in his blood the torture of the man I love."

"'Tis false!" cried Bill; "it was his, and if he escape the bullets of the soldiers, he cannot the hands of the executioners, and i am told that the murder of a mandarin is punished by having the living body of the assassin sawn asunder."

"Oh, loathsome wretch! Oh, vengeful demon!" cried Minnie, aghast, "and you would seek to consign him to such a fate—you would perjure your black soul and shut out all hopes of salvation to inflict such a fearful doom upon him."

"I would!" hissed Bill, "there is no revenge too deep, no sin too black to perpetrate to minister to my vengeance. Had I ten thousand lives at my mercy I would give them all for his, and in the taking of it, if I could inflict ten thousand tortures, by earth and heaven even they would be too small to gratify my revenge.

"Great Heaven!" cried Minnie, in horror raising her clasped hands and eyes upwards. "Is this a man or a devil? Can Hades possess a fiend so foul, so unnatural? Oh, impossible, for even lost souls would rebel at the desecration of such a monster, and hurl him from their midst."

"Ha, ha, ha," laughed Bill, "you see what your obstinacy, your scorn, your derision has made me. Think of it, and tremble for him you love, for him I hate—Ned Nimble."

So saying, he flung open the door, passed out, closed the door behind him and Minnie with a sinking heart heard the bolts shot into their sockets without.

Then with a sob she fell into a chair and wept as if her heart would break.

"Oh, Ned, Ned," she sobbed, "has Heaven indeed deserted us? Must it ever be that when happiness seems to be within our reach, despair is to tear it from our hearts? Oh, Heaven, my heart is breaking!"

She slipped from the chair to the floor, on to her knees, and buried her face on the bamboo bedstead, and her frame shook beneath the powerful emotions that filled her bosom with dismay and despair.

All was silent now.

The firing had ceased, not even a foot-fall broke upon her ears.

Where was Ned, she thought; had he escaped the bullets of the soldiers and fled, or—oh, horror! had he fallen captive into the hands of the Celestials?

Better that he had falllen by bullet or steel in the fight, for too well she felt assured that Bill would denounce him as the murderer of the governor.

The idea of escape for herself did not for a moment find a resting place in her heart.

She thought not of herself now; all her thoughts were for Ned, and her prayers for his safety.

A beautifully-coloured lamp, or rather lantern, hung from the ceiling of the room, and its gorgeous paper sides threw beams of many colours over the walls and floor of the room, a golden ray resting upon her bowed head and shoulders.

Her back was towards the door, and her thoughts so occupied her mind that she neither heard nor saw the narrow door open or the form that crossed its threshold.

It was a stalwart Celestial, a man with a noble carriage and a face far more handsome than the generality of his countrymen.

His features were bronzed almost to the hue of a Spaniard, and his rich robes and jewelled hilted sword and pistols showed him above the ordinary stamp of the inhabitants of the pagoda.

But he was not a mandarin—his dress proclaimed that fact.

He started on seeing the kneeling form of the young girl, but recovering himself in a moment, he stepped softly across the matted floor and placed his hand on her shoulder.

With such a cry as the sting of a serpent might have called forth, Minnie turned her face towards him.

She had expected that her eyes would have encountered the features of Bill Boaster; great then was her surprise to find a stranger bending over her.

She sprang to her feet, recoiled a pace, then falling on her knees, cried—

"Oh, if you be human, save me, save me!"

For a moment the man gazed down into her pleading eyes, and then taking her clasped hands in his, he said in a low soft voice—

"Save you girl? From whom—from what?"

"From him, my persecutor! from the wretch who has stolen me from my friends, who has dragged me hither, who seeks to make others suffer by inflicting torture on me. Oh, you at least are human; you will pity and shield a poor suffering, heart-broken girl from the persecutions of a villain."

"Girl, who are you?" he said.

"A miserable, heart-broken English girl torn from her friends and her home by a villain who would force me to become his wife; whose cruelties have driven me to despair—to madness. Oh take me hence, take me anywhere—anywhere from him!"

"What is the name of this man you fear?" asked the Celestial.

"Boaster—William Boaster," she replied.

The other smiled.

"And you are she then whom he forced to witness the torture of a prisoner?"

Minnie started.

How knew he that?

What could she say?

What could she do to shield Ned?

If he had fallen into the hands of the Chinese, might not one word of hers consign him to a fearful doom?

Oh, how she longed to ask the man before her if he knew whether Ned was captured, killed, or escaped.

But she dared not.

Perhaps he knew not of his escape from the dungeon, of the fight in the pagoda—and yet, vain hope, how could that be possible?

Surely he must know all, since he knew that she had been forced to witness the torture of her lover.

So she gasped out with a burst of sobs—

"Alas, I am she."

"And this man, who could force you to witness such a scene, where is he?" he asked.

"I know not; he went out from here just now, after threatening me as only a villain and a monster could do."

"He is your foe, then, as well as your lover?"

"A bitter one, indeed."

"'DON'T BE SO FOOLISH, SALLY!' CRIED JACK."

"And you would escape him?"

"Heaven knows how gladly," she replied.

"For what purpose?" he asked.

"That I might join my——"

She paused—she felt it unsafe to mention Ned.

He looked at her curiously for a moment, and then said—

"Girl, I will save you from this man if you are willing to go on board my vessel. I know more of you and that man than you imagine, and I know also that he who was submitted to the torture was the one you love and the one you would seek."

Minnie looked at him in surprise, but was silent.

"If your lover, aided by friends, has escaped from this pagoda he will not remain long at liberty. The governor has fallen by the hands of one of the barbarians, and all who sought to aid him and you will be captured and slain."

"Oh Heaven!" gasped Minnie.

"But you at least may escape, for I can get you on board my junk unseen, and before the authorities are on the alert."

"If Ned must die, then let me die with him," cried Minnie.

The man looked hard in her lovely face and his eyes showed the admiration he felt for the girl before him.

But Minnie observed not his looks or she would have shrunk from him; she only heard his soft mellow tones as holding her hands in his, he whispered in her ear—

"Girl, I pity you and will protect you. Fear not; trust yourself with me, and if it be possible I will save your lover."

"Oh bless you, bless you!" cried Minnie. "Oh, who—what shall I call my friend?"

"I am Captain Chow-Woo. Come, every moment increases your danger, and your persecutor may return. Trust to me; my boat is ready, and if you get hence ere the authorities are aroused you are safe."

"I will trust you, and Heaven reward you as you act towards me."

He supported her on his arm and descended to the vault and through it to the channel, where his boat lay moored.

The appearance of the men with which the boat was manned terrified Minnie, and she drew back from the edge of the platform.

"Fear nothing, girl," said Chow-Woo, "My men may look fierce, but not one of them would dare offer you harm or indignity. Go with them without fear. I will remain and seek for your lover that I may restore him to you. Trust me, and all will yet be well."

"Oh, come you not with me?" cried Minnie. "I dare not go alone with these fearful-looking men. With you I feel safe, but with them——"

"Well, well," he said, interrupting her, "I will accompany you, and then return and look for your lover. Now, let me assist you into the boat."

He raised her in his arms and lowered her into the boat.

The men seized the oars, while one threw off the rope.

Chow-Woo made a move as if to spring into the boat, when Loogee dashed through the opening on to the platform, and seizing her husband's arm, cried—

"Chow-Woo, my husband! Oh, I feared—Ah! what is this? Why are you here? and who is that girl?"

She pointed to Minnie, who was calling to Chow-Woo not to desert her as she felt the boat glide from the platform.

The captain turned in surprise and annoyance at the words of his wife, and gave a start as a pair of small folding doors at the side of the platform flew open, and the figure of Bill Boaster appeared.

Minnie caught sight of the villain and uttered a loud cry.

The next moment the boat shot round into the darkness of the channel, and with a moan she sank down, wailing out the cry—

"Lost! betrayed—betrayed!"

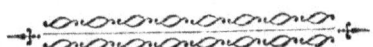

CHAPTER XXXI.

IN WHICH BILL BOASTER FINDS THE PIRATE CAPTAIN ONE TOO MANY FOR HIM.

HOLDING the doors in his hands, Bill Boaster stood, as it were, for a moment paralysed with surprise and consternation.

In one brief glance he had taken in all his surroundings, and realised the whole truth of the scene before him.

The gorgeously-attired man on the platform was the celebrated pirate chief; those in the boat were some of his crew and the girl in their charge was none other than Minnie Sash, whom he had left locked in the little chamber but a few minutes before ; and the man who stood confused, and surprised, and amazed before the upbraiding woman, must have released her, not out of pity for her sufferings, but to serve some purpose of his own.

Like lightning these thoughts flashed through his brain, and then he drew his revolver from his belt, and sprang before Chow-Woo and Loogee.

"Villain!" he cried, "call back that boat, or I'll stretch you dead at my feet!"

And he levelled the weapon at the pirate's head.

Loogee uttered a cry and flung herself before her husband.

Not a muscle of Chow-Woo's face changed.

His voice was as calm as ever, as he said—

"What mad barbarian is this?"

"Call back that boat!" cried Bill. "That girl is mine, and no man shall take her from me."

"Be it as you wish," said Chow-Woo. "What care I for the girl? If she belongs to you, you shall have her. She sought my aid to escape from the pagoda, and I bade my men take her hence and put her ashore. She is naught to me, and right glad am I to be rid of her."

Loogee breathed a sigh of relief.

And in her heart she deeply upbraided herself for suspecting her husband.

"Then call her back," said Bill, "and surrender her to me. I have the governor's promise that none should molest her or myself."

"The governor's word is enough for me," said Chow-Woo. "I will summon my men to return with her at once."

He placed his hand in his bosom and drew forth a small ivory whistle, which he applied to his lips.

He blew it loudly, and the channel and vault echoed and re-echoed with the sound.

"That will be understood by my men," he said. "And now, young fire-eating barbarian, perhaps you will lower that pistol since it alarms my wife."

Bill thrust the pistol back into his belt.

"Loogee," said the pirate, "I was coming to you when the poor girl implored me to get her out of the pagoda, where strange and terrible scenes have been transpiring. Go, sweet one, and I will join you directly. Go, and comfort Fee-Woo-Ta, for her heart will be heavy."

"What means my husband?" cried the young woman.

"Some accursed barbarian has robbed the governor of his life," he whispered. "Go, break the news gently to her ere I come."

A look of horror overspread the woman's face, and she cast a shivering look towards Bill as he stood glancing along the channel in search of the boat he expected to return.

"Not he, I think," said Chow-Woo, in a whisper. "But leave me; I will come soon. So go to Fee-Woo-Ta."

"Fum-Fum dead—slair!" cried Loogee wringing her hands. "Oh poor Fee-Woo-Ta, poor stricken dove, how shall I tell her, how wring her gentle heart with the sad, sad story?"

Then clasping her husband's hand, and looking up into his face with tear-bedimmed eyes, she cried—

"Oh, my love, my lord, light of my life, sun of my heart, come with your poor Loogee to Fee-Woo-Ta. I dare not speak the words that will kill her.

Let yours be the tongue to utter words that will sink like black despair to her heart."

"Better your gentle voice than my rough tones pronounce the fate of her husband," said Chow-Woo; "so go my sweet bird. From your lips she will better hear the awful news, and on your bosom she will find comfort for her agony and despair."

Gently he drew her through the doorway into the vault, urged her forward on her sad errand, and watched her as she hurried away.

Then, as footsteps broke upon his ears, he smiled grimly and laid his hands on the jewelled butts of the pistols he wore at his belt.

As Chow-Woo spoke, he led Loogee through the doorway into the vault.

Bill, in his eagerness to catch sight of the boat, did not observe the absence of Chow-Woo from the platform.

And when, after a moment or two, surprised at the delay of the boat, he turned to accost him, he started on seeing him just within the vault, holding in each hand a jewelled revolver, levelled at his head.

Instinctively Bill's hand went to his belt.

But ere it reached it the voice of Chow-Woo rang out like a clarion cry—

"Hold up your hands, or I'll lay your head low, dog of a barbarian! Up with them, I say, or in another moment there will be a dead body in that channel beneath you!"

"Traitor!" cried Bill, as he held up his hands.

"Dog," was the reply, "keep your mouth closed. The man who defies Chow-Woo the pirate seldom lives to tell that he has done so."

There was a hurried tramp of feet, and several men came rushing into the vault.

"Seize and bind that dog of a barbarian!" said the captain, addressing the men.

In a moment Bill was pounced upon by the rough pirates.

His revolver was taken from him, his arms tied behind his back, and he was flung on to the platform at the captain's feet.

"Is this the murderer of the governor?" asked Zanara of his chief.

"I know not," was the reply. "He is a barbarian, that is sufficient, and the people will demand a victim for that deed, so he will do as well as any one else."

"True," said Zanara, "and it is as well that one has been secured, though the rest have escaped. What shall we do with him?"

"Let him lie where he is for the present, and guard him close. I have business on hand and will return when the boat comes back. See that he is not left alone."

"Your orders shall be obeyed, captain," said Zanara.

The captain entered the vault and made his way to the upper part of the pagoda.

On entering the room in which the struggle had taken place, and where the body of Fum-Fum had been carried, a sad and heartrending scene met his gaze.

On the large table the dead body of the governor had been placed, and over it lay the weeping and shrieking Fee-Woo-Ta, while around her neck Loogee had thrown her arms, and sought in vain to assuage her grief at the fate of her husband.

"Oh, woe is me!" cried the poor wife of the dishonourable governor. "The sun of my life has gone out, and the darkness of night has fallen on the soul of Fee-Woo-ta. Oh, woe is me—woe is me!"

And wringing her hands, she bathed the face of the dead governor in tears.

The pirates and attendants of Fum-Fum had disappeared, leaving the two women alone to their grief.

On entering the apartment, the pirate captain joined with his wife in comforting Fee-Woo-Ta, but in this they could not succeed.

More and more violent her grief became, till finally flinging up her arms, she uttered a piercing shriek, and fainted on the body of her dead husband.

Then Chow-Woo raised her in his strong arms, and speaking hurriedly to his wife, bore the insensible form across the apartment, behind the curtain and up another flight of stairs to the rooms occupied by the ladies of the pagoda.

From behind the image the concealed friends had watched the terribly sad scene, and heard all that had transpired, and when the room was left alone to the dead, they raised the curtain and issued forth.

On bringing in the body of the governor the pirates had closed the shutter and secured it ; but 'Dolf instantly withdrew the bolts, saying—

"There's no knowing but what we may have to escape that way."

"Now is our time," said Harry, "to make a further search for Minnie and Boaster, though I fear that they have got out of the place, for Bill would not like to be mixed up with the governor's death."

"I do not believe either of them are here now," said Jack. "The villain had plenty of opportunities to carry her off while we were engaged with the soldiers besides, if he had the chance to do so, it is hardly likely he'd remain to confront us. He's no coward I admit, but he's as artful as the evil one himself."

"I guess he's tooked his hook," said Jumbo.

"And so, I expect, have the pirates by this time," said Harry. "But as I know how to get to their storehouse, suppose I go there and see if it is so. We have little to fear from the soldiers or attendants, and much from pirates. If they have left the pagoda, we'll then chance meeting with the others and search it from top to bottom. How say you, Ned ?"

"As you will, dear boy ; but you must not go to the vaults alone."

"Yes, it will be better that I do," said Harry. "Leave me alone for being careful not to betray my presence if any of the pirates are still down there."

So saying, he drew his knife and left the room.

"Guess dey's a bery bad lot what libs in dis yer 'ouse," said Jumbo.

"Almost as bad as yourself," said Charley.

"Dat's trufe," was the reply.

Ned stood beside the body of the governor.

"His villainies are ended for ever," he said. "Cruel as he has been to me, I freely forgive him."

"That's kind of you, Ned," said Jack.

"It is wrong to bear animosity towards the dead," said Ned. "Providence has taken his punishment into its own hands now."

"But how 'bout dat ar angelic angel ob a woman, what tooked on so 'bout him," said Jumbo. "Golly, if dat ar gal was de wife ob dis yer magernanermous inderwiderel, I reckons as how i'd neber go an' get killed and make her cry dem ar eyes ob her'n out, bressed if I would."

"Hush !" said Jack, "don't talk so loud."

They became silent and waited anxiously Harry's return.

They were begining to fear that some harm had befallen him, when he came hurriedly back.

"Ned," he said quickly, "the pirates are still below."

A look of disappointment passed over every face.

"They are waiting for their captain to join them, the man we saw here but a few minutes ago."

"Is he their captain ?" said Ned.

"Yes. But I have something else to tell you, dear boy."

"What ?"

"Promise you'll be calm, Ned."

"Go on, old boy, don't keep me in suspense."

"Then to stay here longer is useless," said Harry.

"Why ?"

"Minnie !"

"Yes. What of her ? Speak, quick —Harry. What of Minnie ?"

"She is not in the pagoda."

"Where is she ?"

Harry took hold of Ned's arm and looked into his face.

"Ned, dear friend, be calm," he said. "Minnie has been taken on board the pirate junk."

"Minnie—my Minnie, taken aboard a pirate !" gasped Ned.

"Yes, sent there by the pirate-captain; and Bill Boaster is a bound prisoner in the hands of the pirates in the vault."

"Minnie taken on board the pirate, and Boaster a prisoner ! what does it all mean ?"

"I know not for certain, but I suspect much," replied Harry; "but one thing is certain. Here we can neither get possession of Minnie nor Bill. We must leave this place and lay our plans outside, for to remain here longer would be madness; and while we could do no good, may only cause our ruin."

"That's true," said 'Dolf.

"With Minnie on board the pirate, and Bill a prisoner in their hands, our place is no longer here," said Jack, "so I vote that we make off while we've got the chance."

"So say all of us," remarked Charley.

"But Bill—why have they taken him prisoner? That I can't understand," said Ned, passing his hand over his forehead wearily.

"I know not, but from what I overheard one of the pirates say as I laid concealed behind the merchandize, I fancy they imagine that it was he who killed the governor, and that they intend to kill him for doing so."

"And serve him right too," said Jumbo.

"Minnie on board the pirate," murmured Ned, vacantly. "Oh, Heaven, why have they taken her there?"

"That we may rescue her," said Harry. "So come, dear boy, come."

He drew Ned towards the window.

"Oh, Harry, Harry, are you sure she is not here still?" he asked, stopping suddenly.

"I am sure from what I heard in the vaults that she is not."

"From whom, Harry—the pirates?"

"No, from Bill himself. He was cursing the pirate-captain for sending her there, and swearing that when he got his liberty he would tear her from the junk and kill the man who made him a prisoner."

"Then Heaven help her!" sighed Ned. "Poor Minnie, how cruelly is she tried —how bitterly are we both made to suffer!"

Harry did not reply, but urged him to the window.

'Dolf threw back the shutter.

Charley got out first, and Jumbo followed him.

Jack and Harry helped Ned over the sill, and those outside lowered him to the ground.

"Go on, Jack," said Harry.

"After you," replied Jack, "I'll be first."

Harry sprang through the opening.

Jack looked round the apartment, and then put his long legs over the sill and dropped down beside the others.

Thrusting his arm in at the window, he pulled close the shutter, and the next minute they were making their way with sad hearts in the direction of the wharfs off which, at some distance from the shore, rode the pirate junk to which Minnie had been taken.

CHAPTER XXXII.

IN WHICH CHOW-WOO COMES TO A DECISION, AND BILL BOASTER MEETS AN OLD ACQUAINTANCE ON BOARD THE PIRATE JUNK.

To keep the fate of the governor Fum-Fum a secret was impossible, for even if those about the pagoda did not betray it, yet his absence must soon be missed, and inquiries as to its cause set on foot.

And these inquiries might lead to the discovery that the trusted servant of the emperor was in league with the pirates, and the vaults of the pagoda were used for the storage of stolen property.

No one knew this better than the pirate-captain himself, and none more dreaded the discovery than he did.

Of the governor's attendants he had little fear, since they were interested themselves, nor had he much fear of whoever might be decided upon to fill

the post of the deceased Fum-Fum, since those in power were ever ready to be bribed.

But Chow-Woo's fear was lest the doings at the pagoda should reach the emperor's ears.

True, he might escape in his junk, and bid defiance to the emperor himself, but then he must lose his share of the plunder stored in the large vaults of the pagoda.

Having succeeded in averting the suspicions of his wife as to his intentions regarding Minnie, and having somewhat calmed the grief of Fee-Woo-Ta, at the loss of her lord and husband, he held counsel with them as to the best means to pursue to prevent any overhauling of the pagoda, and any suspicions being fixed upon Fum-Fum and himself.

After much thought and many suggestions, it was at last decided that it should be given out that the governor had been slain by an English barbarian while trying to extort a confession from a prisoner, and that, on the alarm being given, the captain of a merchant junk lying off the pagoda, had landed with some of his men and secured the assassin, taken him red-handed and imprisoned him on board his vessel till he should know the will of the authorities respecting him.

The soldiers who had fallen in the fight were of so little consequence that no mention was to be made of them while those who survived were little to be feared since they would be sure to remain silent lest they were executed for not saving the governor's life, or for their own cowardice.

Having arranged that Fee-Woo-Ta and Loogee should despatch messengers with this information to the various mandarins around and forward an account of Fum-Fum's death to the emperor, the captain decided to have the vaults secured from intrusion from above, and go on board his vessel with the prisoner and there await the will of the Chinese nobles.

"Why, not remain here with me?" asked Loogee. "After so long an absence it is cruel to leave me so soon."

"I know it is, sweet dove," replied Chow-Woo, "but my presence here might excite suspicion. I must seem what I pretend to be—the captain of a trading junk—and you must not be known as my wife till this sad affair is over, and I have arranged with the new governor to follow the tactics of the old one."

"Then let me accompany you, and share your perils and your hardships?" said Loogee. "Are you not my husband, the sun of my life?"

"Ay, sweetest; but would you desert poor Fee-Woo-Ta in her hours of grief? Who shall comfort and console her now if her friend and companion Loogee desert her while the black clouds have closed over her brain and heart?"

"Oh, my husband, you teach me my duty to friendship. I will remain with the wounded dove till you bid me come."

"It's ever like my own sweet bird," he said with a look of relief.

He drew her to his bosom and kissed her.

"Go to her," he said; "let your voice be music in her ears, and your deeds fall like oil upon her troubled heart. Let your presence be like sunshine piercing the black clouds, and then will Chow-Woo love you the more."

She smiled through her tears, and embraced him again and again.

At length he tore himself away, after enjoining her to be careful neither by word nor deed to betray her relationship to himself till such a time as he bid her do so.

Then he sought his men in the vault.

The boat had returned and awaited him.

Calling Zanara aside, he told him his intentions respecting their prisoner and the governor's death.

"But where is the man who slew him?" asked Zanara. "There were several barbarians in the pagoda."

"What matters that?" said Chow-Woo. "The law will demand a victim, so as well one barbarian as another. So far from this man having killed the governor, I believe him to have purchased Fum-Fum's friendship; but he will appease the wrath of the emperor and the people, and by giving him up we prevent search for others that might lead to a betrayal of the secrets of the pagoda."

"True," said Zanara. "Then what's your will?"

"See that all entrances from above are secured so that none may discover these vaults and their contents, and then let's get on board."

"And the prisoner?"

"We take him with us, and by surrendering him up as the assassin at the proper time, purchase favour for ourselves and ward off all suspicion as to our true character."

"But the inmates of the pagoda," said Zanara doubtfully.

"Have no fear of them; those in our secrets will keep them; those who know them not will be silent lest their tongues bring danger on their own heads."

"You know best, captain," said Zanara.

"Take some of the men with you, and see that all is made secure at once."

Zanara ordered some of the pirates to follow him, and the captain approached the spot where Bill lay, bound hand and foot.

"You will repent this outrage," said Bill, addressing the pirate captain.

"Indeed," replied the other with a smile.

"I don't pay twelve thousand pounds to Fum-Fum to secure my safety, and that of another, and then let one of his myrmidons treat me thus without knowing the reason why."

"You gave the governor twelve-thousand?" said Chow-Woo in surprise.

"Yes, and I have been robbed and cajoled; and if you are not a bare-faced villain, you will release me and bring back the girl you sent off in that boat."

"Are you then Bill Boaster?"

"I am," said Bill.

"And that was the girl you abducted?"

"Yes," replied Bill, thinking that perhaps the pirate had mistaken him for Ned, and so made him prisoner.

"Then you do not well to call another a villain," said Chow-Woo, turning on his heel, and passing into the vault.

"Curse you, you pirate dog!" hissed Bill, "but I'll be even with you yet."

After awhile the captain returned, and with him the pirates.

"Is all secure?" he asked.

"All," replied Zanara; "even the steps to the vaults are concealed, and none will discover them but by the aid of a traitor."

"Which I fear not," said Chow-Woo. "Are our men all here?"

Zanara looked round.

"All," he said.

"Then lift the prisoner into the boat."

"What are you going to do with me?" asked Bill, as the men bent over him.

"Take you on board," was the reply.

"On board what?"

"You'll know when you get there," said one.

"I will not go! I defy you to kidnap me! I am a British subject, and you shall rue this work."

"Silence, or I will have you gagged," said the captain.

"You dare not, you Chinese dog!" cried Bill fiercely.

One of the men thrust the barrel of his pistol into Bill's mouth.

"Hold your noise," he hissed, "or I'll blow your brains out."

Bill's face that had grown red with passion. now became pale as death.

He saw the fellow meant what he threatened, and his heart sank within him.

The pistol prevented him from giving utterance to any more threats just then, but even had it been removed he would have remained silent.

They lifted him by the arms and legs and lowered him to the men in the boat.

These took him and placed him in the bottom of the vessel.

The captain then sprang from the platform, and his men followed him.

"Barbarian," said Chow-Woo. "If you are tired of your life you will speak; if not, you will be silent. I never threaten but I perform, remember that."

Bill made no reply.

Zanara bent forward and whispered to the captain, while he pointed to the lanterns hanging over the platform.

"They will go out ere daylight." said Chow-Woo, and the gate will open at the signal."

Zanara sat down.

"Cast off," he said.

The rope was cast off, and the boat drifted from the side.

The men dropped their oars into the water.

"Give way," was the order.

The boat shot along till it reached the bend, and then turned into darkness.

From this moment the men counted their strokes, so as to know when again to turn the boat.

Bill felt a cold perspiration break out over his face and body.

"Where were they—where were they going?"

Then came the fear that they intended to fling him overboard, and his heart almost stood still.

Then he heard a shrill whistle.

Was that the signal for his doom.

He tried to rise.

But a foot pressed him down and a voice said—

"Beware! a move—a word and you die!"

Then there was a noise as of chains rattling above his head.

"Steady, ship oars," came the order.

And then the boat glided out of the dense darkness, and Bill saw the light of the stars in the black sky above.

Again he breathed more freely.

Again the oars were put out, and the men bent to their work.

But there was scarce a sound as they fell into the water.

Silently but swiftly the boat glided along, and as his eyes got accustomed to the darkness, Bill saw looming up out of the water the huge dark hull of a vessel.

Nearer and nearer to this approached the boat.

At last it rounded the bows of the phantom-like ship, and was rowed alongside.

"Boat ahoy!"

"Ay, ay ; make fast there."

Down dropped a rope-ladder into the boat, and while some held fast to the ropes, others grasped the ladder and held it taut.

Chow-Woo sprang on to the strands, and hastily mounted to the deck.

"Stand by to haul up," he said addressing those at the side, "a prisoner coming aboard."

"Bound ?" asked one.

"Yes."

The men each grasped a rope that hung over the side.

Zanara ordered the men to sling Bill, and they secured a rope under his arms, and another round his waist.

"On deck there," he said when this operation was completed.

"Ay, ay," came from above.

"Haul up."

The men on deck began to haul at the ropes, and Bill was drawn from the boat and hung in the air.

He would have been dashed against the side of the junk but Zanara caught hold of his feet, and mounted the ladder, holding him off as he rose.

In a few moments he was seized by those above, and lowered to the deck.

"Clap him in irons," said Chow-Woo; "he will be safer there than anywhere else."

They lifted Bill on to his feet.

"Wretches," he cried, "how dare you? I am wounded and bleeding. My head is cut and the blood is trickling from it, and I am wounded in the leg. Do you want to kill me ?"

A lantern was unmasked and the captain gazed at him by its light.

The wound in Bill's head was again open and bleeding, and the pirate gave orders to take off his bonds and convey him to the sick bay.

Closely guarded, Bill was taken to that part of the vessel devoted to invalids.

By the light of the lantern that swung in the centre he looked around the place and a cry broke from his lips.

Scarce had he uttered it when a man sprang from his bunk, and stood before him with clenched hands and blazing eyes.

It was the pirate Tom Stockton!

CHAPTER XXXIII.

IN WHICH SALLY GETS OUT OF SORTS, AND CHING-FOW IS FLUNG OUT OF THE DOORWAY.

WITH anything but pleasant feelings, Ned and his friends pursued their way to their lodgings, where, wearied and dispirited, they were not long in seeking their couches.

Excitement had thus far kept them up, but now this was over they began to experience the full force of their toils and sufferings.

Gladly would Sally and Tilda have had their curiosity gratified about all that had happened, but they had to wait awhile for that, and so both retired in anything but a good humour.

The following day neither Jumbo nor Ned could leave their couches.

Both were too ill and sore, and Harry's head ached as if it would split.

Poor Ned was the worst of the lot.

His throat was sore from the terrible pressure to which it had been put, and he could articulate with difficulty.

Jumbo's neck was too stiff to allow him to turn his head, and Harry's temples throbbed fearfully.

Tilda still felt the effects of the pillory, but not to an extent to compel her to keep her bed, and she and Sally did all they could for the sufferers.

Jack, Charley, and 'Dolf only enjoyed their usual health, and felt little or no effects from the struggle of the night before.

But they were greatly concerned about Ned, who in his sleep had kept murmuring the name of Minnie, and callling upon Boaster to release her.

They also felt ill at ease lest they might be called to account for the work of the previous night.

"If the others were able," said Jack addressing 'Dolf and Charley, "I should persuade them to shift our quarters, for I expect there'll be a regular flare up about the governor's death."

"But Ned is too ill to be moved," said 'Dolf.

"I know he is, so we must take our chance, and trust to Providence. What is to be, will be."

"Lor'," said Charley, "as if any fool didn't know that."

"Did you?" asked Jack.

"Rather."

"Then you know you are a fool," said Jack quietly.

"If you was Jumbo, I'd——"

"What?"

"Punch your head," said Charley.

"But I ain't Jumbo," said Jack.

"And so I don't punch," replied Charley.

"We had enough punching last night," said 'Dolf.

"It's been nothing else since we left England," said Jack. "It riles me, it does, to see one man defeat the lot of us time after time. Here are six of us, and ever since that fellow Phinicky Phopps got his quietus, I'm blest if Bill Boaster hasn't got the best of us, single handed at every turn."

"He seems to have the devil's luck and his own too," said 'Dolf.

"But I think its turned, now," said Charley. "Leastways, if what Harry told us is right."

"That fellow's half demon, half snake," said Jack, "and he'll find a way to wriggle out of any mess he gets into."

"The Devil always helps his own," said 'Dolf.

"I should like to help him," said Charley, "to a berth in the next world."

"And that poor girl," said Jack. "My heart bleeds for her. So young, so beautiful, and so pure."

"What's that?"

Jack looked round.

"What's that you've got to say about some girl being young and beautiful?" said Sally. "You didn't think I was so near you, did you?"

"My dear——" began Jack.

"Don't you dear me, sir. I ain't your dear. How dare you talk about another woman being young and beautiful, in hearing of your own wife? Tell me that if you dare?"

"Why, Sally, what's the matter with you?"

"Don't talk to me, sir," cried Sally. "No wonder you didn't want me to go with you last night. Oh, dear no I am not young and beautiful. Of course, I'm old and ugly, I am."

"Dat's trufe, as Jumbo says," remarked Tilda, who had come into the room.

"Bravo Tilda! Many a true word spoke in a jest, you know," cried Charley, laughing.

Sally's face grew purple.

"You audacious, imperdent minx!" cried Sally, turning on Tilda. "How dare you——"

"My dear, my dear," said Jack, "what on earth has bit you that you fly into this passion for nothing?"

"Perhaps it am a flea," said Tilda. "Dey's bery annoying, dey is, sometimes."

"And so are you, you ugly black cat!" cried Sally. "I'd have you to know——"

And choking with rage, Sally made a dash and a grab at the surprised negress.

Jack sprang forward and placed his hand on his wife's arm.

"I must have you to know, Sally," he exclaimed angrily, "that such goings on as this is not only ridiculous but annoying to me, and must prove painful to our sick friends. I'm ashamed of you?"

"Oh, of course, of course, you are," cried Sally. "I'm not young and beautiful; you've found that out, have you?"

"Sally, what do you mean?" asked Jack. "Are you going mad?"

"No wonder if I do, when the man who swore to love and obey me turns against me for a young and beautiful rat-eating Chinese gal."

"I like the 'obey,'" said Charley. "I'd never say as others say, 'Love, honour, and obey.' No, no; not I."

"Guess dat's what yer said yerself,

Mrs. Jones," said Tilda. " Yer's got mixed up a bit, ain't yer, an' is a-going ober de burial serbice ob yer husband ?"

"Sally," said Jack, "you ought to have more sense."

"I ought to have had, I know I ought than to marry a man who tells me to my face that he loves a young and beautiful girl, and don't care for me because I'm old and ugly."

"Oh woman's imagination," said Jack, "what a strange thing it is."

"And this is my reward," said Sally, "for sitting here hour after hour a-worrying about you last night, and a-thinking as how if you was killed, I'd break my heart, and go and drown myself for grief."

"Walker," said Charley.

"And now to be told that——"

"Wait, wait a bit," said Jack. "Your imagination is running away with you, ain't it ?"

"That's more than I'd do," said Charley. "And if I did I know I'd drop her like a hot potato afore long."

Sally burst into tears.

Jack wasn't proof against this weapon.

His anger vanished in a moment, and he took his wife's hand in his own.

"What a silly little woman you are," he said.

"Fourteen stone," said Charley. "I like the little !"

"Be quiet," said 'Dolf.

"Why, Sally, what ails you," said Jack, "that you talk in such a silly manner because I said what I'm sure you yourself would say, that poor Minnie is young, beautiful, and pure ?"

"Was it Minnie you meant ? " cried Sally, looking at him through her tears.

"Of course it was."

"I thought it was some other—some nasty Chinese girl you was talking of."

"What nonsense, Sally. What care I for any other than yourself, do you think ? "

"Not much," said Charley. "One of her sort's enough to last a fellow his lifetime."

Jack scowled at him.

"Oh, if it was only Minnie. You are sure, now, you ain't deceiving me, your own dear faithful wife ? " asked Sally. "You know what sort of a woman I am, Jack."

"Of course, Sally, and I wonder, that you could for a moment doubt me."

And Jack drew her head down on his bosom.

Sally gave vent to a copious flood of tears.

"As plentiful as a water-cart you true lovers all," sang Charley.

Sally, who had passed hours of anxiety on the previous night, was low-spirited and nervous, but Charley's taunts roused her.

She sprang away from Jack, and making a dart at Charley, caught that interesting youth by the hair.

"You tormenting wagerbone," she cried, "don't you jeer me, or I'll show you the sort of woman I am !"

"Here, Jack, your wife's gone mad," said Charley. "Just use your authority and make her let go my hair, will you ? "

"I'll learn you, I will," cried Sally.

And she gave his hair a tug that brought Charley to his knees.

"Let go !" cried Charley. "I don't want to lose my wool, and be turned into a nigger. Go and pull Jack's."

"I'll twist your head off if you insult me," said Sally.

"Who's a-insulting of you ? " said Charley.

"Didn't you call me a water-cart ? " cried Sally. "What do you say I am, eh ? "

And she gave his hair another pull.

"A tug, that's what you are. Here stow it, will you ? "

Jack drew her back.

"Don't be so foolish, Sally," he said, "and as for you, Charley, you'd better shut up, or I shall take you in hand."

"You ain't big enough," said Charley, rising, "and I don't care to take advantage of your size."

"It I was Jack I'd smash you," said Sally.

"But then you ain't Jack, you see," said Charley. "Oh, woman, woman, thy name is Sally Jones."

"Yes," cried Sally, "and I'd like to see the man who said it wasn't. I'd soon show him what sort of a woman I am."

"Jack would swear to it," said Charley.

"Swear to what, you jackanapes ? " cried Sally.

"That your name was Jones, of course. I reckon he's found that out before now."

"There, there, don't take any notice of him," said Jack; "he will have his say."

"And so will I," said Sally.

"Dat's trufe," said Tilda.

"I won't be talked to by any man, I won't," cried Sally. "I never was and I never will be, not me!"

"Oh, Jack, I never thought you made love to such an angel in dumb show," said Charley. "Well, perhaps it ain't very surprising, seeing that Sally can do enough jawing for twenty, let alone two."

"Jack, I shall kill him, I know I shall."

"Better take no notice of him," returned Jack; "it's not worth while."

"Notice of him!" said Sally. "He's beneath my notice, he is."

"Guess he wasn't when yer'd got ole ob dat ar hair of his'n," said Tilda.

"Perhaps you'll mind your own business," said Sally.

"Ob course, ma'am," said Tilda, freezeingly. "I forgot as how I war speaking to my 'feriors."

"Your inferiors, indeed," cried Sally, with a toss of the head. "I'd have you to know that I'm not a nigger, but a free-born English woman."

"Guess I don't care what yer am," said Tilda; "but if yer is English I don't fink much ob yer."

And Tilda left the room.

"Come, Sally," said Jack, "all this is very foolish, and if ever there was a time when each should strive to cheer the other surely it is now, when illness and danger assail us. We know not what last night's work may bring about, and instead of quarrelling among ourselves, we ought rather to seek to make things as comfortable as possible."

"Well, ain't I doing it?" said Sally. "I'm sure there's not a woman in the world that's more kind than I am."

"You have got a rum way of showing it," said Charley. "I like your kindness

when you scalp a fellow. Learnt that dodge afore you met Jack in the woods, didn't yer?"

"Hold your tongue, will you?" said Jack.

"Can't," said Charley, "had some fat bacon for breakfast, and it's slippery."

"There, go and see if you can't be of some use in Ned's room," said Jack. "Poor fellow, he is very ill, and must have suffered terribly yesterday."

"I'd like to have the willains what tried to choke him," said Sally. "If I didn't show 'em what sort of a woman I am, my name ain't Sally Jones."

And Sally started off to attend upon Ned.

Jack was about to upbraid Charley for vexing his wife, when he was stopped by the entrance of Ching-Fow the younger.

"Why don't you learn to knock before you come in, you ill-mannered chopstick?" said 'Dolf.

"No time for knockee," said the Celestial. "Not muchee time to tellee what I come to sayee."

"What have you got to say?" asked Jack.

"Got muchee," said Ching-Fow, his little eyes gleaming fiercely. "Somebody killee Chinee governee, and people say it was English manees what killee the manderinee."

"It's a lie!" roared Jack. "Get out of this."

"No kickee," cried the Celestial. "Givee muchee monee and Ching-Fow sabee; if no gibee monee sabee, and Chinee manee catchee English menee, and English manee all be hangee."

Jack sprang upon the young Chinaman, and grasping him by the shoulder and the hip raised him from the floor, and flung him out of the door way.

The Celestial picked himself up, and shaking his fists at Jack, cried fiercely—

"I'll hangee English manee—I swear I'll hangee! You hitee Chinee manee, and Chinee manee killee—hangee!"

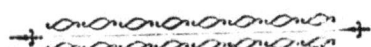

CHAPTER XXXIV.

IN WHICH CHING-FOW'S KNOWLEDGE PROVES DANGEROUS TO HIMSELF.

ANNOYED at the Celestial's threats, Jack made a dash after him, but paused suddenly and became thoughtful.

It might be no idle threat that Ching-Fow made.

The governor had been slain and the pagoda overrun by Englishmen, and if they were accused of being the men who had done so much execution in protecting Ned, it was certain that they would be made to suffer, even though they had simply defended one who had been unjustly illused.

Jack knew that Chinese justice was undeserving of the name.

That the Celestials hated foreigners with an ineradicable hatred, and that even the smallest offence would only be too sure to be magnified into a fearful crime.

Suspicion alone in their case would be magnified into certainty, and that hatred of the barbarians or foreign devils would ensure punishment even without guilt.

Knowing and feeling this Jack felt far from comfortable as to his own or his friend's safety.

They had had reason to suspect Ching-Fow the younger of a bad feeling towards them before, and this feeling Jack could not help experiencing he had increased by flinging the Celestial out of the room.

He remembered also the fellow's suspicious presence and behaviour on the occasion when discovered by them in their apartments, and Jumbo's belief that another than Ching-Fow himself had been present.

Jack felt sorry that he had allowed his indignation and annoyance to get the better of him, and wished that he had treated the fellow's words as uttered in jest and laughed at the idea of their having been in or near the pagoda.

But his anger had gone far to confirm the fact that they were really those who had played havoc with the inmates of the temple.

"Confound the fellow," said Jack, "I am afraid he'll make things unpleasant for us."

"I don't like the beggar," said Charley.

"And I've had a suspicion of him all along," said 'Dolf.

"What was he sneaking about our rooms for, pretending to look for Ned?" said Charley.

"There's no doubt that Sally made an enemy of him at first," said Jack, "when she laid into him with the bamboo for trying to make love to her."

"If he'd known her as well as you do, old man, he wouldn't have done it, I reckon," said Charley.

"I tell you what," said Jack, "I'm precious sorry Ned's an invalid just now."

"Why now?" asked Charley.

"Because if he was allright I should advise him that we stepped it from this place."

"Why?"

"Because I expect that we shall get arrested for that affair last night."

"I don't see that," said Charley. "Who's to know that it was really we who were at the pagoda? I reckon we didn't give the chopsticks much chance to recognise us, for we were down on 'em like a load of bricks, and they hooked it before they could tell what we were like."

"They could see we were foreigners, though," said Jack.

"Well, suppose they could, there's more here than ourselves, and we were all dressed like sailors, you know."

"That's true; but this fellow I believe has been spying and listening, and will be able to convict us out of our own mouths. How do we know what he has seen and heard?"

"That's true," said 'Dolf; "you may depend upon it he knows more than we think."

"And will use his knowledge to our harm I fear, since we, or rather I, refused to give him money."

"For his silence?" said Charley.

"Exactly."

"I don't like the idea of buying a fellow's silence; it looks cowardly," said 'Dolf.

"So it does," said Jack, "and yet the illness of Harry, Ned, and Jumbo prevent us doing what we might—either be off before an attempt is made to secure us, or serving those who attempt to molest us as we did the myrmidons of the governor."

"It will never do for us to fall into the hands of the Chinese authorities," said 'Dolf; "that would not only mean destruction to ourselves, but to the poor girl whom we have struggled so long and so hard to obtain the release of."

"So it would," said Jack. "What do you propose, 'Dolf, for the best?"

"I hardly know what to propose," said 'Dolf.

"Twist the neck of Ching-Fow, say I," put in Charley.

"Or give him something to keep him silent," said 'Dolf.

"Yes, one on the nob," said Charley.

"It would serve the skunk right," said Jack; "but that won't do, and hang me if I like to buy a fellow's silence and my own safety with money."

"Nor I," said 'Dolf; "but more than our lives perhaps depend on keeping that wretch's tongue quiet."

"Yes, and that I suppose must decide us. I'll summon the beast and see what he has got to say."

Jack struck the gong.

A servant entered.

"Look here, yellow-skin," said Jack; "where's that pig-eyed rascal, young Ching-Fow?"

"He washee him facee, 'cos him nosee bleedee."

"Washing his face because his nose is bleeding, is he?"

"Yessee, massee."

"Then when he's done washing his face tell him I want him."

"S'pose he no comee," said the Celestial. "He no likee kickee—no likee punchee; makee bleedee."

"If he won't come we'll jolly soon fetch him," said Charley. "Just you tell him that he had better come, or I'll drag him here by his pigtail."

"No, no," said Jack, "don't tell him that. Say that if he comes and behaves himself we will give him what he asked, and something over for plaister for his nose."

And Jack took a dollar from his pocket and placed it in the man's hand.

"There," he said, "you may keep that for yourself."

"Muchee tankee," cried the man; "me tellee and he comee sharpee, 'cos he likee monee; it make him heart gladee."

And the fellow went dancing off in search of his young master.

"You don't think he'll come, do you?" asked Charley.

"That will depend upon which is the strongest, his love of gold or his desire for revenge," said Jack, "and I ain't no judge of character if the fellow wouldn't sell his soul for gold."

"I wouldn't trust him too far," said Charley.

"I don't mean to," replied Jack.

They waited some time, and then the servant returned.

"Ching-Fow no comee, 'less English manee say he no killee, no kickee, no chuckee," said the fellow.

"Tell him we promise not to harm him if he comes at once; but that if he does not come we will fetch him, and if we do we won't leave a whole bone in his body."

"Me no tell him that 'less me get 'noder dollar," said the fellow, holding out his hand.

"What?" cried Jack.

"Me telle Ching-Fow beatee. No get beatee 'less get payee. Ching-Fow no payee, then English manee payee poor Chinee manee."

"Pay him over the head, Jack," said Charley.

"You greedy cur," said Jack, "if you ain't off and tell Ching-Fow what I say, I'll double you up and put you in your own pocket in two twos."

He made a pretence to seize hold of him, but the fellow turned and hurried off.

They waited some five minutes, when Ching-Fow appeared with his blouse held to his nose, and looking as if doubtful whether to advance or retreat.

"Come in," said Jack.

"English manee no hurtee," whined the Celestial.

"I will not—I give you my promise."

Ching-Fow slowly entered, but kept close to the doorway, ready to run if need be.

"Look you," said Jack. "When you threaten an Englishman you must expect to get your head broken. You have no one but yourself to blame for what you got. What do you mean about a governor being killed and we being made to suffer for his death unless we give you money, eh?"

"English manee killee mandarinee, and English manee get killee if he no payee."

"How do you know that he was killed by Englishmen?" asked Jack.

"Me know muchee."

"What do you know?" cried Jack.

The Celestial made a step backwards and ran up against Charley, who, to prevent the fellow's retreat, had worked his way between him and the door.

"No, you don't," said Charley, pushing him further into the room. "We are so fond of your company that we can't spare it just yet."

"You no hurtee?" cried Ching-Fow.

"That will depend upon yourself," said Charley, "so just mind what you are after."

And Charley drew his revolver and tapped it significantly.

Ching-Fow began to tremble.

The fellow was an arrant coward.

"Come now," cried Jack, "what do you know?"

"Yes, what do you know?" echoed Charley placing his revolver to the Chinaman's ear.

Ching-Fow gave a terrified leap, and then fell on his knees.

"Mercee—no killee—no shootee!" he whined.

"Then speak up plainly and truthfully," said Jack. "What do you mean by demanding money for your silence? Silence about what? Out with it."

"And no lies," said Charley, "or down goes your house. The truth, the whole truth and nothing but the truth, or you're a gone Chinaman."

"I know mandarin be killee, I know soldiers be killee, and I know who killee."

"Who killed him?" asked Jack.

"English manees."

"How do you know?"

There was no reply.

"Was you there to see?" asked Jack.

"No, no."

"Then speak up. Why do you accuse us?"

"Me know. English manee go to pago-da, fightee with soldiers, killee Chinee manee."

"But you say you know that we are the Englishmen. How do you know that?"

"Because me hear English manees talkee 'bout killee—talkee talkee while in bedee."

"You infernal villain!" cried Jack, seizing him by the throat, "you have been listening—hiding and listening. Speak, you despicable cur, is it not so?"

"Chinee manee hear all English manee sayee, and Chinee manee know English manee got muchee monee, and he want payee so he no tellee and English manee get killee."

"You are a despicable cur," said Jack, "to stoop to listen to other men's conversation; but you have overreached yourself. We have no money, or, at least, very little."

The Celestial shook his head.

"Chinee manee know English manee got muchee monee."

"It is false."

"No falsee—all true. Chinee manee see muchee monee—lots of monee."

"Where?" asked 'Dolf, quickly.

"In big boxee, all shinee."

"You infernal rascal!" said Jack. "You have been overhauling our property in our absence."

"No stealee," cried the Celestial, recoiling from the pistol that Charley again pressed to his ear, "no stealee. Chinee manee swearee no stealee."

Charley, Jack and 'Dolf exchanged glances.

"English manee got monee," said Ching-Fow. "Chinee manee no want killee English manee, so let English manee pay Chinee manee and Chinee manee no tellee."

"And what if we refuse, you infernal dog?" cried Jack.

"Then Chinee manee hab all English manees monee, and English manees all be killee with long ropee, so better pay, and be sabee."

"How do we know that if we pay you to be quiet we can get away safely?" asked 'Dolf.

"Me no telle."

"But perhaps you have already told what you know, and then we should be paying for nothing," said Jack.

"'REMEMBER YOUR TREACHERY. DIE, TRAITOR, DIE!' CRIED TOM STOCKTON."

"Hear Chinee manee swear he no telle nobodee what he knowee."

And Ching-Fow held his right hand aloft.

"You swear you have not yet told any one your suspicions that it was us who were engaged in the fight at the pagoda?"

"Me swear me no telle."

"And you never will?" said Jack.

"Not if gibee monee—muchee monee."

"And if we won't?"

"Then tellee, and English manee be killee," said Ching-Fow, believing that he had things all his own way now.

Jack seized him by the throat and shook him as a dog does a rat.

"You dirty, despicable cur," he cried, "not only shall you never have a penny, but I'll ensure your silence. I'd blow your brains out but you are not worth the bullet. Gag him, Charley, and you, 'Dolf, throw out everything from my big chest. This fellow is too contemptible to pay and too despicable to kill; but his silence must be ensured till we are beyond the reach of his malice or his greed."

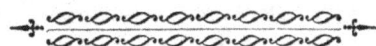

CHAPTER XXXV.

IN WHICH ONE RASCAL GETS BOXED UP AND ANOTHER TAKEN DOWN.

In vain Ching-Fow struggled and tried to cry out.

Jack's fingers pressed his windpipe so tightly that the small eyes of the Celestial fairly started from his head.

Twisting his silk handkerchief, Charley thrust it into the open mouth of Ching-Fow, and then tearing off his neckcloth, bound it tightly over the fellow's lips.

'Dolf flung the articles from a large box which Jack had purchased for his clothing on to the floor in a heap.

The chest was an extra large one, being quite four feet in length by two and a half in height, and as soon as it was emptied Jack dragged the terrified and half-strangled Celestial to it.

"Now, you dirty cur," he said, "this shall be your resting-place till we can get away. You know too much, and our safety necessitates that you be rendered powerless to do us that harm your heart would prompt you to do."

So saying, Jack lifted him off his feet and sat him down in the box.

It was too short for Ching-Fow to lie at full length, and too low for him to sit upright, and for a moment Jack looked puzzled.

"Lay him on his back," said Charley, "and draw his legs up, then the lid will shut down close."

Jack forced the Celestial's legs up and his head down.

Ching-Fow still struggled.

"Keep quiet," hissed Jack, "or I'll make this chest your coffin. If he moves again, Charley, put your pistol to his head, and give him his final sleeping dose."

Charley levelled his pistol at the pleading eyes of the now horrified Celestial.

Ching-Fow struggled no longer.

But the look he gave must have excited their pity but for the danger they felt they would run by suffering him to go free.

Charley kept the Chinaman motionless with his pistol, while Jack shut down the lid and locked the chest.

"Poor devil," he said, rising, "there's no help for it. We dare not remove the gag, or his cries would bring some one to his aid before we can get away from here."

Bang, bang, bang, from the box, but the sound was very slight, and would not reach beyond the apartment.

"That must be with his hands," said Jack, for he cannot move his legs to kick in the position they are."

Bang, bang! louder than before.

"That must be stopped," said Jack. "I don't like to torture a fellow, let him be as bad as he may, but it must be done. Find something, Charley, to tie his arms to his sides."

"This will do," said Charley, holding up a piece of grass rope that had been used to secure one of their boxes.

Jack opened the chest.

The eyes of Ching-Fow flashed for a

moment with hope, but when they rested on the rope their expression changed to a look of despair.

Jack soon had his arms secured to his sides, so that he was powerless to move them.

"Now, Ching-Fow, listen to me," he said, "for though you can't speak, you can hear! you have learned much, and suspect more, and are therefore dangerous to us. But whether this chest will become your coffin or only a temporary residence will depend upon how far you have used your knowledge or suspicions to injure us. Rest as you are; we have no desire to kill you, but our own safety is paramount, and in our safety lies your own.

Saying this, Jack again closed and locked the chest.

"Will he be able to breathe?" asked 'Dolf in a whisper.

"I'll make sure of that," said Jack.

And taking his knife, he cut with some difficulty a hole in the side of the chest.

Then he rose to his feet.

"Bring those things, and come with me," he said.

Charley and 'Dolf gathered up the articles that had been flung out of the chest and followed Jack into the apartment where Ned, Harry and Jumbo lay.

Ned was sitting up in bed, and Sally was holding a cup of water to his lips.

"How do you feel, Ned?" asked Jack.

"Awfully queer," replied Ned. "My joints seem all out of their sockets, and my throat is so swollen I can scarcely swallow."

"Au' mine ditter," said Jumbo. "Dis yer winepipe ob mine am dat ar sore dat my bret scratches it like a currycomb does a sore on a horse's leg."

"I'm sorry for you, Ned," said Jack.

"I don't care much for myself," said Ned. "I wouldn't care what I suffered if Minnie was only safe—if I could only manage to get on board that pirate, that Harry says lays just off the pagoda, and where they have taken her. Oh! it is cruel hard to be cooped up here and she so near. Can't anything be done Jack?"

"'Dolf, keep your eyes on the next room," said Jack. "Don't let us be surprised and overheard."

The footman took up a position so as to command the outer apartment and its entrance.

"Ned," said Jack, "you know nothing that could be done would be left undone by us, who, thank Heaven, preserve our health and strength. At present we can do but one thing, and even how that is to be done is a puzzle to me.

"What's that, Jack?" asked Ned.

"Get away from this place at once."

What do you mean?"

"That we are in fearful danger here."

Jack told Ned how Ching-Fow had learned that it was they who had been engaged in the fight in the pagoda, and had resolved to hand them over to the authorities unless his silence was purchased, and what they had done to ensure that silence till they could get out of reach of the law.

"Better, perhaps buy his silence," said Ned after-awhile.

"Yes," said Jack, "if we could only be sure that he alone is acquainted with the fact that we were at the pagoda, or that he would keep silence after being paid. But I believe that he was in league with whoever sent that letter to lure you to the pagoda; in fact, that he is hand and glove with the pirates, and only seeks to get the gold which he well knows the authorities would secure."

"It may indeed be so," said Ned.

"There have been many suspicious circumstances, Ned," said Jack; "his pryings and his threats, his knowledge of our means, and remarks he has made on previous occasions, all point to the fact that we are sitting on a mine that may explode at any moment."

Harry had been listening, and he now said—

"Ned, ill or well, we must get out of this somehow, and at once. Even if there were no proof of it being us who were in the pagoda, yet the knowledge that we have a good deal of wealth may induce the wretches who inhabit this place to swear that it was indeed us, and so fix the governor's death upon us in order to get our valuables, for you may rest assured that young Ching-Fow has at least made his father acquainted with what he has discovered."

"An' dat oder feller dat was in dis yer room wid him, what he swored was neber here at all, though I knowed dese yer eyes ob mine seed him," said Jumbo,

"That was evidently a mistake of yours, Jumbo," said Jack.

"Yer may say what yer like 'bout dat," said Jumbo, "but I guess I sees what I sees."

"What was him like, den?" said Tilda.

"He was 'bout as tall as dis yer chile, but he wasn't so good-looking, mind yer."

"Ob course not; guess as how dar's nobody what's dat but me own self," said Tilda.

"Dat's trufe; an' he wasn't quite so big as dis inderwideral."

"He would be tall for a Chinaman if he was as tall as you," said Jack.

"Guess he was all dat, an' he had splendifferous close, an' he was browner nor most ob 'em. A'cos I seed his face I did."

"Gammon," said Charley.

"No, 'tain't gammon neider, an' he wore a hat what wasn't a hat, wid a fevver like a shabing brush all black a-sticking out ob de top ob it, an' he had a cemetary at his side, and silber mounted 'voivers in a green sash roun' his waist. Now say I didn't see him; guess if I didn't I'se a liar."

"Dat's trufe," said Tilda.

"What's trufe—dat it's a lie?"

"Get out, didn't I say I guess de lie was a trufe?"

"Den dere's where yer iggerant," said Jumbo. "It's de trufe what's de lie, dat's what it am."

There was a strange expression on Harry's face as he leaned forward and said—

"Bronzed face; about Jumbo's height, splendid attire, and black brush in his cap."

"Dat's de werry dogerantyke ob de inderwideral what wanished like a flash ob funder frue de floor or up de chimney when I looked at him, de wery instant dat he seed me."

"And no wonder," cried Charley; "he must have thought you was the devil."

"I reckon dat's trufe," said Jumbo.

"By Heavens, the very portrait!" cried Harry.

"Of whom?" asked Ned and Jack in a breath.

"The pirate captain whom I saw in the vault; whom we saw when hidden behind the idol in the pagoda."

"The same," cried the others in a breath.

"But," said Ned suddenly, "we forget that Jumbo also saw him bending over the body of the mandarin, and trying to console the Chinese ladies."

"Yes, and he has given this portrait to the man he fancied he saw in company with Ching-Fow in this apartment," said Jack.

"It must be so."

"Jus' yer 'ole on dar, will yer?" said Jumbo; "guess dars a lot more trufe in dis yer chile's obserwations dan dar am in yers. I reckons I sees what I does see, an' I don't see what I don't see, does I?"

And Jumbo looked round for an answer.

None came, as there could be no dispute as to the fact.

"Now, as consent gibes silence, I perceeds," said Jumbo. "De obserbant obserbations ob dis extinguished inderwideral can't be did in de dark, an' if ye'll all just scratch dem heads ob yourn ter let de sense get frue de pores ob de skin, ye'll know as how dis chile didn't see not nuffin ob de sight in der pargodar what yer did, acos he was down at de bottom ob de steps in dat ar hole ahind de idol."

"That's true," said 'Dolf; "Jumbo could not see what transpired in that room while the pirate was present."

"He certainly could not," said Jack.

"Den yer see dat mysterious mystery am solbed," said Jumbo.

"It's as plain as pitch," said Charley.

"Ob course it am," said Jumbo.

"If Jumbo really did see that man here," said Jack, "it's plain that he and young Ching-Fow are in league together, and it is more than probable that he had a hand in prevailing upon Ned to go to the pagoda, and there could have been but one object, getting us all out of the way so as to rob us of our valuables, the existence of which must have been learned; whether they were also in league with Boaster it is difficult to say. But one thing is certain, that we are in danger here, and if we would save ourselves, and eventually rescue Minnie, we must get out of this before it is too late."

"It is too late now!" cried a loud voice in the doorway of the apartment.

'Dolf sprang round, for his attention

had been drawn off the outer apartment by the conversation transpiring in the inner room, and the others started in surprise and gazed at the intruder.

In the doorway stood a tall Celestial, his yellow cheeks bronzed almost to the hue of a Spaniard, his figure poised in a graceful attitude, and with his hand clasped over the jewelled hilt of a curved sword.

Surprise for the moment held all dumb.

"It is too late now to escape," cried the man again, "and in the name of the emperor, whose slave I am, I summon you to surrender on the charge of killing and slaying Fum-Fum, governor and mandarin, and several of his guards, in the Purple Pagoda."

"Who are you that dare charge us with this?" cried Ned.

"The servant of my sovereign," was the reply. "Resistance is useless, escape impossible, for I have many without who, at a word, will come to my side, unless——"

"What?" asked Ned.

"Life is dear, and youth will sacrifice much to keep it," was the reply, "You have gold and jewels in plenty, but blood is more precious than gold, and life more beautiful than riches. In a word assassins, murderers, though you be, you have the chance of purchasing existence by surrendering your wealth. But there must be no delay. I give you your choice while I have the power. Which shall it be, your gold or death? Quick, decide! one stamp of my foot and all chance is gone—one moment's hesitation and you are lost!"

"'Tis you who are lost, pirate!" cried Jack, springing forward and grasping the man in his powerful arms. "Villain, you are no servant of the emperor, but Chow-Woo, the accomplice of Fum-Fum, and captain of the pirate junk!"

CHAPTER XXXVI.

IN WHICH BILL BOASTER ESCAPES FROM THE PIRATE JUNK, AND TOM STOCKTON BIDS FAREWELL TO LIFE.

FOR a moment or two Bill Boaster stood confronting the bearded ruffian unable to utter a word or move a limb, so great was the shock he had experienced in the sudden and unexpected appearance of Tom Stockton.

With eyes blazing with fury, and with lips quivering with rage, Tom glared upon Bill through the semi-darkness, the while grinding his teeth, and working his fingers spasmodically.

"At last—at last!" hissed the pirate.

And then he launched himself upon Bill, and made a grasp at his throat with both hands.

With a cry of horror Bill sprang aside, and Tom, grasping the air, fell heavily upon his face.

With the yell of a wounded tiger, the man bounded to his feet, but in the exertion the wound in his shoulder burst afresh, and he staggered faint and sick across the floor of the sick bay.

"Save me!—keep him off!" cried Bill. "He is mad!"

"Traitor—cur!" yelled Tom, "you shan't escape me! Keep back there, or I'll kill you all!"

This last was addressed to the pirates, who placed themselves between the furious man and the terrified Bill.

The expression on Tom's face was fearful, and the pirates recoiled as he advanced.

"Keep back!" yelled Tom, "keep back! Let me get at the villain! I've sworn to kill him, and I'll have his blood, if I drink it!"

And dashing forward again, Tom, fairly maddened with pain and rage, hurled the pirates aside as if they had been children, shouting, and grinding his teeth, and showing symptoms of madness the while he sought to reach Bill Boaster.

Bill's usual courage seemed to have deserted him.

He retreated, keeping the pirates between himself and Tom, and eagerly looking for an opportunity to reach the steps leading to the deck.

The yells, shouts, and oaths that were uttered brought Zanara into the sick bay to learn the cause of the commotion.

"What means this?" he cried, as he descended the steps.

"The Englishman, Tom, has gone mad," cried one.

"You lie——you lie!" thundered Tom. "Stand aside, or I'll kill you! The first man that tries to prevent me taking my revenge on that traitor cur, dies!"

"Back there yourself," cried Zanara, levelling a pistol at Tom's head. "Back to your bunk, fool, or you will bleed to death!"

"What care I so that I kill him ere I die?" cried Tom. "Back yourself, or it will be the worse for you!"

"Seize him and bind him. The man is mad," said Zanara, and will do himself an injury. He knows not what he says or does."

"It's a lie!" roared Tom. "I know that villain to be the wretch who robbed me and my mates of our share of the booty, and then betrayed us to the American authorities. He is Bill Boaster, whom, instead of slaying, we made our captain, and in return he handed us over to the law. I alone escaped, and sought to kill him, but I was taken, and sent to prison for life, and only escaped by killing my gaoler—escaped that I might hunt him down, the coward, the dog, the traitor! that I might kill him, and avenge myself and messmates in his blood!"

On hearing this the pirates drew back. They no longer felt any desire to shield Boaster from Tom's fury.

But Zanara still confronted Stockton, and held his pistol levelled at the pirate's head.

"Back to your bunk, Tom," he said. "Your revenge will soon come."

"It shall, and now," cried Tom.

"No, no, you must not harm him. The captain has designs which will ensure his fate. I dare not permit you to thwart the intentions of Chow-Woo. So to your bunk, man. You but endanger your own life by acting as you do. To your bunk, I say."

"When I have had that dog's blood, and my revenge. Till then, never!" cried Tom.

And Tom sprang forward, and seizing the barrel of Zanara's pistol, tried to wrest it from his grasp.

But Zanara was a powerful man, and together they struggled over the sick bay.

"Seize the madman!" cried Zanara.

The pirates hurried to their officer's aid, and tried to tear Tom away.

But the fury of the English pirate increased, and he struggled so desperately that he flung the pirates from him one after the other, and turned again upon Zanara.

"Curse you! if you will have it, take it!" cried the lieutenant, and pulled the trigger of the pistol he still managed to retain in his hand.

The ball cut its way along the flesh of Tom's arm, and buried itself in the wall of the sick bay.

Bill Boaster reached the steps, and forgetful of his own wounds, dashed up them.

The pirates tried to intercept him, and Tom Stockton, uttering a mingled yell of pain and fury, dashed them aside and reached the steps.

He made a grasp at Bill's leg, but missed it, and then, with a fearful oath, he dashed up the steps, to the deck, followed by Zanara and the pirates.

Scarcely had he reached the deck, than Bill struck his foot against a coil of rope and fell prostrate.

He gave himself up for lost.

But fear lent him strength.

He bounded to his feet, and dashed onwards in the darkness.

But he had scarcely taken a dozen steps when Tom Stockton was upon him.

Desperate, he turned to struggle with his former foe.

"You don't escape me!" hissed Tom.

And he flung Bill round as if he had been an infant.

"Remember your treachery," hissed Tom. "Ha, ha! but you shan't remember it long. Die accursed dog—traitor, die!"

In his mad fury he lifted Bill from his feet, and bore him to the side of the junk.

"Seize him—strike him down!" cried Zanara.

The pirates dashed towards the two men.

But too late.

Ere they could reach them, Tom flung Bill over the side of the vessel, and dashed his fist into his face.

Bill held on to the brawny ruffian, and as the men sought to grasp Tom, he swung himself over the rail, and with a splash they both went into the water, locked in each other's embrace.

Down, down they went, grasped in a death struggle.

Then up they came to the surface, locked in each other's arms.

Lanterns flashed from the junk's deck, and threw a glare over the water.

Then the light was shut out from their eyes, as once more they sank beneath the surface.

Suddenly Bill felt Tom's hold relax, and mustering all his strength, he dashed his fist into the pirate's face and was free.

Up like a cork he shot.

Again the lights met his half-blinded gaze, and he struck out feebly for the shore.

But every moment he expected to feel the grasp of Tom Stockton on his body.

He could not swim faster, though he tried, for he was weak as an infant.

He felt certain that if Tom should again seize him he must succumb now.

But he need not have feared anything from the pirate.

The fellow was in a worse plight than himself.

His exertions, and the opening of the wound in his shoulder had proved fatal.

He had sunk fainting beneath the surface, and from that faint he would never more awaken.

He had died without consummating his revenge.

And though exhausted, wounded, and almost powerless, his would-be victim was slowly making his way to the shore through the darkness of the night.

As the moments passed Bill began to realise that he had indeed escaped from Tom.

But then came a new fear.

The pirates would launch a boat and search for him.

Then fear for a time gave him fresh strength.

He swam more rapidly.

But his wounds began to tell upon him.

Slower and slower grew his strokes, slower and slower his progress.

He cast a backward look towards the junk.

The lights had disappeared from its deck.

Had they launched a boat?

Were the pirates on his track, and if so would they overtake him, or would he escape them in the darkness?

All these thoughts flashed through his mind with lightning-like rapidity.

But he could answer none.

He could only hope, for too well he knew that recapture would mean a cruel death.

For he had learned enough to know the pirate captain's intentions regarding him.

He shuddered.

If handed over to the Chinese authorities as the murderer of Fum-Fum his fate would indeed be a dreadful one.

And of what avail would be his denial of the crime?

None!

Oh, how he longed for more strength —how he panted to reach the shore!

Once there he would secure his ill-gotten treasure and get away from those parts.

At length he reached the shore.

But he could not land, as the walls were too high.

He must swim some distance ere he could leave the water.

But as he could hear nothing of pursuit, he took heart and bent to his work.

It was fearful work, ill and faint as he was.

But escape meant liberty—life, and he persevered.

At last his perseverance was crowned with success.

He crawled up the beach and tottered on towards the town.

He looked towards the pagoda and saw lights gleaming in its windows, proclaiming to all who gazed that something unusual had transpired there.

But not towards the temple did he wend his way.

He made his way in the direction of the place where he had lived since he had forced Minnie to accompany him to these parts.

But as he walked, or rather staggered onwards, his thoughts went to the poor girl, and he cursed the pirate who had taken her from him, and vowed to possess her again, and kill the man who had robbed him of the girl he had vowed to destroy, and whose destruction was to form, at least one portion of his revenge on Ned Nimble.

But not now dared he think of attempting Minnie's rescue.

Life was even dearer to him than revenge, though to obtain revenge he had so often perilled his life.

He must bide his time.

It might be long, it might be short, but it would come.

"Now I must forget everything but escape," he muttered. "Dead, I am powerless to harm her or Ned. Alive, and I will find means to do both. Could I forego revenge I might not care to die; but revenge is what I have lived for, and I will drink it to the dregs."

On through the darkness, from one narrow street to another, till at last he paused before a house close to where Tom Stockton had observed him, and from whence he had given him chase.

Bill made his way into the square yard, and thrust back a door that opened from it, and passing into a dark passage, closed it behind him.

He groped his way into an apartment, and from a shelf on one side procured the means of obtaining a light.

He lit a small lamp and staggered with it in his hand into an inner apartment furnished as a bed-chamber.

"I must dress these wounds as best I can," he said, "and then disguise myself and get away from here before morning, lest search is made for me."

He washed and bound up the wounds in his head and leg, and then flung himself on the bed to rest.

For some time he tried to sleep, but in vain.

After tossing restlessly from side to side, he arose, went to a recess, and brought out a suit of clothes, and attired himself in them.

Then he took from a small bag hanging in the recess a paper parcel, which he opened and drew forth a quantity of light hair.

"I shall not be recognised with these on," he muttered.

They were large false whiskers and moustache, and a flaxen wig.

These he adjusted to his face and head.

The change was wonderful.

He looked forty years old, and so completely did the whiskers and moustache disguise his features, that none could have recognised Bill Boaster in the fair, middle-aged man that he now appeared to be.

A light-coloured frock coat, vest, and trousers, and brown soft felt hat with a wide brim, rendered the metamorphosis more complete.

Bill selected a couple of small revolvers from a box and a supply of cartridges, together with a long, thin stiletto in a velvet sheath.

These he hid in his breast and coat pockets.

This done he turned up the bed, and took from under it a beautiful, inlaid casket, the same that he had stolen from the tent of Dost Mahomed on his flight from Bokhara.

This he fastened to a strap and slung round his waist beneath his coat.

"Now I am ready," he muttered. "Necessity bids me fly; but revenge will burn the fiercer that circumstances have delayed it. I have now another foe in the pirate captain, and he, like Minnie Sash and Ned Nimble, shall yet feel the vengeance of Bill Boaster!"

CHAPTER XXXVII.

IN WHICH MINNIE BEGINS TO UNDERSTAND SHE HAS PLACED HER FAITH ON A ROTTEN REED.

MINNIE'S feelings were not at all enviable as the boat swept into the darkness of the channel.

She felt that she had been deceived and betrayed by the handsome stranger who had promised to defend her and protect her lover, and in whose truth and friendship she had so far trusted as to suffer herself to be placed in the boat.

One moment she felt inclined to fling herself from the boat into the dark waters, but the next she realised that it was impossible for her to do so, as she felt a hand on her arm and heard a voice say—

"Keep still. We shall be out of this darkness directly. You must not attempt to move."

"What does this mean?" she asked.

To this question she only received the reply—

"Keep still and wait. When the captain comes you will know all."

Then she saw a difference in her surroundings, and the boat shot out into the river and the stars twinkled overhead.

She breathed a sigh of relief.

But still terrible fears assailed her heart.

Fain would she have learned something of the man in whom she had trusted, but when she thought of the forbidding features of the rowers, her tongue failed her and she remained silent.

The junk was soon reached and a chair was lowered, into which she was lifted and raised to the deck.

Not a light was to be seen.

She was hurried along and then down a short flight of matted stairs.

A door was opened, a flood of light burst on her vision, nearly dazzling it, and a voice said—

"Captain Chow-Woo will soon come aboard."

Before she could reply the door was closed behind her and she was alone.

It was a splendid apartment in which she found herself.

The cabin or state-room was sumptuously furnished.

The walls were hung with pink silk, and the furniture chased and carved most elaborately.

The table that stood in the centre was inlaid with pearl and of beautiful design, and the lamp which hung suspended over it threw bars of coloured light over every article in the place.

For a moment Minnie gazed upon her surroundings with admiration; then turned and tried the door.

It was fast, and her heart sank lower than ever.

"It is as I feared," she gasped. "I am a prisoner."

She sat down on a couch and wrung her hands in despair.

"Oh, who and what is this man—what is this vessel?" she muttered. "My heart misgives me. Oh, Heaven! Have I surrendered myself into the hands of one as base as he from whom I begged his aid to escape? Have I but eluded one fiend to find myself in the power of another? This magnificence which surrounds me appals my heart, and I dread to acknowledge even to myself the horrors it suggests."

She rose and examined the apartment.

She saw that it had evidently been occupied by a female at some recent date, and one highly cultivated, as the musical instruments, paintings and embroideries attested.

But despite this she could not shake off the fears that possessed her.

Evidently she was on board no merchant junk.

On no trading ship could such a cabin be found.

"Oh, horror!" she cried suddenly, "can this vessel be a pirate?—can that man be a pirate—these Celestials who brought me hither be some of the cruel and bloodthirsty pirates of the Chinese seas? Alas, alas! I fear it is so. This cabin—those men—the absence of all lights on deck—that dark tunnel through which we came—that merchandise in the vaults of the pagoda—Oh, mercy! it must be so, and I am lost, lost!"

Again she sank upon the silken couch and buried her face in her hands.

And while she gave way to grief and tears, while horror upon horror chased through her brain and heart, the door of the cabin was flung open and Chow-Woo appeared.

Minnie looked up, dashed her tears away and rose and stood before him.

"Weeping?" said Chow-Woo in that soft, silvery voice he could assume when it pleased him. "Is the golden-haired dove disappointed in its nest?"

And he pointed round the apartment.

"Tell me," she cried, "what ship is this to which I am brought by your orders, and what are you? This is no trading vessel nor Chinese war ship."

"True, sweet bird," he replied. "This is no Chinese war junk, if you mean a fighting ship of the emperor's—nor a trader, as the term is understood with merchants, but my junk is both a war ship and a trader."

"Say rather a pirate," cried Minnie.

"If the term pleases you better, fair hair," said the captain, "then my ship is a pirate."

"Oh, Heaven! I thought so," she gasped; "and you?"

"Am a pirate," was the reply.

"Then Heaven help me!" moaned Minnie, sinking down on the couch.

Chow-Woo gazed at her in silence for some moments, then advanced and placed his hand on her shoulder.

She turned from him as if a serpent had stung her.

"Why that start?" he asked. "What does the fair-haired bird fear?"

"You," replied Minnie.

"I?" he said. "Wherefore should you fear me?"

"You are a pirate."

"True."

"And therefore a villain," said Minnie.

He looked at her as if he fancied that he could not have heard aright.

"A villain?" he said at last.

"Yes; a coldhearted bloodthirsty villain—a robber, a murderer, for is not a pirate all these?"

And springing from the couch, Minnie stood before him, her cheeks pale with horror, but her eyes flashing with disgust.

"Deny it if you dare," she cried. "You are a pirate, and therefore a villain, a robber, and a murderer!"

Chow-Woo fixed his gaze upon Minnie and said—

"What I take I fight for and expose my life to my opponent's shot or slash. A murderer does not give his foe the chance to take his life if he can—he kills unawares. A robber I am, but not a murderer."

"So you think perhaps," said Minnie; "but you are a murderer, for you sacrifice the lives of innocent men who only wish to defend their own from your rapacious claws, and that you are a villain behold the proof in my presence here on board your accursed junk."

"Has the gentle dove I found in the Purple Papoda changed itself into a fierce eagle?" said Chow-Woo.

"You have deceived me—lied to me,' cried Minnie; "and, fool that I was, I believed you. Rather had I remained to be tortured by the villain who has persecuted me so long and so cruelly than have trusted myself to the mercy of a Chinese pirate."

"Think you, fair hair, that the mercy of a Chinese executioner were more tender than the mercies of myself?" he asked. "Is this place more hateful than a prison cell, the rolling of my junk less to be endured than the sling, the chances of death by a bullet or cannon ball more to be dreaded than strangulation by the executioner's rope or pressure to death between boards?"

"What had I to fear, who have done no wrong?" she asked; "at least from the executioners of Chinese laws? I did not seek to fly from them, but from the persecutions of a villain, and in trusting you I have but escaped one danger to fall into another."

"Wherefore do you say this?" he asked.

"Is it not so?" she cried quickly, "Oh, say it is not and I will bless you. Oh, if I have wronged you forgive me; I have suffered so much and so long that I fear and suspect all men."

"Then why did you seek my aid?" he asked.

"Because—because you looked so kind, so noble, so true," she replied; "but, but——"

She paused.

"But what, fair hair?" he asked.

"I knew not then you were a pirate," she replied; "I thought you an honest man, and when you spoke of your ship I thought you must be an honest merchant willing to aid a poor girl; but when you placed me in charge of that fearful crew, when I discovered your junk was a piratical craft, I could but fear the worst for myself."

"What could be worse than the fate that would have overtaken you in the pagoda?" he asked. "If left to the mercies of your persecutor would he have spared you—if found by the officers of the law in the place where the governor was slain by your countryman, would they have spared you? No, either way you must have suffered. I gave you the chance to escape your persecutor and his vengeance, and in return you upbraid me.

Is this English justice—English gratitude?"

"Am I free to leave this ship when I will?" asked Minnie.

"You would rush into the danger," he replied. "Your presence in the pagoda was known to the attendants, your presence even in the torture chamber where Fum-Fum was slain. No, if I suffered you to leave this junk you would be instantly arrested. I promised to save you and I will do so by putting to sea as quickly as possible and taking you far beyond the reach of those who would slay you. As for the Englishman you feared and sought to escape from he never more can harm you."

"How?" cried Minnie eagerly; "is he dead then?"

"No, but to-morrow I shall surrender him into the hands of the officers of the law, to be dealt with for the murder of Fum-Fum and the defenders of the pagoda."

"You surrender him! Is he then in your power?" asked Minnie.

"He is on board my junk, brought hither a prisoner by me to be handed over to suffer for the mandarin's death.'

"But, but," she cried, "he did ——"

She paused.

Much as she hated Bill, much as he deserved death, yet could she allow him to die on a false charge, knowing that it was her own hand and not Boaster's that had robbed Fum-Fum of life.

And yet, if she denied his guilt, dare she place it on her own shoulders?

If she did would the pirate captain give her up to justice?

No, rather would he make the knowledge a stepping-stone to his own purposes.

She dared not reveal the truth, and yet she felt she could not, bad as he was suffer Boaster to be charged and executed for a crime he never committed.

What could she do?

How should she act?

While her mind was torn with conflicting thoughts, there came the hurrying of feet along the deck, and the shouts of many voices.

The captain sprang to the door and flung it open.

"Lower a boat, quick, or they will both be drowned! Hoist the lanterns and throw lights on the water—there they rise, there they are!"

As these words reached the captain's ears he sprang through the doorway, pulled the door after him, bounded up the stairs and reached the deck.

"What is this?" he cried.

"The Englishmen!" cried one.

"What Englishmen?" asked the Captain.

"Both of them—there, there!"

The captain followed the indications of the men, and saw in the ray of light cast by one of the lanterns being held over the side what appeared to be two heads just above the water and at some distance from the ship.

Zanara came to his side.

In hurried tones he explained all that had transpired.

Several of the pirates were launching one of the boats.

The captain called out to them to stop.

"It's no use," he said, turning to the lieutenant; "neither Tom nor the young fellow will ever reach the shore wounded as they are, and before a boat could come up with them they will be lying dead at the bottom of the river. Let them go."

"But the authorities will demand him in the morning," said Zanara. "How will you account for his escape from your custody—for said you not your wife would inform them you had brought him here?"

"True; he leaped overboard and was drowned; if they don't believe it let them search for his body at the bottom of the river. Perhaps it will be better that he drowns, then he could not delay our departure, and I have no desire to give evidence against him."

"It might lead to something unpleasant," said Zanara, "and I for one should be glad to be out at sea when the inquiry as to Fum-Fum's death takes place."

"And I also," said Chow-Woo.

"But your wife," said Zanara, "she may need your presence and your comfort at such a time?"

"Loogee is wise," he replied, "and I have another to comfort and console. I shall go ashore in the morning for a short time, so have everything ready for sailing by my return."

"On what errand, captain?" asked the lieutenant.

"No matter," was the reply, as Chow-Woo turned and strode towards the after part of the vessel.

Having despatched an old woman to attend upon Minnie, Chow-Woo strode to his own cabin, and the next morning with a well-armed boat's crew went ashore.

CHAPTER XXXVIII.

IN WHICH CHOW-WOO IMAGINES HE DOES A GOOD STROKE OF BUSINESS, BUT NED AND HIS FRIENDS DO NOT.

No sooner had Jack seized the pirate by the throat, recognised and denounced him, than Ned, forgetful of the presence of Sally and Tilda, bounded out of bed on to the floor.

Then as suddenly recollecting himself he bounded in again.

"Villain!" he shouted, "where is the girl, you conveyed on board your piratical junk? By Heaven, if ill has come to her you die!"

And placing his hand under his pillow, he drew forth his revolver and levelled it at the pirate.

But he dared not have fired, for Jack stood between him and Chow-Woo.

"Be off," he cried, addressing Sally and Tilda. "Go to your own room."

The women hurried off.

And then Ned, Harry, and Jumbo sprang from their couches, and hurriedly drew on their trousers.

They quite forgot all their sufferings in the knowledge that the man who held Minnie in his power was now in theirs.

Powerful as Jack was, the pirate was no mean adversary.

He grappled with the Englishman, and they struggled through the doorway and into the apartment where Ching-Fow lay coiled up in Jack's big box, unable to cry out or make the least sound.

Down on to the floor went Jack and the pirate, and over and over they rolled till Charley seizing one leg and Jumbo the other, he lay on his back with Jack's keen pressed on his chest, and Jack's fingers tightened round his throat.

By this time Ned joined them.

He levelled his revolver at the pirate's head.

"Give up the girl you took from the pagoda last night," he cried, "or you die."

Chow-Woo struggled hard to speak, but could not.

Harry and Jumbo each seized an arm of the pirate.

"Let go his throat, Jack," said Ned. Jack obeyed.

"Now speak," said Ned. "Where is the girl you took from the pagoda last night? Don't lie for we have proof that you sent her off in your boat through the channel. If you have harmed her, beware."

"Fools!" said the pirate. "Why should I harm the girl?"

"Why did you take her away?"

"Listen, idiots of Englishmen that you are. Barbarians, is this your gratitude for saving a girl of your nation from one who persecuted her and who would have handed her over to the authorities for slaying the governor, or being accessory to his murder."

"What do you mean?" said Ned.

"The girl appealed to me to save her from the man who had taken her against her will to the pagoda to witness the torture of a lover, during which torture the governor was slain, probably by the Englishman himself, but he had sworn to fix the guilt upon her, and hence her danger being twofold, she implored me to save her, and I did so."

"And the wretch Boaster, the man she feared, he too was taken by you to your ship?" said Harry.

"He was," said the pirate.

"And they are there now; and by Heaven, if you surrender them not both up to us, you die."

"I have braved death too many times to fear it now," said Chow-Woo, "therefore your threats have no terrors for me. You are in greater danger than I am, defenceless though you hold me here."

"You are in no danger," said Ned, "if you surrender the girl and her persecutor to me, but if you fail to do that your fate is as sure as death."

"The man is already beyond my power," said Chow-Woo, "and ere long will be beyond yours or any one else's."

"What do you mean?" asked Harry.

"At midday he will be sawn asunder for slaying, or aiding in the murder of Fum-Fum the governor," was the reply. "But an hour since I surrendered him into the keeping of those who will make justice both swift and sure."

They looked at him in doubt, but so calm and truthful were his features, that they believed him.

"Is this really true," asked Ned.

"By the bones of my father I swear it," was the reply.

"And the girl?" asked Jack.

"Is safe."

"With you?" said Ned.

"Yes," replied Chow-Woo, "and it rests with you whether she ever leaves my junk alive. If I return with the gold I know you to possess, the girl is free—if I return not, she dies, while you cannot escape death for your work in the pagoda last night."

And the pirate unflinchingly turned his gaze from one to the other.

"Villain," said Ned, you think you have us at your mercy?"

"I know I have," was the reply, "though lying here as I do now, you imagine I am at yours. Blow my brains out. What then? You have not got the girl, you cannot save your gold or your own lives. If I am suffered to go free, and loaded with your wealth, the girl's life is safe, also your own lives. Go one of you, to the courtyard if you doubt me, and there see whether I speak truly or not."

"Go, Charley," said Ned.

Charley let go the pirates arm, and went out.

In a minute he returned.

"A dozen of the bloodthirstiest looking varmints I ever saw," he whispered to Ned.

Though Chow-Woo did not hear the words he guessed what Charley had said, and burst out laughing.

"You are satisfied?" he said.

"Yes," replied Ned, "you are well prepared. But so are we. Englishmen are not afraid of double their number."

"I know their courage," said Chow-Woo, "and I know their sense, but you seem to be badly in want of that commodity with which the general run of your countrymen are gifted."

"What's yer mean by dat ar?" asked Jumbo. "Say as dis nigger ain't got no sense?"

Ned motioned him to be silent.

"Hark you, Englishman," said Chow-Woo. "Since I failed to persuade you that I was an officer of justice, and induce you to purchase your safety with your gold, by acting on your fears, I will reason with your common sense if you will permit me to sit up."

"I reckons as how we'll fust take care ob yer wolvers and cemetary," said Jumbo.

"I am at your mercy," said the pirate captain.

"Guess dat's no lie," said Jumbo, as he took the pistols from Chow-Woo's belt, and drew his scimitar from its scabbard.

"Dar, now, if de ladies and genlem—leastways dar's no ladies here now—am willing, yer can get up."

They suffered Chow-Woo to sit up, but Ned kept him covered with his pistol.

"Now what have you to say?" asked Ned.

"Simply this," replied Chow-Woo, "that men of my profession are not particular how they obtain wealth so that they get it."

"Dat's trufe," said Jumbo.

"I had learned that you were possessed of considerable wealth, and desired to possess it. How I obtained that information is little matter. I only needed the means and opportunity to get it."

"You're very kind," said Charley sarcastically.

"The opportunity came on discovering that it was you who made an attack upon the inmates of the pagoda, and I resolved to take advantage of it, and failing to obtain it either through your fear or unwillingness to part with it, I have arranged to hand you over to justice and take what you refuse to give. That I am prepared to do so you know from having seen my followers without."

"How did you know we were possessed of wealth?" asked Jack.

The pirate shrugged his shoulders.

"I have spies," he said.

"Ching-Fow," said Charley.

"You are not far wrong," was the reply. "It was either he or I. We might have stolen it, but I prefer to earn it. Anyhow, you cannot keep it. If you shoot me, as you can, you certainly die, and lose your gold, and the girl to boot. If you hand over your riches you escape a fearful fate, have the girl restored to you, and live. The choice is in your own hands, but there must be no delay as my junk sails in an hour."

The coolness of Chow-Woo surprised them.

With the pistols levelled at his head he met their gaze unflinchingly, and his voice was as calm as if not the slightest danger assailed him.

Ned saw that despite the position of the pirate, their own danger was great, and that of Minnie terrible.

What should they do—how act?

To slay the pirate would be to slay Minnie and probably lose their own lives.

But Minnie must be saved at any cost.

"Say what will satisfy you—what will purchase the poor girl's safety and our own?" asked Ned at last. "Remember we are in a foreign country, thousands of miles from home, and need a large sum to reach our native land."

"I am not unmindful of the fact that you will need gold to live and travel with," said Chow-Woo, "but I may as well tell you that I know exactly what you possess. I had arranged to share it with another, but I have reason to believe that other would have taken it all for himself had he possessed the courage, and only sought my aid when he found he could not work alone. Now, since it is the coward who turns traitor, and not the brave man, I somewhat mistrust him, and therefore, though it is against my principle, I have no objection to leave him out. So that makes things more pleasant for you. Surrender half your wealth to me, and you silence the tongues that could condemn you to the hands of the executioners."

"And you will surrender the girl?"

"Yes, if she be willing."

"That I know she will be," said Ned, "and it is for her sake I consent, for I tell you, pirate, that were it only to save my own life, I'd shoot you through the head where you sit. Friends, are you willing to give up half your possessions?"

"I am," said Harry.

"And I, and I," said the others.

"But I reckons dis coon ain't a-goin' ter be fooled," said Jumbo. "We has dat ar lubly Minnie fust, afore we gibs up de tin."

"Do you doubt me?" said Chow-Woo, angrily.

"I guess I always doubts a liar," said Jumbo.

"Liar!" echoed the pirate captain.

"Guess dat's what dis chile said. Didn't yer say as yer was a orsifer ob de emperor's an' wasn't dat ar a lie? Jus' tell me dat ar."

"It was said for a motive," replied the pirate.

"An' so may be de gettin' ole ob our money, but I reckons we hab dat ar gal fust, an' den we hands ober, and not afore."

"Certainly not," said Ned. "Let him place Minnie in our charge, and I swear that he shall have half our wealth."

"I am not alone, remember," said the pirate captain. "Though I may trust to your word my men may refuse."

"Then we will hold you as hostage till the girl is brought to us," said Ned.

"And if they refuse to surrender her till they possess the gold—what then?" asked Chow-Woo.

"You die, by Heaven!" said Ned.

"And seal your own doom," was the reply. "It is not your life we seek, but your gold. Dead you are worthless. And what care we whether you live or not? Your wealth is all we require, therefore surrender it, and save the girl and yourselves."

"I will make a bargain with you," said Charley. "A portion of the treasures shall be taken on board by your men, and one of us will go with them to bring away the girl, and when she is here safe and sound the rest of the money shall be paid over to you."

"Agreed," said the captain, "but I must go on board to give the order for her release."

"No," said Ned, "you can write that order to your officer in command."

"Be it so, then," said the pirate. "Give me paper and ink."

It was placed before him, and on top of the box in which Ching-Fow was confined he wrote the order.

"Call in my men," he said, and let

them take this box on board with this order."

"Why that box ?" asked Ned.

"Because," said the pirate, "in that box is much of the wealth you own. Deny it not, for here on the lid is the marks placed by myself and Ching-Fow in your absence."

And with a smile the pirate pointed to a scratch on the lid.

"Be it so, then," said Ned. "but if you are disappointed, blame not us."

"I am content: Call in my men and I will bid them take this box and paper. No words. I am determined they take that box or none."

And the pirate pointed to the box and smiled grimly.

CHAPTER XXXIX.

IN WHICH JOY IS TURNED TO SORROW AND JACK JONES MEETS WITH A SAD FALL.

NED and his friends exchanged glances, and a smile hovered round Jack's lips.

"I will go on board with the pirates and receive Minnie," he said; "if that will be agreeable to you, Ned."

"Quite," replied Ned.

"Then call in your men," said Jack, addressing the pirate. "Stay, we will send for them. Charley, tell those without their captain wants two of them; no more must enter, and they will be able to carry the box despite the heaviness of its contents."

"Guess dey don't know what a lot dar is in dat chest," said Jumbo.

The pirate captain smiled.

Little did he dream that the treasures which he and Ching-Fow had seen on the day when the friends so suddenly returned and put an end to their examination, had been removed by Sally and Tilda to other hiding places, or the actual contents of that iron-bound chest at that moment.

Charley now returned with two of the pirate crew, who looked no little astonished at seeing their captain capless and deprived of his weapons.

For a moment they evidently fancied they had been betrayed into an ambush but the smiling face of their commander reassured them.

"Take this chest on board," he said, pointing to the box, "and give this to Zanara, and bid him see that my orders are complied with without hesitation. This barbarian will accompany you. Ask no questions, but get the chest on board as quickly as possible."

"And our messmates ?" asked one.

"Will go with you."

"All of them ?"

"All; they can return with the boat and the barbarian."

The man took the paper with the strange hieroglyphics scrawled thereon thrust it into his belt, and then assisted his companion to lift the chest.

"It is heavy," said one.

"I know it," said the captain, "see that you do not let it fall or get overboard, or you will suffer for your carelessness."

"Are you not going on board, captain?"

"Not yet, I shall be ready when you return," was the reply.

It was with no little difficulty that the pirates bore the box out of the room.

"Be on your guard, Jack," whispered Ned. "There's no knowing what may happen."

"Trust me," replied Jack in a low tone. "Don't fail to keep a sharp look out on the captain. I don't half like his coolness, it don't seem natural under the circumstances."

"I hope no suspicion will arise as to the real contents of the chest," whispered Ned.

"Leave me to prevent that," said Jack, as he nodded to the others and followed the pirates to the courtyard.

He found the men both looking and speaking their surprise at the captain remaining behind.

"Now then, lads," cried Jack; "heave a-head, as they say on ship board, and get that chest afloat and yourselves too."

He was at once obeyed.

"' DOG, I'LL TRAMPLE THE LIFE OUT OF YOU! SHOULDER TO SHOULDER, BOYS! DOWN WITH THE PIRATES!' CRIED JACK."

www.ingramcontent.com/pod-product-compliance
Lightning Source LLC
Chambersburg PA
CBHW081153170626
46813CB00009B/3183